'The G...
its my... ...by disease event... ...ire
consequenc... ...superb performance'   *...y Morning Herald*

'Richly satisfying ... as immersive a reading experience as its pre-
decessor, finding all the necessary imaginative depth within the
more realistic confines of its world ... Revolutionary'   *Atlantic*

'*The Glass Hotel* may be the perfect novel for your survival bunker ...
That Mandel manages to cover so much, so deeply is the abiding
mystery of this book'   *Washington Post*

'The question of what is real—be it love, money, place or memory—
has always been at the heart of Ms. Mandel's fiction ... Certainties
are blurred, truth becomes malleable and in *The Glass Hotel* the con
man thrives ... Ms. Mandel invites us to observe her characters
from a distance even as we enter their lives, a feat she achieves with
remarkable skill'   *Wall Street Journal*

'An eerie, compelling follow-up ... Like all Mandel's novels,
The Glass Hotel is flawlessly constructed'   *Boston Globe*

'A mysterious and delicate book ... *The Glass Hotel* beautifully
depicts the many lives impacted by the collapse of an ambitious
Ponzi scheme'   *Elle Magazine* (USA)

'A flawless tale of schadenfreude and Ponzi schemes, greed, depression and addiction. I loved the main setting on Vancouver
Island, a place wild and safe and sinister at the same time'
          Sunday Times (South Africa)

'Mandel's wonderful novel follows a brother and sister as they
navigate heartache, loneliness, wealth, corruption, drugs, ghosts,
and guilt ... This ingenious, enthralling novel probes the tenuous
yet unbreakable bonds between people and the lasting effects of
momentary carelessness'   *Publishers Weekly*

THE GLASS HOTEL

Emily St. John Mandel was born in Canada and studied dance at The School of Toronto Dance Theatre. Her previous novels are *Last Night in Montreal*, *The Singer's Gun*, *The Lola Quartet* and *Station Eleven*. She lives in New York City with her husband and daughter.

Also by Emily St. John Mandel

Last Night in Montreal
The Singer's Gun
The Lola Quartet
Station Eleven

EMILY ST. JOHN MANDEL

THE GLASS HOTEL

PICADOR

First published in the USA 2020 by Alfred A. Knopf, a division of
Random House, Inc., New York, and in Canada by HarperCollins Publishers Ltd

First published in the UK 2020 by Picador

This edition published 2021 by Picador
an imprint of Pan Macmillan
The Smithson, 6 Briset Street, London ECIM 5NR
Associated companies throughout the world
www.panmacmillan.com

ISBN 978-1-5098-8283-0

3 5 7 9 8 6 4

A CIP catalogue record for this book is available from the British Library.

Printed and bound by CPI Group (UK) Ltd, Croydon, CRO 4YY

Visit **www.picador.com** to read more about all our books
and to buy them. You will also find features, author interviews and
news of any author events, and you can sign up for e-newsletters
so that you're always first to hear about our new releases.

For Cassia and Kevin

Contents

PART ONE

PART ONE

I

VINCENT IN THE OCEAN

December 2018

1

Begin at the end: plummeting down the side of the ship in the storm's wild darkness, breath gone with the shock of falling, my camera flying away through the rain—

2

Sweep me up. Words scrawled on a window when I was thirteen years old. I stepped back and let the marker drop from my hand and still I remember the exuberance of that moment, that feeling in my chest like light glinting on crushed glass—

3

Have I risen to the surface? The cold is annihilating, the cold is all there is—

4

A strange memory: standing by the shore at Caiette when I was thirteen years old, my brand-new video camera cool and strange in my hands, filming the waves in five-minute intervals, and as I'm filming I hear my own voice whispering, "I want to go home,

I want to go home, I want to go home," although where is home if not there?

5

Where am I? Neither in nor out of the ocean, I can't feel the cold anymore or actually anything, I am aware of a border but I can't tell which side I'm on, and it seems I can move between memories like walking from one room to the next—

6

"Welcome aboard," the third mate said the first time I ever boarded the *Neptune Cumberland*. When I looked at him, something struck me, and I thought, *You*—

7

I am out of time—

8

I want to see my brother. I can hear him talking to me, and my memories of him are agitating. I concentrate very hard and abruptly I'm standing on a narrow street, in the dark, in the rain, in a foreign city. A man is slumped in a doorway just across from me, and I haven't seen my brother in a decade but I know that it's him. Paul looks up and there's time to notice that he looks terrible, gaunt and undone, he sees me but then the street blinks out—

I ALWAYS COME TO YOU

1994 and 1999

1

At the end of 1999, Paul was studying finance at the University of Toronto, which should have felt like triumph but everything was wrong. When he was younger, he'd assumed he'd major in musical composition, but he'd sold his keyboard during a bad period a couple years back and his mother was unwilling to entertain the idea of an impractical degree, for which after several expensive rounds of rehab he couldn't really blame her, so he'd enrolled in finance classes on the theory that this represented a practical and impressively adultlike forward direction—*Look at me, learning about markets and the movements of money!*—but the one flaw in this brilliant plan was that he found the topic fatally uninteresting. The century was ending and he had some complaints.

He'd expected that at the very least he'd be able to slip into a decent social scene, but the problem with dropping out of the world is that the world moves on without you, and between the time spent on an all-consuming substance and the time spent working soul-crushing retail jobs while he tried not to think about the substance and the time spent in hospitals and rehab facilities, Paul was twenty-three years old and looked older. In the first few weeks of school he went to parties, but he'd never been good at striking up conversations with strangers, and everyone just seemed so young to him. He did poorly on the midterms, so by late October he was spending all his time either in the library—reading, struggling to take an interest in finance, trying to turn it around—or in his room, while the city grew colder around him. The room was a single, because one of the very few things he and his mother had agreed on was that it would be disastrous if Paul had a roommate and the roommate was into opioids, so he was almost always alone. The room was so small that he was claustrophobic unless he sat directly in front of the window. His interactions with other people were few and superficial. There was a dark cloud of exams on the near horizon, but studying was hopeless. He kept trying to focus on probability theory and discrete-time martingales, but his thoughts kept sliding toward a piano composition that he knew he'd never finish, this very straightforward C-major situation except with little flights of destabilizing minor chords.

In early December he walked out of the library at the same time as Tim, who was in two of his classes and also preferred the last row of the lecture hall. "You doing anything tonight?" Tim asked. It was the first time anyone had asked him anything in a while.

"I was kind of hoping to find some live music somewhere." Paul hadn't thought of this before he said it, but it seemed like the right direction for the evening. Tim brightened a little. Their one previous conversation had been about music.

"I wanted to check out this group called Baltica," Tim said, "but I need to study for finals. You heard of them?"

"Finals? Yeah, I'm about to go down in flames."

"No. Baltica." Tim was blinking in a confused way. Paul

remembered something he'd noticed before, which was that Tim seemed not to understand humour. It was like talking to an anthropologist from another planet. Paul thought that this should have created some kind of opening for friendship, but he couldn't imagine how that conversation would begin—*I can't help but notice that you're as alienated as I am, can we compare notes?*—and anyway Tim was already walking away into the dark autumn evening. Paul picked up copies of the alternative weeklies from the newspaper boxes by the cafeteria and walked back to his room, where he put on Beethoven's Fifth for company and then scanned the listings till he found Baltica, which was scheduled for a late gig at some venue he'd never heard of down at Queen and Spadina. When had he last gone out to hear live music? Paul spiked his hair, unspiked it, changed his mind and spiked it again, tried on three shirts, and left the room before he could make any further changes, disgusted by his indecisiveness. The temperature was dropping, but there was something clarifying about the cold air, and exercise was a therapeutic recommendation that he'd been ignoring, so he decided to walk.

The club was in a basement under a goth clothing store, down a steep flight of stairs. He hung back on the sidewalk for a few minutes when he saw this, worried that perhaps it would turn out to be a goth club—everyone would laugh at his jeans and polo shirt—but the bouncer barely seemed to notice him and the crowd was only about 50 percent vampires. Baltica was a trio: one guy with a bass guitar, another guy working an array of inscrutable electronics attached to a keyboard, and a girl with an electric violin. Whatever they were doing onstage sounded less like music than like some kind of malfunctioning radio, all weird bursts of static and disconnected notes, the kind of scattered ambient electronica that Paul, as a lifelong Beethoven fanatic, absolutely did not get, but the girl was beautiful so he didn't mind it at all, if he wasn't enjoying the music he could at least enjoy watching her. The girl leaned into the microphone and sang, *"I always come to you,"* except there was an echo—the guy with the keyboard had pressed a foot pedal—so it was

I always come to you, come to you, come to you

—and it was frankly discordant, the voice with the keyboard notes and the bursts of static, but then the girl raised her violin, and this turned out to be the missing element. When she drew her bow, the note was like a bridge between islands of static and Paul could hear how it all fit together, the violin and the static and the shadowy underpinning of the bass guitar; it was briefly thrilling, then the girl lowered her violin and the music fell apart into its disparate components, and Paul found himself wondering once again how anyone listened to this stuff.

Later, when the band was drinking at the bar, Paul waited for a moment when the violinist wasn't talking to anyone and swooped in.

"Excuse me," he said, "hey, I just wanted to tell you, I love your music."

"Thanks," the violinist said. She smiled, but in the guarded manner of extremely beautiful girls who know what's coming next.

"It was really fantastic," Paul said to the bass player, in order to confound expectations and keep the girl off balance.

"Thanks, man." The bass player beamed in a way that made Paul think he was probably stoned.

"I'm Paul, by the way."

"Theo," the bass player said. "That's Charlie and Annika."

Charlie, the keyboardist, nodded and raised his beer, while Annika watched Paul over the rim of her glass.

"Can I ask you guys kind of a weird question?" Paul wanted so badly to see Annika again. "I'm kind of new to the city, and I can't find a place to go out dancing."

"Just head down to Richmond Street and turn left," Charlie said.

"No, I mean, I've been to a few places down there, it's just hard to find anywhere where the music doesn't suck, and I was wondering if you could maybe recommend . . . ?"

"Oh. Yeah." Theo downed the last of his beer. "Yeah, try System Sound."

"But it's a hellhole on weekends," Charlie said.

"Yeah, dude, don't go on the weekends. Tuesday nights are pretty good."

"Tuesday nights are the best," Charlie said. "Where are you from?"

"Deepest suburbia," Paul said. "Tuesday nights at System, okay, thanks, I'll check it out." To Annika, he said, "Maybe I'll see you there sometime," and turned away fast so as not to see her disinterest, which he felt like a cold wind on his back all the way to the door.

On the Tuesday after exams—three C's, one C–, academic probation—Paul went down to System Soundbar and danced by himself. He didn't really like the music, but it was nice to stand in a crowd. The beats were complicated and he wasn't sure how to dance to them so he just kind of stepped back and forth with a beer in his hand and tried not to think about anything. Wasn't that the point of clubs? Annihilating your thoughts with alcohol and music? He'd hoped Annika would be here, but he didn't see her or the other Baltica people in the crowd. He kept looking for them and they kept not being there, until finally he bought a little packet of bright blue pills from a girl with pink hair, because E wasn't heroin and didn't count, but there was something wrong with the pills, or something wrong with Paul: he bit one in half and swallowed it, just the half, didn't feel anything so he swallowed the other half with beer, but then the room swam, he broke out in a sweat, his heart skipped, and just for a second he thought he was going to die. The girl with the pink hair had vanished. Paul found a bench against the wall.

"Hey, man, you okay? You okay?" Someone was kneeling in front of him. Some significant amount of time had passed. The crowd was gone. The lights had come up and the brightness was terrible, the brightness had transformed System into a shabby room with little pools of unidentifiable liquid shining on the dance floor. A dead-eyed older guy with multiple piercings was walking around with a garbage bag, collecting bottles and cups, and after the force of all that music the quiet was a roar, a void. The man kneeling in front of Paul was club management, in the regulation jeans/Radiohead T-shirt/blazer that club management always wore.

"Yeah, I'm okay," Paul said. "I apologize, I think I drank too much."

"I don't know what you're on, man, but it doesn't suit you," the management guy said. "We're closing up, get out of here." Paul rose unsteadily and left, remembered when he got to the street that he'd left his coat at the coat check, but they'd already locked the door behind him. He felt poisoned. Five empty cabs cruised by before the sixth finally stopped for him. The cabbie was a proselytizing teetotaler who lectured Paul about alcoholism all the way back to campus. Paul wanted desperately to be in bed so he clenched his fists and said nothing until the cab finally pulled up to the curb, when he paid—no tip—and told the cabdriver to stop fucking lecturing him and fuck off back to India.

> "Listen, I want to be clear that I'm not that person anymore," Paul told a counsellor at a rehab facility in Utah, twenty years later. "I'm just trying to be honest about who I was back then."

"I'm from Bangladesh, you racist moron," the cabdriver said, and left Paul there on the sidewalk, where he knelt carefully and threw up. Afterward he stumbled back to the dorm building, marvelling at the scale of the disaster. Against all odds he had clawed his way up into an excellent university, and here it was only December of his first year and it was already over. He was already failing, one semester in. "You must gird yourself against disappointment," a therapist had told him once, but he couldn't gird himself against anything, that had always been the problem.

Fast-forward two weeks, past the non-event of the winter holidays—his mother's therapist had advised distance from her son, taking time for herself, and giving Paul a chance to be an adult, etc., so she'd gone to Winnipeg to be with her sister for Christmas and hadn't invited Paul; he spent Christmas Day alone in his room and called his dad for an awkward conversation in which he lied about everything, just like old times—and all the way to December 28, the nadir of that dead week between Christmas and New Year's, when he dressed up and walked back down to System Soundbar on another Tuesday night, hair slicked back, wearing a button-down shirt that he'd purchased specially. He was wearing the jeans he'd been wearing last time he was here and didn't remember till he got to the club that the little packet of blue pills was still in a front pocket.

He walked into System and there were the Baltica people, Annika and Charlie and Theo, standing together at the bar. They must have just wrapped up a gig nearby. It was like a sign. Had Annika become more beautiful since he'd seen her last? It seemed possible. His university life was almost over, but when he looked at her he could see a new version of reality, another kind of life he might lead. He felt that he was not, objectively speaking, a bad-looking individual. He had some talent in music. Maybe his past made him interesting. There was a version of the world wherein he dated Annika and was in many ways a successful person, even if he wasn't cut out for school. He could get back into retail, take it more seriously this time and make a decent living.

> "Look," he told the counsellor in Utah, twenty years into
> the future, "obviously I've had some time to think about
> this, and of course I realize that that line of thinking was
> insane and self-centred, but she was so beautiful, and I
> thought, *She's my ticket out of this,* meaning my ticket out
> of feeling like a failure—"

It's now or never, Paul thought, and he approached the bar in a blaze of courage.

"Hey," Theo said. "You. You're that guy."

"I took your advice!" Paul said.

"What advice?" Charlie asked.

"System Soundbar on Tuesdays."

"Oh right," Charlie said, "yeah, of course."

"Good to see you, man," Theo said, and Paul felt a flush of warmth. He smiled at all of them, with particular focus on Annika.

"Hi," she said, not unkindly, but still with that irritating wariness, like she expected everyone who looked at her to ask her out, although of course that was exactly what Paul was planning to do.

Charlie was saying something to Theo, who leaned down to hear him. (Brief portrait of Charlie Wu: small guy with glasses and a generic office-appropriate haircut, dressed in a white button-down shirt with jeans, standing there with his hands in his pockets, and the light reflecting off his glasses so that Paul couldn't see his eyes.)

"Listen," Paul said, to Annika. She looked at him. "I know you don't know me, but I think you're really beautiful, and I wondered if you'd let me take you to dinner sometime."

"No thank you," she said. Theo's attention had shifted from Charlie to Paul, and he was watching Paul closely, like he was worried that he might have to intercede, and Paul understood: their evening had been fine until Paul came along. Paul was the problem. Charlie was cleaning his glasses, apparently oblivious, nodding his head to the music as he polished the lens.

Paul forced himself to smile and shrug. "Okay," he said, "no problem, no hard feelings, just figured it couldn't hurt to ask."

"Never hurts to ask," Annika agreed.

"You guys into E?" Paul asked.

"—I don't know," he told the counsellor, twenty years later, "to tell you the truth I don't know what I was thinking, in memory my mind is like this terrifying blank, I didn't know what I was going to say before I said it—"

"It's not really my thing," Paul said, because they were all looking at him now, "I mean, no judgment, I've just never been that into it, but my sister gave these to me." He flashed the little packet in the palm of his hand. "I don't really want to sell them, that's not my thing either, but I feel like it'd be kind of a waste to flush them down the toilet, so I just wondered."

Annika smiled. "I think I tried those last week," she said. "Same exact colour."

> "You can see why I've never told this story before," Paul told the counsellor, twenty years after System Sound-bar. "But I didn't know the pills were bad. I thought I'd maybe just had a bad reaction, you know, like maybe my system was kind of messed up from coming off opioids or something, like not a thing where every single person who tried those pills would automatically get sick or whatever, let alone—"

"Anyway, they're yours if you want them," he said, to this group that like all of the other groups he'd ever encountered in his life was going to reject him, and Annika smiled and took the packet from his hand. "I'll see you around," he said, to all of them but especially to her, because sometimes *no thank you* means *not at the present moment but maybe later,* although the pills, the pills, the pills—

"Thank you," she said.

> "Well, just the way she reacted," Paul told the counsellor. "I can see the way you're looking at me, but I really thought she'd tried the same pills, the previous week, like she said, and the way she smiled, it made me think she'd had a good trip, she'd obviously really liked them, so what happened to me when I tried them seemed like

definitely just a weird reaction, like I said, not something that would necessarily . . . look, I know I'm being repetitive but what I need you to understand is that I couldn't possibly have predicted, I mean I know how it sounds but I seriously had no idea—"

After Paul walked away, Annika took one pill and gave the other two to Charlie, whose heart stopped a half hour later on the dance floor.

2

It's easy to dismiss Y2K hysteria in retrospect—who even remembers it?—but the risk of collapse seemed real at the time. At the stroke of midnight on January 1, 2000, the experts said, nuclear power plants might go into meltdown while malfunctioning computers sent flocks of missiles flying over the oceans, the grid collapsing, planes falling from the sky. But for Paul the world had already collapsed, so three days after Charlie Wu's death he was standing by a pay phone in the arrivals hall at the Vancouver airport, trying to reach his half sister, Vincent. He'd had enough money to flee Toronto, but there wasn't enough left over for anything else, so his entire plan was to throw himself on the mercy of his aunt Shauna, who in hazy childhood memory had an enormous house with multiple guest bedrooms. Although he hadn't seen Vincent in five years, since she was thirteen and he was eighteen and Vincent's mother had just died, and he hadn't seen Shauna since he was, what, eleven? He was running through all of this while the phone rang endlessly at his aunt's house. A couple walked by wearing matching T-shirts that said PARTY LIKE IT'S 1999, and only then did he remember that it was actually New Year's Eve. The last seventy-two hours had had a hallucinatory quality. He hadn't been sleeping much. His aunt seemed not to have an answering machine. There was a telephone directory on the shelf under the phone, where he found the law firm where she worked.

"Paul," she said, once he'd cleared the hurdle of her secretary. "What a lovely surprise." Her tone was gentle and cautious. How much had she heard? He assumed he must have come up in conversation over the years. *Paul? Oh, well, he's in rehab again. Yes, for the sixth time.*

"I'm sorry to bother you at work." Paul felt a prickling behind his eyes. He was extremely, infinitely sorry, for everything. (Try not to think of Charlie Wu on the stretcher at System Soundbar, an arm dangling limp over the side.)

"Oh, it's no trouble at all. Were you just calling to say hello, or . . . ?"

"I've been trying to reach Vincent," Paul said, "and for some reason she hasn't been picking up at your home number, so I wondered if she'd maybe gotten her own phone line, or . . . ?"

"She moved out a year ago." A studied neutrality in his aunt's voice suggested that the parting hadn't been amicable.

"A year ago? When she was sixteen?"

"Seventeen," his aunt said, as if this made all the difference. "She moved in with a friend of hers from Caiette, some girl who'd just moved to the city. It was closer to her job."

"Do you have her number?"

She did. "If you see her, say hi to her for me," she said.

"You're not in touch with her?"

"We parted on strained terms, I'm afraid."

"I thought she was supposed to be in your care," he said. "Aren't you her legal guardian?"

"Paul, she isn't thirteen anymore. She didn't like living in my house, she didn't like going to high school, and if you'd spent more time with her, you'd know that trying to get Vincent to do anything she doesn't want to do is like arguing with a brick wall. If you'll excuse me, I have to run to a meeting. Take care."

Paul stood listening to the dial tone, clutching a boarding pass with Vincent's phone number scrawled on the back. He'd harboured fantasies of being absorbed into an extra guest bedroom, but the ground was shifting rapidly underfoot. His headphones were dangling around his neck, so he put them on, hands shaking a little; pressed play on the CD in his Discman; and let the Brandenburg Concertos settle him. He only listened to Bach when he was desperate for order. *This is the music that will get me to Vincent,* he thought, and set out to find a bus to take him downtown. What kind of apartment would Vincent be living in, and with whom? The only friend of hers he remembered was Melissa, and only because she'd been there when Vincent wrote the graffiti that got her suspended from school:

Sweep me up. Words scrawled in acid paste on one of the school's north windows, the acid marker trembling a little in Vincent's gloved hand. She was thirteen years old and this was Port Hardy, British Columbia, a town on the northernmost tip of Vancouver Island that was somehow less remote than the place where Vincent actually lived. Paul came around the corner of the high school too late to stop her, but in time to see her do it, and now the three of them—Vincent, Paul, Melissa—were silent for a moment, watching thin trails of acid dripping down the glass from several letters. Through the words, the darkened classroom was a mass of shadows, empty rows of desks and chairs. Vincent had been wearing a man's leather glove that she'd found who knows where. Now she pulled it off and let it drop into the trampled winter grass, where it lay like a dead rat, while Paul stood useless and gaping. Melissa was giggling in a nervous way.

"What do you think you're doing?" Paul wanted to sound stern, but to his own ears his voice sounded high and uncertain.

"It's just a phrase I like," Vincent said. She was staring at the window in a way that made Paul uneasy. On the other side of the school, the bus driver honked his horn.

"We can talk about this on the bus," Paul said, although they both knew they wouldn't talk about it at all, because he wasn't especially convincing as an authority figure.

She didn't move.

"I should go," Melissa said.

"Vincent," Paul said, "if we miss that bus we're hitchhiking back to Grace Harbour and paying for a water taxi."

"Whatever," Vincent said, but she followed her brother to the waiting school bus. Melissa was sitting up front by the driver, ostensibly getting a head start on her homework, but she glanced up furtively as they passed her seat. They rode the bus in silence back to Grace Harbour, where the mail boat waited to take them to Caiette. The boat careered around the peninsula and Paul stared at the massive construction site where the new hotel was going up, at the clouds, at the back of Melissa's head, at the trees on the shore, anything to avoid looking into the depths of the water, nothing he wanted to think about down there. When he glanced at Vincent, he was relieved to see that she wasn't looking at the water either. She was looking at the darkening sky. On the far side of the peninsula was Caiette, this place that made Port Hardy look like a metropolis in comparison: twenty-one houses pinned between the water and the forest, the total local infra-structure consisting of a road with two dead ends, a small church from the 1850s, a one-room post office, a shuttered one-room elementary school—there hadn't been enough children here to keep the school open since the mid-eighties—and a single pier. When the boat docked at Caiette, they walked up the hill to the house and found Dad and Grandma waiting at the kitchen table. Normally Grandma lived in Victoria and Paul lived in Toronto, but these were not normal times. Vincent's mother had disappeared two weeks ago. Someone found her canoe drifting empty in the water.

"Melissa's parents called the school," Dad said. "The school called me."

Vincent—give her credit for courage—did not flinch. She took a seat at the table, folded her arms, and waited, while Paul leaned awkwardly against the stove and watched them. Should he come to the table too? As the responsible older brother, etc.? As ever and always, he didn't know what he was supposed to do. In the way Dad and Grandma stared at Vincent, Paul heard everything they were all refraining from mentioning: Vincent's new blue hair, her plummeting grades and black eyeliner, her staggering loss.

"Why would you write that on the window?" Dad asked.

"I don't know," she said quietly.

"Was it Melissa's idea?"

"No."

"What were you thinking?"

"I don't know what I was thinking. They were just some words I liked." The wind changed direction, and rain rattled against the kitchen window. "I'm sorry," she said. "I know it was stupid."

Dad told Vincent that she'd been suspended for all of next week; it would've been a much longer suspension, but the school was making allowances. She accepted this without comment, then rose and went up to her room. They were quiet in the kitchen, Paul and Dad and Grandma, listening to her footsteps on the stairs and her door closing quietly behind her, before Paul joined the other two at the table—the grown-up table, he couldn't help thinking—and no one pointed out the obvious, which was that he'd ostensibly come back from Toronto to look out for her, which presumably should ideally involve not letting her write indelible graffiti on school windows. But when had he ever been in a position to look out for anyone? Why had he imagined that he could help? No one brought this up either, they just sat quietly listening to rain dripping into a bucket that Dad had placed in a corner of the room, Vincent represented by a ceiling vent that Dad and Grandma seemed not to realize was a conduit into her bedroom.

"Well," Paul said finally, desperate for a change of scene, "I should probably get started on my homework."

"How's that going?" Grandma asked.

"School? Fine," Paul said, "it's going fine." They thought he'd made a noble sacrifice, leaving all his friends behind in Toronto and coming out here to finish high school in order *to be there for your sister,* but if they'd been paying more attention or were on speaking terms with his mother, they'd have known he wasn't going to be allowed back to his old school anyway, and also that his mother had kicked him out of the house. But does a person have to be either admirable *or* awful? Does life have to be so binary? Two things can be true at the same time, he told himself. Just because you used your stepmother's presumed death to start over doesn't mean that you're not also doing something good, being there for your sister or whatever. Grandma was giving him a flat stare—could she possibly have spoken to his mother?—but Dad was gearing himself up to say something, a gradual process that involved shifting around in his chair, some throat-clearing, lifting his tea halfway to his mouth and putting it down again, so Paul and Grandma broke off their staring contest and waited for him to speak. Grief had lent him a certain gravitas.

"I have to go back to work soon," Dad said. "I can't take her with me to camp."

"What are you suggesting?" Grandma asked.

"I'm thinking about sending her to live with my sister."

"You've never gotten along with your sister. I swear you and Shauna started arguing when you were two and she was a baby."

"She drives me crazy sometimes, but she's a good person."

"She works a hundred hours a week," Grandma said. "Wouldn't it be better for Vincent if you got a job nearby?"

"There are no jobs nearby," he said. "Nothing I could live on, anyway."

"What about the new hotel?"

"The new hotel will be a construction site for at least another year, and I don't know anything about construction. But look, it's not just . . ." He went quiet for a moment, staring into his tea. "Financial considerations aside, I'm not sure living here is really the best thing for Vincent. Every time she looks at the water . . ." He ended the thought there. And Paul thought it went in the good column that he thought of Vincent first when Dad said that, that his first thought wasn't of the goddamn haunted inlet that he was trying not to look at through the kitchen window, but of the girl listening upstairs at the vent.

"I'm going to go check in on Vincent," Paul said. He liked the way they looked at him—*Look how Paul has matured!*—and disliked himself for noticing. At the top of the stairs, his nerve almost failed him, but he did it, he knocked softly on Vincent's bedroom door and let himself in when he heard no answer. He hadn't been in this room in a long time and was struck by how shabby it was, embarrassed for noticing and embarrassed for Vincent, although did she notice? Unclear. Her bed was older than she was and had paint chipping off the headboard; opening the top drawer of her dresser required pulling on a length of rope; the curtains had previously been sheets. Maybe none of it bothered her. She was sitting cross-legged by the vent, as predicted.

"Is it okay if I sit here with you?" he asked. She nodded. *This could work out,* Paul thought. *I could be more of a brother to her.*

"You shouldn't be in grade eleven," she said. "I did the math." Christ. There was a flash of pain that had to be acknowledged, because his thirteen-year-old half sister had noticed what his own father apparently hadn't.

"I'm repeating a grade."

"You failed grade eleven?"

"No, I missed most of it the first time around. I spent some time in rehab last year."

"For what?"

"I had a drug problem." He was pleased with himself for being honest about it.

"Do you have a drug problem because your parents split up?" she asked, in tones of genuine curiosity, at which point he wanted desperately to get away from her, so he rose and brushed off his jeans. Her room was dusty.

"I don't have a drug problem, I *had* a drug problem. That's all behind me now."

"But you smoke pot in your room," she said.

"Pot isn't heroin. They're completely different."

"Heroin?" Her eyes were very wide.

"Anyway, I've got a lot of homework." *I don't hate Vincent,* he told himself, *Vincent has never been the problem, I have never hated Vincent, I have only ever hated the* idea *of Vincent.* A kind of mantra that he found necessary to repeat to himself at intervals, because when Paul was very young and his parents were still married, Dad fell in love with the young hippie poet down the road, who quickly became pregnant with Vincent, and within a month Paul and Paul's mother had left Caiette, "fleeing that whole sordid soap opera" was how she put it, and Paul spent the rest of his childhood in the Toronto suburbs, shuttling out to British Columbia for summers and every second Christmas, a childhood of flying alone over prairies and mountains with an UNACCOMPANIED MINOR sign around his neck, while Vincent got to live with both of her parents, all the time, until two weeks ago.

He left her there in her bedroom and went back to the room where he'd been sleeping—he'd stayed there as a kid, but it had been repurposed for storage in his absence and didn't feel like his anymore—and his hands were shaking, he was besieged by unhappiness, he rolled a joint and smoked it carefully out the window, but the wind kept blowing the smoke back inside until finally there was a knock on his door. When Paul opened it, Dad was standing there with a look of unbearable disappointment, and by the end of the week Paul was back in Toronto.

The next time he saw Vincent was on the last day of 1999, when he took a bus downtown from the airport with the Brandenburg Concertos playing on his Discman and found Vincent's address in the sketchiest neighbourhood he'd ever seen, a rundown building across the street from a little park where users stumbled around like extras from a zombie movie. While Paul waited for Vincent to answer the door, he tried not to look at them and not to think of the general preferability of being on heroin, not the squalid business of trying to get more of it and getting sick, but the thing itself, the state in which everything in the world was perfectly fine.

Melissa answered the door. "Oh," she said, "hey! You look exactly the same. Come in." This was somehow reassuring. He felt marked, as if the details of Charlie Wu's death were tattooed on his skin. Melissa did not look exactly the same. She'd obviously gone deep into the rave scene. She was wearing blue pants made of fun fur and a rainbow sweatshirt, and her hair, which was dyed bright pink, was in the same kind of pigtails he remembered Vincent wearing when she was five or six. Melissa led him down the stairs and into one of the worst apartments he'd ever walked into, a semi-finished basement with water stains on the cinder-block walls. Vincent was making coffee in a tiny kitchenette.

"Hey," she said, "it's great to see you."

"You too." The last time he'd seen Vincent she'd had blue hair and was writing graffiti on windows, but she seemed to have pulled back from that particular edge. She didn't seem to be a raver, or if she was, she saved the costumes for the raves. She was wearing jeans and a grey sweater, and her long dark hair was loose around her shoulders. Melissa was talking a little too fast, but hadn't she always? He remembered her as a nervous kid. He studied Vincent closely for signs of trouble, but she seemed like a reserved, put-together person, someone who'd conducted herself carefully and avoided the land mines. How did she get to be like that, and Paul like *this*? This question had all the markers of the kind of circular thinking he was supposed to be avoiding—why are you *you*?—but he couldn't stop the spiral. *You've never hated Vincent, just remember that. It isn't her fault she doesn't have the same problems as you.* They sat around in a living room with dust bunnies the size of mice, Paul and Vincent on a thirty-year-old couch and Melissa on a grimy plastic lawn chair, trying to come up with topics of conversation, but the conversation kept stalling so they kept drinking instant coffee and not quite meeting one another's eyes.

"Are you hungry?" Vincent asked. "We're a little low on groceries, but I could make you some toast or a tuna sandwich or something."

"Nah, I'm good. Thanks."

"Thank god," Melissa said. "This is the last four days before payday and rent's due tomorrow, so it's probably literally bread or canned tuna."

"If you need groceries that badly, just dip into your beer money," Vincent said.

"I'm going to pretend I didn't hear that."

"Next paycheque, I'm going to remember to buy lightbulbs," Vincent said. "I keep forgetting when I have money." The living room was lit by three mismatched floor lamps, and the one in the far corner was flickering. Vincent rose, switched it off, and returned to the couch. Now the room was halfway dark, shadows crowding in around the periphery.

"Aunt Shauna says hi," Paul said after a while.

"She's fine," Vincent said, answering a question he hadn't asked, "but probably wasn't equipped to take in a traumatized thirteen-year-old."

"She made it sound like you'd dropped out of school."

"Yeah, high school was tedious."

"That's why you left?"

"Pretty much," she said. "It turns out getting straight A's isn't the same thing as being motivated enough to drag yourself to school in the mornings."

He didn't know what to say to this. As ever and always, he wasn't sure what his role was. Was he supposed to counsel her to go back to school? He was in no position to tell anyone to do anything. Charlie Wu's funeral was today. Charlie Wu was absolutely not standing in the darkest corner of the room, but there was still no need to look in that direction.

"Are you in school?" he asked Melissa.

"I'm going to UBC in the fall."

"Good for you. That's a good school."

Melissa raised her coffee cup. "Here's to a lifetime of student-loan debt," she said.

"Cheers." He raised his coffee cup and couldn't quite meet her eyes. Paul's mother had paid for his university tuition.

"We have to go out dancing tonight," Melissa said finally. "I've got a couple places in mind."

"I know people who are holed up in remote cabins with supplies in case civilization collapses," Vincent said.

"That seems like a lot of trouble to go to," Paul said.

"Do you find yourself sort of secretly hoping that civilization collapses," Melissa said, "just so that something will happen?"

Later that night they got into Melissa's beat-up car and drove to a club. Vincent wasn't legal but the doorman chose not to notice, because when you're eighteen and beautiful all the doors are open to you, or so it seemed to Paul as he watched her flit through ahead of him. The doorman scrutinized Paul's ID very carefully and gave him a searching look, which made Paul want to say something snappy, but he decided against it. The new century was a new opportunity, he'd decided. If they survived Y2K, if the world didn't end, he was going to be a better man. Also if they survived Y2K he hoped never to hear the term *Y2K* again. At the coat check, Paul saw that Vincent was wearing a sparkly thing that was really only half a shirt, like the front was a normal shirt but the back was missing, just two pieces of string tied in a bow under her naked shoulder blades, making her back seem horribly vulnerable.

"I need a drink," Melissa said, so Paul accompanied her to the bar, where they ordered beer instead of hard liquor, pacing themselves—responsible adults here—and when he looked back at the dance floor, Vincent was already dancing by herself, eyes closed, or maybe she was just looking at the floor, alone in a very fundamental sense: *lost in her own little world* was the phrase Paul remembered Vincent's mother using, whenever someone was trying to get her attention while she read a book or stared unreachably into space.

"She's so spacey," Melissa said, actually shouted, because the music was quieter by the bar but still not quiet enough to talk.

"She's always been spacey," Paul shouted back.

"Well, what happened with her mom, that would mess any-one up," Melissa shouted, possibly mishearing him. "It was just such a tragic—" Paul didn't hear the last word, but he didn't have to. They were quiet for a moment, contemplating Vincent and also the Tragedy of Vincent, which was a separate entity. But Vincent didn't strike him as a tragic figure, she struck him as someone who had her life more or less together, a composed person with a full-time job busing tables at the Hotel Vancouver, and as such he felt somewhat ill at ease around her.

After two beers he went to join her on the dance floor and she smiled at him. *I'm trying,* he wanted to tell her, *I'm really trying, everything's gone wrong but the new century's going to be different.* He ingested nothing except beer and danced hard for a while under the influence of nothing—*almost* nothing, beers don't count—until he looked up and saw Charlie Wu in the crowd and the night skipped a beat. Paul froze. Of course it wasn't Charlie, of course it was just some random kid who looked a little like him, a kid with a similar haircut and glasses that reflected the lights, but the vision was so appalling that he couldn't stay here for even long enough to tell Vincent and Melissa he was going, so he stumbled out onto the street and that was where they found him a half hour later, shivering under a streetlight. Nothing, he told them, he just didn't really like the music and suddenly needed a little air, did he mention he got claustrophobic in crowds sometimes, also he was really hungry. Twenty minutes later they were staring at menus in a diner where all the other customers were drunk. The lights were so bright that it was possible to be certain that he hadn't actually seen a ghost. Everyone looks alike in strobe lighting. There are doppelgängers everywhere.

"So why did you come here for New Year's?" Melissa asked. He'd been a little vague about how long he was staying. "Aren't the clubs better in Toronto?"

"I'm actually moving here," Paul said.

Vincent looked up from the menu. "Why?" she asked.

"I just really need a change of scene."

"Are you in trouble or something?" Melissa asked.

"Yeah," he said, "maybe a little."

"Well come on," Melissa said, "you have to tell us."

"There was some bad E going around. It seemed like I was maybe going to get blamed for it."

"Well, because there was just no reason not to be sort of honest," he told the counsellor in Utah, in 2019. "Of course I didn't tell them anything else, but I already knew I was going to get away with it. I was on academic probation, so it wasn't weird that I'd withdrawn from school. *Paul* must be one of the most common names in the world, and that was the only name the Baltica people knew—"

"Oh wow," Melissa said. "That's awful," and he thought, *You have no idea.* He couldn't help but notice how disinterested Vincent seemed. She'd returned to the menu without comment. None of the possibilities here were great: either she didn't care about Paul at all, or getting in trouble was something that she'd come to expect from him, or she was acquainted with trouble herself. *I don't hate Vincent,* he told himself silently, *I've only ever hated Vincent's incredible good fortune at being Vincent instead of being me, I only hate that Vincent can drop out of high school and move to a terrible neighbourhood and still somehow miraculously be perfectly fine, like the laws of gravity and misfortune don't apply to her.* When they'd finished their burgers, Melissa glanced at her watch, a big plastic digital thing that looked like it should belong to a child.

"Eleven-fourteen," Melissa said. "We've still got forty-four minutes to kill before the end of the world."

"Forty-six minutes," Paul said.

"I don't think it's gonna end," said Vincent.

"It'd be exciting if it did," Melissa said. "All the lights going out, like *poof*—" She spread her fingers like a magician casting a spell.

"Ugh," Vincent said. "A city with no lights? Thank you, no."

"It'd be kind of creepy," Paul said.

"Dude, *you're* kind of creepy," Melissa said, so he threw a French fry at her and then they all got kicked out. They stood shivering and dehydrated on the street for a few minutes, debating where to go, and then Melissa remembered another club where she thought Vincent probably wouldn't get carded, another club in another basement, not that far from here—so they set out, got lost twice, eventually found themselves in front of an unmarked door through which the bass pulsed faintly from below. It was somehow still 1999. They descended another set of stairs into another permanent night, and Paul heard the lyrics as the door opened,

I always come to you, come to you, come to you—

—and for a second he couldn't breathe. The song had been remixed into dance music, Annika's voice layered over a deep house beat, but he recognized it immediately, he'd have known it anywhere.

"You okay?" Melissa shouted in Paul's ear.

"Fine!" he shouted back. "I'm good!"

They dispensed with their coats and were absorbed into the dance floor, where the Baltica track was shifting into another song, a song about being blue that was playing on all of the dance floors of 1999, of which only a few minutes remained. *Last song of the twentieth century,* Paul thought, and he was trying to dance but there was something bothering him, a sense of movement in his peripheral vision, a feeling of being watched. He looked around wildly, but there was only a sea of anonymous faces and none of them were looking at him.

"You sure you're okay?" Melissa shouted.

The lights began to strobe, and just for a flash Charlie Wu was there in the crowd, hands in his pockets, watching Paul, there and then gone.

"Fine!" Paul shouted. "I'm totally fine!" Because that was actually the only option now, to be fine despite the awful certainty that Charlie Wu was somehow here. Paul closed his eyes for a moment and then forced himself to dance again, pretending desperately. The lights didn't go out when 1999 changed to 2000, the hours rolling forward until sunrise, when they emerged into the cold street and the new century and piled into Melissa's beat-up wreck of a car, cold with sweat, Paul in the passenger seat and Vincent curled up in the back like a cat.

"We got through the end of the world," she said, but when he looked over his shoulder, she was sleeping and he wondered if he'd imagined it. Melissa was red-eyed and speedy, driving too fast, talking about her new job selling clothes at Le Châ-teau while Paul only half listened, and somewhere on the drive back to their apartment he found himself seized by a strange, manic kind of hope. It was a new century. If he could survive the ghost of Charlie Wu, he could survive anything. It had rained at some point in the night and the sidewalks were gleaming, water reflecting the morning's first light.

"No," Paul told the counsellor, "that was only the first time I saw him."

3

THE HOTEL

Spring 2005

1

Why don't you swallow broken glass. Words scrawled in acid paste on the glass eastern wall of the Hotel Caiette, etched trails of white dripping from several letters.

"Who would write something like that?" The only guest to have seen the vandalism, an insomniac shipping executive who'd checked in the day before, was sitting in one of the leather armchairs with a whisky that the night manager had brought him. It was a little past two-thirty in the morning.

"Not an adult, presumably," the night manager said. His name was Walter, and this was the first graffiti he'd seen in his three years on the property. The message had been written on the outside of the glass. Walter had taped a few sheets of paper over the message and was presently moving a potted philodendron to cover the paper, with the assistance of Larry, the night porter. The bartender on duty, Vincent, was polishing wineglasses while she watched the action from behind the bar at the far end of the lobby. Walter had considered recruiting her to help move the planter, because he could use another set of hands and the night houseman was on a dinner break, but she didn't strike him as a particularly robust person.

"It's unnerving, isn't it?" the guest said.

"I don't disagree. But I think," Walter said, with more confidence than he felt, "that this could only have been the work of a bored adolescent." In truth, he was deeply shaken and was taking refuge in efficiency. He stepped back to consider the philodendron. The leaves almost but not entirely covered the taped paper. He glanced at Larry, who gave him a this-is-the-best-we-can-do shrug and went outside with a garbage bag and a roll of tape to cover the message from the other side.

"It's the specificity of it," the guest said. "Disturbing, isn't it?"

"I'm so sorry you had to see it, Mr. Prevant."

"No one should have to see a message like that." A quaver of distress in Leon Prevant's voice, which he covered with a quick swallow of whisky. On the other side of the window, Larry had folded the garbage bag into a neat strip and was taping it over the message.

"I agree completely." Walter glanced at his watch. Three in the morning, three hours remaining on his shift. Larry had resumed his post by the door. Vincent was still polishing glasses. He went to speak to her, and saw when he did that she had tears in her eyes.

"You okay there?" he asked softly.

"It's just so awful," she said, without looking up. "I can't imagine what kind of person would write something like that."

"I know," he said. "But I'm standing by my bored-teenager theory."

"You believe that?"

"I can convince myself of it," he said.

Walter went to see if Mr. Prevant needed anything—he didn't—and then returned to his inspection of the glass wall. Only one more guest was expected that night, a VIP, his flight delayed. Walter lingered by the glass wall for a few minutes, looking out at the reflection of the lobby superimposed on the darkness, before he returned to the desk to write the incident report.

2

"The property's in the middle of nowhere," Walter's general manager had told him, at their first meeting in Toronto three years ago, "but that's precisely the point."

This first meeting was in a coffee shop by the lake, the coffee shop actually built on the pier, boats bobbing nearby. Raphael, the general manager, lived on the property of the Hotel Caiette, along with almost everyone else who worked there, but had come to Toronto to attend a hospitality conference and poach talent from other hotels. The Hotel Caiette had been open since the mid-nineties, but had recently been redone in what Raphael called Grand West Coast Style, which seemed to involve exposed cedar beams and enormous panes of glass. Walter was studying the ad campaign photos that Raphael had slid across the table. The hotel was a glass-and-cedar palace at twilight, lights reflected on water, the shadows of the forest closing in.

"What you said earlier," Walter said, "about it not being accessible by car?" He felt he must have misunderstood something in the initial presentation.

"I mean exactly that. Access to the hotel is by boat. There are no roads in or out. Are you somewhat familiar with the geography of the region?"

"Somewhat," Walter lied. He'd never been that far west. His impression of British Columbia was akin to a series of postcards: whales leaping out of blue water, green shorelines, boats.

"Here." Raphael was shuffling through papers. "Take a look at this map." The property was represented as a white star in an inlet at the north end of Vancouver Island. The inlet nearly broke the island in half. "It's wilderness up there," Raphael said, "but let me tell you a secret about wilderness."

"Please do."

"Very few people who go to the wilderness actually want to experience the wilderness. Almost no one." Raphael leaned back in his chair with a little smile, presumably hoping that Walter might ask what he meant, but Walter waited him out. "At least, not the people who stay in five-star hotels," Raphael said. "Our guests in Caiette want to come to the wilderness, but they don't want to be *in* the wilderness. They just want to *look* at it, ideally through the window of a luxury hotel. They want to be wilderness-adjacent. The point here"—he touched the white star with one finger, and Walter admired his manicure—"is extraordinary luxury in an unexpected setting. There's an element of surrealism to it, frankly. It's a five-star experience in a place where your cell phone doesn't work."

"How do you bring in guests and supplies?" Walter was having some difficulty grasping the appeal of the place. It was undeniably beautiful but geographically inconvenient, and he wasn't sure why your average executive would want to vacation in a cellular dead zone.

"On a speedboat. It's fifteen minutes from the town of Grace Harbour."

"I see. Aside from the undeniable natural beauty," Walter said, trying a different tack, "would you say there's a distinguishing factor that sets this hotel apart from similar properties?"

"I was hoping you'd ask me that. The answer's yes. There's a sense of being outside of time and space."

"Outside of . . . ?"

"A figure of speech, but it's not far off." Raphael loved the hotel, Walter could see that. "The truth of the matter is, there's a certain demographic that will pay a great deal of money to escape temporarily from the modern world."

Later, walking home through the autumn night, temporary escape from the world was an idea that Walter couldn't let go. In those days he was renting a cramped one-bedroom on a street that felt somehow between neighbourhoods. It was the most depressing apartment he'd ever seen, which for reasons he refused to articulate was why he'd chosen it. Elsewhere in the city, the ballet dancer to whom Walter had been engaged until two months ago was setting up house with a lawyer.

Walter stopped into the usual grocery store on his way home that evening, and the thought of stopping into this store again tomorrow, and then the day after that, and then the day after that, slow strolls down the frozen-food aisle interspersed with shifts at the hotel where he'd been working for the past decade, a day older every time, the city closing in around him, well, it was unbearable, actually. He placed a package of frozen corn in his basket. What if this was the last time he ever performed this action, here in this particular store? It was an appealing thought.

He'd been with the ballet dancer for twelve years. He hadn't seen the breakup coming. He'd agreed with his friends that he shouldn't make any sudden moves. But what he wanted in those days was to disappear, and by the time he reached the checkout counter he realized that he'd made his decision. He accepted the position; arrangements were made; on the appointed day a month later he flew to Vancouver and then caught a connecting flight to Nanaimo on a twenty-four-seat prop plane that barely reached the clouds before descending, spent the night in a hotel, and set off the next day for the Hotel Caiette. He could have saved considerable time by flying into one of the tiny airports further north, but he wanted to see more of Vancouver Island.

It was a cold day in November, clouds low overhead. He drove north in a grey rental car through a series of grey towns with a grey sea intermittently visible on his right, a landscape of dark trees and McDonald's drive-throughs and big-box stores under a leaden sky. He arrived at last in the town of Port Hardy, streets dim in the rain, where he got lost for a while before he found the place to return the rental car. He called the town's only taxi service and waited a half hour until an old man arrived in a beat-up station wagon that reeked of cigarette smoke.

"You're headed to the hotel?" the driver asked when Walter requested a ride to Grace Harbour.

"I am," Walter said, but found that he didn't particularly feel like making conversation after all of these hours of travelling in solitude. They drove in silence through the forest until they reached the village of Grace Harbour, such as it was: a few houses here and there along the road and shoreline, fishing boats in the harbour, a general store by the docks, a parking lot with a few old cars. He saw a woman through the window of the general store, but there was no one else around.

Walter's instructions were to call the hotel for a boat. His cell phone didn't work up here, as promised, but there was a phone booth by the pier. The hotel promised to send someone within the half hour. Walter hung up and stepped out into cool air. It was getting on toward evening and the world was shifting to monochrome, the water pale and glassy under a darkening sky, shadows accumulating in the forest. He walked out to the end of the pier, luxuriating in the silence. This place was the opposite of Toronto, and wasn't that what he'd wanted? The opposite of his previous life? Somewhere back in the eastern city, the ballet dancer and the lawyer were at a restaurant, or walking the streets holding hands, or in bed. *Don't think of it. Don't think of it.* Walter waited, listening, and for a while there was only the soft lapping of water against the pier and the occasional cry of a seagull, until in the distance he heard the vibration of an outboard motor. A few minutes later he saw the boat, a white fleck between the dark banks of forest, a toy that grew steadily until it was pulling up alongside the pier, the motor obscenely loud in all that quiet, wake splashing against pylons. The woman at the stern looked to be in her mid-twenties and wore a crisp, vaguely nautical uniform.

"You must be Walter." She disembarked in a single fluid motion and lashed the boat to the dock. "I'm Melissa from the hotel. May I help with your bags?"

"Thank you," he said. There was something startling about her, an air of apparition. He was almost happy, he realized, as the boat pulled away from the pier. There was a cold wind on his face, and he knew this was a voyage of no more than fifteen minutes, but he had an absurd sense of embarking on an adventure. They were moving so rapidly, darkness falling. He wanted to ask Melissa about the hotel, how long she'd been here, but the motor was prohibitively loud. When he glanced over his shoulder, the wake was a silver trail leading back to the scattered lights of Grace Harbour.

Melissa piloted them around the peninsula and the hotel was before them, an improbable palace lit up against the darkness of the forest, and for the first time Walter understood what Raphael had meant when he'd talked about an element of surrealism. The building would have been beautiful anywhere, but placed here, it was incongruous, and its incongruity played a part in the enchantment. The lobby was exposed like an aquarium behind a wall of glass, all cedar pillars and slate floors. A double row of lights illuminated the path to the pier, where a doorman—Larry—met them with a trolley. Walter shook Larry's hand and followed his luggage up the path to the hotel's grand entrance, to the reception desk, where Raphael stood waiting with a concierge smile. After introductions, dinner, and paperwork, Walter eventually found himself in a suite on the top floor of the staff lodge, whose windows and terrace looked out into trees. He closed the curtains against the darkness and thought about what Raphael had said, about the hotel's existing outside of time and space. There's such happiness in a successful escape.

By the end of his first year in Caiette, Walter realized that he was happier here than he'd ever been anywhere, but in the hours following the graffiti, the forest outside seemed newly dark, the shadows dense and freighted with menace. Who stepped out of the forest to write the message on the window? *The message was written backwards on the glass,* Walter wrote on the incident report, *which suggests it was meant to be viewed from the lobby.*

"I appreciate the clarity of the report," Raphael said when Walter came to his office the following afternoon. Raphael had lived twenty years in English Canada but retained a strong Quebec City accent. "Some of your colleagues, I ask for a report and they hand in a dog's breakfast of typos and wild speculations."

"Thank you." Walter valued this job more than he'd ever valued anything and was always vastly relieved when Raphael praised his performance. "The graffiti's unsettling, isn't it?"

"I agree. Just this side of threat."

"Is there anything on the surveillance footage?"

"Nothing very useful. I can show you if you'd like." Raphael swivelled the monitor toward Walter and pressed play on a black-and-white video clip. Security footage of the front terrace at night, cast in the spooky luminescence of the camera's night-vision mode: A figure appears from the shadows at the edge of the terrace, wearing dark pants and an oversized sweat-shirt with a hood. His head is down—or is it a woman? Impossible to tell—and there's something in the gloved hand: the acid marker that defaces the glass. The ghost steps gracefully up onto a bench, scrawls the message, and melts back into the shadows, never looking up, the entire vision transpiring in less than ten seconds.

"It's like he practised it," Walter said.

"What do you mean?"

"Just, he writes it so quickly. And he's writing backwards. Or she. I can't tell."

Raphael nodded. "Is there anything else you can tell me about last night," he said, "that might not have appeared in the report?"

"What do you mean?"

"Anything at all out of the ordinary in the lobby. Any strange details. Something you maybe thought not relevant."

Walter hesitated.

"Tell me."

"Well, I don't like to rat on my colleagues," Walter said, "but it seemed to me that the night houseman was behaving strangely."

The night houseman, Paul, was Vincent's brother—no, Vincent had said he was her half brother, but Walter was unclear on which parent they had in common—and he'd been at the hotel for three months. He'd been living in Vancouver for five or six years but he'd grown up in Toronto, he told Walter, which should have created a bond but didn't, in part because he and Paul were from different Torontos. They tried to compare favourite Toronto restaurants and nightclubs, but Walter had never heard of System Soundbar, whereas Paul had never heard of Zelda's. Paul's Toronto was younger, more anarchic, a Toronto that danced to the beat of music that Walter neither liked nor understood, a Toronto that wore peculiar fashions and did drugs that Walter had never heard of. ("Well, but you know why the raver kids wear soothers around their necks," Paul said, "it's not just bad fashion sense, it's because K makes you grind your teeth," and Walter nodded knowledgeably without having the slightest idea of what "K" was.) Paul never smiled. He did his job well enough but had a way of drifting off into little reveries while cleaning the lobby at night, staring at nothing while he mopped the floor or polished tabletops. It was sometimes necessary to say his name two or three times, but any sharpness in tone in the second or third repetition would trigger a reproachful, wounded expression. Walter found him to be an irritating and somewhat depressing presence.

On the night of the graffiti, Paul returned from his dinner break at three-thirty a.m. He came in through the side door, and Walter looked up in time to see the way Paul's gaze fell immediately to the awkwardly placed philodendron and then to Leon Prevant, the shipping executive, who by then was on his second whisky and reading a two-day-old copy of the *Vancouver Sun*.

"Something happen to the window?" Paul asked as he passed the desk. To Walter's ear, there was something faux-casual about his tone.

"I'm afraid so," Walter said. "Some extremely nasty graffiti."

Paul's eyes widened. "Did Mr. Alkaitis see it?"

"Who?"

"You know." Paul nodded toward Leon Prevant.

"That isn't Alkaitis." Walter was watching Paul closely. He was flushed and looked even more miserable than usual.

"I thought it was."

"Alkaitis's flight was delayed. You didn't see anyone lurking around outside, did you?"

"Lurking around?"

"Anything suspicious. This just happened in the last hour."

"Oh. No." Paul wasn't looking at him anymore—another irritating trait; why did he always look away when Walter was talking?—and was staring at Leon, who was staring at the window. "I'm going to go see if Vincent needs the kegs changed," he said.

"What was unusual?" Raphael asked.

"Inquiring about guests like that. How would he even know who was checking in that night?"

"It's not the worst thing for a houseman to take a look at the guest list, familiarize himself with the lay of the land. Just playing devil's advocate."

"Okay, sure, I'll give you that. But then, the way he looked straight to that point on the glass when he walked in, straight at the potted plant. I just don't think the philodendron was that obvious," Walter said.

"It is obviously out of place, to my eye."

"But is it the first thing you look at? Especially at night? You walk into the lobby from the side door, at night, you look past the double row of pillars, past the armchairs and the side tables, halfway down the glass wall . . ."

"He does clean the lobby," Raphael said. "He'd know better than anyone where the potted plants go."

"I'm not accusing him of anything, to be clear. It's just something I noticed."

"I understand. I'll speak with him. Was there anything else?"

"Nothing. The rest of the shift was completely normal."

The rest of the shift:

By four a.m., Leon Prevant was beginning to yawn. Paul was somewhere back in the heart of the house, mopping floors in the staff corridors. Walter had finished his report and gone through his checklist. He was gazing out into the lobby, trying not to think too much about the graffiti. (What does *Why don't you swallow broken glass* signify, if not *I hope you die*?) Larry was standing by the door with his eyes half-open. Walter wanted to wander over and talk to him, but he knew Larry used the quiet hours to meditate, and that when his eyes were half-open, that meant he was counting breaths. Walter considered going to talk to Vincent, but it wouldn't look right for the night manager to linger by the bar while a guest was present, so he settled for a leisurely inspection of the lobby. He straightened a framed photograph by the fireplace, ran a fingertip over the bookshelves to check for dust, adjusted the leaves of the philodendron so that they better covered the paper taped to the glass. He stepped out for a moment into the cool night air, listening for a boat that he knew was not yet en route.

At four-thirty Leon Prevant rose and drifted toward the elevator, yawning. Twenty minutes later, Jonathan Alkaitis arrived. Walter heard the boat long before it came into view, as always, the motor violently loud in the stillness of night, and then the lights on the stern swung over the water as the boat rounded the peninsula. Larry set off for the pier with a luggage trolley. Vincent put away the newspaper she'd been reading, adjusted her hair, reapplied lipstick, and took two quick shots of espresso. Walter put on his warmest professional smile as Jonathan Alkaitis walked in behind his luggage.

In later years Walter was interviewed three or four times about Jonathan Alkaitis, but the journalists always left disappointed. As a hotel manager, he told them, he lived and died by his discretion, but in truth there wasn't much to tell. Alkaitis was interesting only in retrospect. He'd come to the Hotel Caiette with his wife, now deceased. He and his wife had fallen in love with the place, so when it'd come up for sale, he'd bought the property, which he leased to the hotel's management company. He lived in New York City and came to the hotel three or four times a year. He carried himself with the tedious confidence of all people with money, that breezy assumption that no serious harm could come to him. He was generically well dressed, tanned in the manner of people who spend time in tropical settings in the wintertime, reasonably but not spectacularly fit, unremarkable in every way. Nothing about him, in other words, suggested that he would die in prison.

The best suite had been set aside for him, as always. He was absurdly jet-lagged, he told Walter, and also quite hungry. Could an early breakfast be arranged? (Of course. For Alkaitis, anything could be arranged.) It was still dark outside, but day broke in the kitchen long before sunrise. The morning shift would be arriving by now.

"I'll just take a seat at the bar," Alkaitis said, and within minutes was deep in conversation with Vincent, who was, it seemed to Walter, at her brightest and most engaging, although he couldn't quite make out what they were talking about.

3

Leon Prevant left the lobby at four-thirty a.m., climbed the stairs to his room, and crept into the bed, where his wife was sleeping. Marie didn't wake up. He'd purposefully drunk one whisky too many with the thought that this might make it possible to fall asleep, but it was as if the graffiti had opened a crack in the night, through which all his fears flooded in. If pressed he might have admitted to Marie that he was worried about money, but *worried* wasn't strong enough. Leon was afraid.

A colleague had told him this place was extraordinary, so he'd booked an extremely expensive room as an anniversary surprise for his wife. His colleague was right, he'd decided immediately. There were fishing and kayaking expeditions, guided hikes into wilderness, live music in the lobby, spectacular food, a wooded path that opened into a forest glade with an outdoor bar and lanterns hung from trees, a heated pool overlooking the tranquil waters of the sound.

"It's heavenly," Marie said on their first night.

"I'm inclined to agree."

He'd sprung for a room with a hot tub on the terrace, and that first night they were out there for at least an hour, sipping champagne with a cool breeze in their faces, the sun setting over the water in a postcard kind of way. He kissed her and tried to convince himself to relax. But relaxation was difficult, because a week after he'd booked this extravagant room and told his wife about it, he'd begun to hear rumours of a pending merger.

Leon had survived two mergers and a reorganization, but when he heard the first whispers of this latest restructuring, he was struck by a certainty so strong that it felt like true knowledge: he was going to lose his job. He was fifty-eight years old. He was senior enough to be expensive, and close enough to retirement to be let go without weighing too heavily on anyone's conscience. There was no part of his job that couldn't be performed by younger executives who made less money than he did. Since hearing of the merger he'd lived whole hours without thinking about it, but the nights were harder than the days. He and Marie had just bought a house in South Florida, which they planned to rent out until he retired, with the idea of eventually fleeing New York winters and New York taxes. This seemed to him to be a new beginning, but they'd spent more money on the house than they'd meant to, he had never been very good at saving, and he was aware that he had much less in his retirement accounts than he should. It was six-thirty in the morning before he fell into a fitful sleep.

4

When Walter returned to the lobby the following evening, Leon Prevant was eating dinner at the bar with Jonathan Alkaitis. They'd met a little earlier, in what seemed at the time like a coincidental manner and seemed later like a trap. Leon had been at the bar, eating a salmon burger, alone because Marie was lying down upstairs with a headache. Alkaitis, who was drinking a pint of Guinness two stools down, struck up a conversation with the bartender and then expanded the conversation to include Leon. They were talking about Caiette, which, as it happened, Jonathan Alkaitis knew something about. "I actually own this property," he said to Leon, almost apologetically. "It's hard to get to, but that's what I like about it."

"I think I know what you mean," Leon said. He was always looking for conversations, and it was a pleasure to think about something—anything!—other than financial insolvency and unemployment for a moment. "Do you own other hotels?"

"Just the one. I mostly work in finance." Alkaitis had a couple of businesses in New York, he said, both of which involved investing other people's money in the stock market for them. He wasn't really taking on new clients these days, but he did on occasion make an exception.

The thing about Alkaitis, a woman from Philadelphia wrote some years later, in a victim impact statement that she read aloud at Alkaitis's sentencing hearing, *is he made you feel like you were joining a secret club.* There was truth in this, Leon had to admit, when he read the transcript, but the other part of the equation was the man himself. What Alkaitis had was presence. He had a voice made for late-night radio, warm and reassuring. He radiated calm. He was a man utterly without bluster, confident but not arrogant, quick to smile at jokes. A steady, low-key, intelligent person, much more interested in listening than in talking about himself. He had that trick—and it was a trick, Leon realized later—of appearing utterly indifferent to what anyone thought of him, and in so doing provoking the opposite anxiety in other people: *What does Alkaitis think of me?* Later, in the years that he spent replaying this particular evening, Leon remembered a certain desire to impress him.

"This is slightly embarrassing," Alkaitis said that night, when they'd left the bar and retired to a quieter corner of the lobby to discuss investments, "but you said you're in shipping, and I realized as you said it that I've only the dimmest idea of what that actually means."

Leon smiled. "You're not alone in that. It's a largely invisible industry, but nearly everything you've ever bought travelled over the water."

"My made-in-China headphones, and whatnot."

"Sure, yes, there's an obvious one, but I really mean almost everything. Everything on and around us. Your socks. Our shoes. My aftershave. This glass in my hand. I could keep going, but I'll spare you."

"I'm embarrassed to admit that I never thought about it," Jonathan said.

"No one does. You go to the store, you buy a banana, you don't think about the men who piloted the banana through the Panama Canal. Why would you?" *Easy now,* he told himself. He was aware of a weakness for rhapsodizing on his industry at excessive length. "I have colleagues who resent the general public's ignorance of the industry, but I think the fact that you don't have to think about it proves that the whole system works."

"The banana arrives on schedule." Jonathan sipped his drink. "You must develop a kind of sixth sense. Here you are in the world, surrounded by all these objects that arrived by ship. You ever find it distracting, thinking about all those shipping routes, all those points of origin?"

"You're only the second person I've ever met who guessed that," Leon said.

The other was a psychic, a college friend of Marie's who'd come into Toronto from Santa Fe, back when Leon was still based in Toronto, and the three of them had had dinner downtown at Saint Tropez, Marie's favourite restaurant in their Toronto years. The psychic—Clarissa, he remembered now— was friendly and warm. He liked her immediately. He had an impression that psychics must very often be exploited by their friends and passing acquaintances, an impression not dispelled by Marie's reminiscences about all the times she'd asked Clarissa for free advice, so over the course of the evening Leon went elaborately out of his way to avoid asking her anything, until finally, over dessert, curiosity overtook him: Was it ever deafening, he asked her, being in a crowded room? Was it like being in a room filled with radios tuned to overlapping frequencies, a clamour of voices broadcasting the mundane or horrifying details of dozens of lives? Clarissa smiled. "It's like this," she said, gesturing at the room around them, "it's like being in a crowded restaurant. You can tune in to the conversation at the next table, or you can let that become background noise. Like the way you see shipping," she said, and this remained in memory as one of the most delightful conversations Leon had ever had, because he'd never talked with anyone about the way he could tune in and out of shipping, like turning a dial on a radio. When he glanced across the table at Marie, for example: he could see the woman he loved, or he could shift frequencies and see the dress made in the U.K., the shoes made in China, the Italian leather handbag, or shift even further and see the Neptune-Avramidis shipping routes lit up on the map: the dress via Westbound Trans-Atlantic Route 3, the shoes via either the Trans-Pacific Eastbound 7 or the Shanghai–Los Angeles Eastbound Express, etc. Or further still, into the kind of language he'd never speak aloud, not even to Marie: there are tens of thousands of ships at sea at any given moment and he liked to imagine each one as a point of light, converging into rivers of electric brilliance over the night oceans, flowing through the narrow channels of the Suez and Panama Canals, the Strait of Gibraltar, around the edges of continents and out into the oceans, an unceasing movement that drove countries, a secret world that he loved so much.

When Walter walked within earshot of Leon Prevant and Jonathan Alkaitis, some time later, the conversation had shifted from Leon's work to Alkaitis's, from shipping to investment strategies. Walter understood none of it. Finance wasn't his world. He didn't speak the language. Someone on the day shift had covered the graffiti on the glass with reflective tape, an odd silvery streak of mirror on the darkened window. Two American actors were eating dinner at the bar.

"He left his first wife for her," Larry said, nodding at them.

"Oh?" said Walter, who could not possibly have cared less. Twenty years of working in high-end hotels had cured him of any interest in celebrity. "I wanted to ask you," he said, "just between the two of us, does the new guy seem a little off to you?"

Larry glanced theatrically over his shoulder and around the

lobby, but Paul was elsewhere, mopping the corridor behind Reception in the heart of the house.

"Maybe a little depressed, is all," Larry said. "Not the most sparkling personality I've ever come across."

"Did he ask you about arriving guests last night?"

"How'd you know? Yeah, asked me when Jonathan Alkaitis was arriving."

"And you told him . . . ?"

"Well, you know my eyesight's not great, and I'd only just come on shift. So I told him I wasn't completely sure, but I thought the guy drinking whisky in the lobby was Alkaitis. Didn't realize my mistake till later. Why?" Larry was a reasonably discreet man, but on the other hand, the staff lived together in the same building in the woods and gossip was a kind of black-market currency.

"No reason."

"Come on."

"I'll tell you later." Walter still didn't understand the motive, as he walked back toward Reception, but there was no doubt in his mind that Paul had committed the act. He glanced around the lobby, but no one seemed to require his attention at that moment, so he slipped through the staff door behind the reception desk. Paul was cleaning the dark window at the end of the hall.

"Paul."

The night houseman stopped what he was doing, and in his expression, Walter knew that he'd been correct in his suspicions. Paul had a hunted look.

"Where'd you get the acid marker?" Walter asked. "Is that something you can just buy at a hardware store, or did you have to make it yourself?"

"What are you talking about?" But Paul was a terrible liar. His voice had gone up half an octave.

"Why did you want Jonathan Alkaitis to see that disgusting message?"

"I don't know what you mean."

"This place means something to me," Walter said. "Seeing it defaced like that . . ." It was the *like that* that bothered him the most, the utter vileness of the message on the glass, but he didn't know how to explain this to Paul without opening a door into his personal life, and the thought of revealing anything remotely personal to this shiftless little creep was untenable. He couldn't finish the sentence. He cleared his throat. "I'd like to give you an opportunity," he said. "Pack up your things and leave on the first boat, and we don't have to get the police involved."

"I'm sorry." Paul's voice was a whisper. "I just—"

"You just thought you'd deface a hotel window, for the sake of delivering the most vicious, the most deranged—" Walter was sweating. "Why did you even do it?" But Paul had the furtive look of a boy searching for a plausible story, and Walter couldn't stand to listen to another lie that night. "Look, just go," he said. "I don't care why you did it. I don't want to look at you anymore. Put the cleaning supplies away, go back to your room, pack your bags, and tell Melissa that you want a ride to Grace Harbour as quickly as possible. If you're still here at nine a.m., I'll go to Raphael."

"You don't understand," Paul said. "I've got all this debt—"

"If you needed the job that badly," Walter said, "you probably shouldn't have defaced the window."

"You can't even swallow broken glass."

"What?"

"I mean it's actually physically impossible."

"Seriously? That's your defence?"

Paul flushed and looked away.

"Did you ever think of your sister in all of this?" Walter asked. "She got you the job interview here, didn't she?"

"Vincent had nothing to do with this."

"Are you going to leave? I'm in a generous mood and I don't want to embarrass your sister, so I'm giving you a clean exit here, but if you'd prefer a criminal record, then by all means . . ."

"No, I'll go." Paul looked down at the cleaning supplies in his hands, as if unsure how they'd landed there. "I'm sorry."

"You should go pack before I change my mind."

"Thank you," Paul said.

5

But the horror of it. *Why don't you swallow broken glass. Why don't you die. Why don't you cast everyone who loves you into perdition.* He was thinking about his friend Rob again, forever sixteen, thinking about Rob's mother's face at the funeral. Walter sleepwalked through the rest of his shift and stayed up late to meet with Raphael in the morning. As he passed through the lobby at eight a.m., up past his bedtime and desperate for sleep, he caught sight of Paul down at the end of the pier, loading his duffel bags into the boat.

"Good morning," Raphael said when Walter looked into his office. He was bright-eyed and freshly shaved. He and Walter lived in the same building, but in opposite time zones.

"I just saw Paul getting on the boat with his worldly belongings," Walter said.

Raphael sighed. "I don't know what happened. He came in here this morning with an incoherent story about how much he misses Vancouver, when the kid practically begged me for a change of scenery three months back."

"He gave no reason?"

"None. We'll start interviewing again. Anything else?" Raphael asked, and Walter, his defences weakened by exhaustion, understood for the first time that Raphael didn't like him very much. The realization landed with a sad little thud.

"No," he said, "thank you. I'll leave you to it." On the walk back to the staff lodge, he found himself wishing that he'd been less angry when he'd spoken with Paul. All these hours later, he was beginning to wonder if he'd missed the point: when Paul said he had debts, did he mean that he needed the job at the hotel, or was he saying that someone had paid him to write the message on the glass? Because none of it actually made sense. It seemed obvious that Paul's message was directed at Alkaitis, but what could Alkaitis possibly mean to him?

Leon Prevant and his wife departed that morning, followed two days later by Jonathan Alkaitis. When Walter came in for his shift on the night of Alkaitis's departure, Khalil was working the bar, although it wasn't his usual night: Vincent, he said, had taken a sudden vacation. A day later she called Raphael from Vancouver and told him she'd decided not to come back to the hotel, so someone from Housekeeping boxed up her belongings and put them in storage at the back of the laundry room.

The panel of glass was replaced at enormous expense, and the graffiti receded into memory. Spring passed into summer and then the beautiful chaos of the high season, the lobby crowded every night and a temperamental jazz quartet causing drama in the staff lodge when they weren't delighting the guests, the quartet alternating with a pianist whose marijuana habit was tolerated because he could seemingly play any song ever written, the hotel fully booked and the staff almost doubled, Melissa piloting the boat back and forth to Grace Harbour all day and late into the evening.

Summer faded into autumn, then the quiet and the dark of the winter months, the rainstorms more frequent, the hotel half-empty, the staff quarters growing quiet with the departure of the seasonal workers. Walter slept through the days and arrived at his shift in the early evenings—the pleasure of long nights in the silent lobby, Larry by the door, Khalil at the bar, storms descending and rising throughout the night—and sometimes joined his colleagues for a meal that was dinner for the night shift and breakfast for the day people, shared a few drinks sometimes with the kitchen staff, listened to jazz alone in his apartment, went for walks in and out of Caiette, ordered books in the mail that he read when he woke in the late afternoons.

On a stormy night in spring, Ella Kaspersky checked in. She was a regular at the hotel, a businesswoman from Chicago who liked to come here to escape "all the noise," as she put it, a guest who was mostly notable because Jonathan Alkaitis had made it clear that he didn't want to see her. Walter had no idea why Alkaitis was avoiding Kaspersky and frankly didn't want to know, but when she arrived he did his customary check to make sure Alkaitis hadn't made a last-minute booking. Alkaitis hadn't visited the hotel in some time, he realized, longer than his usual interval between visits. When the lobby was quiet at two a.m., he ran a Google search on Alkaitis and found images from a recent charity fundraiser, Alkaitis beaming in a tuxedo with a younger woman on his arm. She looked very familiar.

Walter enlarged the photo. The woman was Vincent. A glossier version, with an expensive haircut and professional-grade makeup, but it was unmistakably her. She was wearing a metallic gown that must have cost about what she'd made in a month as a bartender here. The caption read *Jonathan Alkaitis with his wife, Vincent.*

Walter looked up from the screen, into the silent lobby. Nothing in his life had changed in the year since Vincent's departure, but this was by his own design and his own desire. Khalil, now the full-time night bartender, was chatting with a couple who'd just arrived. Larry stood by the door with his hands clasped behind his back, eyes half-closed. Walter abandoned his post and walked out into the April night. He hoped Vincent was happy in that foreign country, in whatever strange new life she'd found for herself. He tried to imagine what it might be like to step into Jonathan Alkaitis's life—the money, the houses, the private jet—but it was all incomprehensible to him. The night was clear and cold, moonless but the blaze of stars was overwhelming. Walter wouldn't have imagined, in his previous life in downtown Toronto, that he'd fall in love with a place where the stars were so bright that he could see his shadow on a night with no moon. He wanted nothing that he didn't already have.

But when he turned back to the hotel he was blindsided by the memory of the words written on the window a year ago, *Why don't you swallow broken glass,* the whole unsettling mystery of it. The forest was a mass of undifferentiated shadow. He folded his arms against the chill and returned to the warmth and light of the lobby.

4

A FAIRY TALE

2005–2008

Swan Dive

Sanity depends on order. Within a month of leaving the Hotel Caiette and arriving in Jonathan Alkaitis's absurdly enormous house in the Connecticut suburbs, Vincent had established a routine from which she seldom wavered. She rose at five a.m., a half hour earlier than Jonathan, and went jogging. By the time she returned to his house, he'd left for Manhattan. She was showered and dressed for the day by eight a.m., by which point Jonathan's driver was available to take her to the train station—he repeatedly offered to drive her to the city, but she preferred the movement of trains to gridlocked traffic—and when she emerged into Grand Central Terminal she liked to linger for a while on her way across the main concourse, taking in the constellations of stars on the green ceiling, the Tiffany clock above the information booth, the crowds. She usually had breakfast at a diner near the station, then made her way south toward lower Manhattan and a particular café where she liked to drink espresso and read newspapers, after which she went shopping or got her hair done or walked the streets with her video camera or some combination thereof, and if there was time she visited the Metropolitan Museum of Art for a while before she made her way back to Grand Central and a northbound train, in time to be home and dressed in something beautiful by six p.m., which was the earliest Jonathan would conceivably arrive home from the office.

She spent the evening with Jonathan but always found a half hour to go swimming at some point before bed. In the kingdom of money, as she thought of it, there were enormous swaths of time to fill, and she had intimations of danger in letting herself drift, in allowing a day to pass without a schedule or a plan.

"People clamour to move into Manhattan," Jonathan said when she asked why they couldn't just live in his pied-à-terre on Columbus Circle, where they stayed sometimes when they had theatre tickets, "but I like being a little outside of it all." He'd grown up in the suburbs, and had always loved the tranquility and the space.

"I see your point," Vincent said, but the city drew her in, the city was the antidote to the riotous green of her childhood memories. She wanted concrete and clean lines and sharp angles, sky visible only between towers, hard light.

"Anyway, you wouldn't be happy living in Manhattan," Jonathan said. "Think of how much you'd miss the pool."

Would she miss the pool? She reflected on the question as she swam. Her relationship with the pool was adversarial. Vincent swam every night to strengthen her will because she was desperately afraid of drowning.

Diving into the pool at night: in summer Vincent dove through the lights of the house, reflected on the surface; in cold weather the pool was heated, so she dove into steam. She stayed under-water for as long as possible, testing her endurance. When she finally surfaced, she liked to pretend that the ring on her finger was real and that everything she saw was hers: the house, the garden, the lawn, the pool in which she treaded water. It was an infinity pool, which created a disorienting impression that the water disappeared into the lawn or the lawn disappeared into the water. She hated looking at that edge.

Crowds

Her contract with Jonathan, as she understood it, was that she'd be available whenever he wanted her, in and out of the bedroom, she would be elegant and impeccable at all times—"You bring such grace to the room," he'd said—and in return for this she had a credit card whose bills she never saw, a life of beautiful homes and travel, in other words the opposite of the life she'd lived before. No one actually uses the phrase *trophy wife* in conversation, but Jonathan was thirty-four years older than Vincent. She understood what she was.

There were adjustments to be made. At first, living in Jonathan Alkaitis's house was like those dreams where you find a door in your kitchen that you never noticed before, and then the door leads into a back hallway that opens up into a never-used au pair's suite, which opens into an unused nursery, which is down the corridor from the master bedroom suite, which is larger than your entire childhood home, and then later you realize that there's a way of getting from the bedroom to the kitchen without ever setting foot in either of the two living rooms or the downstairs hall.

In her hotel days, Vincent had always associated money with privacy—the wealthiest hotel guests have the most space around them, suites instead of rooms, private terraces, access to executive lounges—but in actuality, the deeper you go into the kingdom of money, the more crowded it gets, people around you in your home all the time, which was why Vincent only swam at night. In the daytime there was the house manager, Gil, who lived with his wife, Anya, in a cottage by the driveway; Anya, who was the cook, supervised three young local women who kept the house clean and did laundry and accepted grocery deliveries and such; there was also a chauffeur, who had an apartment over the garage, and a silent groundskeeper, who maintained everything outside of the house. Every time Vincent looked up, someone was nearby, sweeping or dusting or talking on the phone to the plumber or trimming a hedge. It was a lot of people to contend with, but at night the staff retreated into their private lives and Vincent could swim in peace without feeling watched from every window.

"I'm glad you're enjoying the pool," Gil said. "The pool design consultant spent so much time on it, and I swear no one ever used it before you got here."

She was in the pool when she first met Jonathan's daughter, Claire. It was a cool evening in April, steam rising from the water. She'd known Claire was coming over that evening, but she hadn't expected to surface and find a woman in a suit staring at her through the steam like a goddamned apparition, standing perfectly still with her hands clasped behind her back. Vincent gasped aloud, which in retrospect wasn't endearing. Claire, who had obviously just come from the office, was a very corporate-looking woman in her late twenties.

"You must be Vincent." She picked up the folded towel that Vincent had left on a lawn chair and extended it in a get-out-of-the-pool kind of way, so Vincent felt that she had no choice but to climb the ladder and accept the towel, which was irritating because she'd wanted to swim for longer.

"You must be Claire."

Claire didn't dignify this with a response. Vincent was wearing a fairly modest one-piece swimsuit but felt extremely naked as she towelled off.

"Vincent's an unusual name for a girl," Claire said with a slight emphasis on *girl* that struck Vincent as uncalled-for. *I'm not that young*, Vincent wanted to tell her, because at twenty-four she didn't feel young at all, but Claire was possibly dangerous and Vincent hoped for peace, so she answered in the mildest tone possible.

"My parents named me after a poet. Edna St. Vincent Millay."

Claire's gaze flickered to the ring on Vincent's finger. "Well," she said, "we can't choose our parents, I suppose. What kind of work do they do?"

"My parents?"

"Yes."

"They're dead."

Claire's face softened a little. "I'm sorry to hear that." They stood staring at one another for a beat or two, then Vincent reached for the bathrobe that she'd left on a deck chair, and Claire said, sounding more resigned than angry now, "Did you know you're five years younger than me?"

"We can't choose our ages either," Vincent said.

"Ha." (Not a laugh, just a spoken word: *ha*.) "Well, we're all adults here. Just so you know, I find this situation absurd, but there's no reason we can't be cordial with one another." She turned away and walked back into the house.

Ghosts

Vincent's mother had read a lot of poetry, having formerly been a poet herself. When Edna St. Vincent Millay was nineteen years old, in 1912, she began writing a poem called "Renascence" that Vincent must have read a thousand times in childhood and adolescence. Millay wrote the poem for a competition. The poem didn't win, but it nonetheless carried an electric charge that transported her from the drudgery of New England poverty to Vassar College, from there into the kind of bohemia that she'd dreamed of all her life: a different kind of poverty, the Greenwich Village–variety, poverty but with late-night poetry readings and dashing friends.

"The point is she raised herself into a new life by sheer force of will," Vincent's mother had said, and Vincent wondered even at the time—she would have been about eleven—what that statement might suggest about how happy Vincent's mother was about the way her own life had gone, this woman who'd imagined writing poetry in the wilderness but somehow found herself sunk in the mundane difficulties of raising a child and running a household in the wilderness instead. There's the *idea* of wilderness, and then there's the unglamorous labour of it, the never-ending grind of securing firewood; bringing in groceries over absurd distances; tending the vegetable garden and maintaining the fences that keep the deer from eating all the vegetables; repairing the generator; remembering to get gas for the generator; composting; running out of water in the summertime; never having enough money because job opportunities in the wilderness are limited; managing the seething resentment of your only child, who doesn't understand your love of the wilderness and asks every week why you can't just live in a normal place that isn't wilderness; etc.

What Vincent's mother probably wouldn't have imagined: a life—an *arrangement*—in which Vincent wore a wedding ring but was not actually married. "I want you close," Jonathan said, at the beginning, "but I just don't want to get married again."

His wife, Suzanne, had died only three years earlier. They never said her name. But while he didn't want to marry Vincent, he did feel that wedding rings created an impression of stability. "In my line of work," he said, "managing other people's money, steadiness is everything. If I take you out to dinner with clients, it's better for you to be a beautiful young wife than a beautiful young girlfriend."

"Does Claire know we're not married?" Vincent asked the night Claire appeared by the pool. By the time Vincent had come in and showered, Claire had already left. She found Jonathan alone in the south living room with a glass of red wine and the *Financial Times*.

"Only two people in the world know that," he said. "You and me. Come here." Vincent came to stand before him in the lamplight. He ran his fingertips down the length of her arm, and then turned her around and slowly unzipped her dress.

But what kind of man lies to his daughter about being married? There were aspects of the fairy tale that Vincent was careful not to think about too much at the time, and later her memories of those years had an abstracted quality, as if she'd stepped temporarily outside of herself.

Accomplices

They had cocktails at a bar in Midtown with a couple who'd invested millions in Jonathan's fund, Marc and Louise from Colorado. At that point Vincent had only been in the kingdom of money for three weeks, and the strangeness of her new life was acute.

"This is Vincent," Jonathan said, his hand on her lower back.

"It's so lovely to meet you," Vincent said. Marc and Louise were in their forties or fifties, and after a few more months with Alkaitis she would come to recognize them as typical of a particular western subspecies of moneyed people: as wealthy as their counterparts in other regions, but prematurely weathered by their skiing obsession.

"It's so great to meet you," they said, and Louise caught sight of Vincent and Jonathan's rings in the round of handshakes. "Oh my goodness, Jonathan," she said, "are congratulations in order?"

"Thank you," he said, in such a convincing tone of bashful happiness that for a disorienting moment Vincent entertained the wild thought that they were somehow actually married.

"Well, cheers," Marc said, and raised his glass. "Congratulations to the both of you. Wonderful news, just wonderful."

"Can I ask . . . ?" Louise said. "Big wedding, small . . . ?"

"If we'd made any to-do about it at all," Jonathan said, "you'd have been the first names on the guest list."

"Would you believe," Vincent said, "that we actually got married at city hall?"

"Good lord," Marc said, and Louise said, "I like your style. Donna's getting married—that's our daughter—and my god, the logistics, the complications, all the drama, the *headache* of it, I'm tempted to suggest they follow your lead and elope."

"There's a certain efficiency to elopement," Jonathan said. "Weddings are such elaborate affairs. We just didn't want all the hoopla."

"I had to convince him to take the day off work," Vincent said. "He wanted to just go down there on his lunch break." They were laughing, and Jonathan put his arm around her. She could tell he appreciated the improvisation.

"Was there a honeymoon?" Marc asked.

"I'm taking her to Nice next week, and then on to Dubai for the weekend," Jonathan said.

"Ah, right," Marc said, "I remember you telling me that you love it there. Vincent, have you been?"

"To Dubai? No, not yet. I can't wait." And so on and so forth. She didn't want to be a liar but his expectations were clear. As a former bartender, she was accustomed to performing. The lies were troublingly easy. On the night when Jonathan had walked into the bar at the Hotel Caiette, someone had written terrible graffiti on the window, and she was standing there polishing glasses, counting the minutes till the end of her shift, wondering why she'd ever thought it was a good idea to come back here, trying to imagine the rest of her life and getting nowhere because of course she could leave and go work in another bar, and then another bar after that, and another, and another, but leaving Caiette wouldn't change the underlying equation. The problems of Vincent's life were the same from one year to the next: she knew she was a reasonably intelligent person, but there's a difference between being intelligent and knowing what to do with your life, also a difference between knowing that a college degree might change your life and a willingness to actually commit to the terrifying weight of student loans, especially since she'd worked alongside enough bartenders with college degrees to know that a college degree might not change anything at all, etc., etc., and she was spiralling through that familiar territory, sick of her thoughts and sick of herself, when Jonathan walked into the bar. In the way he spoke to her, his obvious wealth and his obvious interest, she saw an opening into a vastly easier life, or at least a *different* life, a chance to live in a foreign country, a life of something other than bartending in a place other than here, and the opportunity was irresistible.

Lying about being married troubled her conscience, but not enough to make her want to flee. *I'm paying a price for this life,* she told herself, *but the price is reasonable.*

Variations

Jonathan never talked about Suzanne, his real wife, but the past wasn't entirely off the table. Sometimes in a certain mood he liked to hear stories about Vincent's life. She doled them out carefully: "When I was thirteen," she told him once, lying in the bed on a Sunday morning, "I dyed my hair blue and got suspended from school for writing graffiti on a window."

"Really. What did you write?"

"Would you believe I wrote a philosopher's last words? I came across them in a book somewhere and loved them."

"Precocious, but morbid," he said. "I'm afraid to ask."

"*Sweep me up.* It has a certain beauty, don't you think?"

"Maybe if you're a temperamental thirteen-year-old girl," he said, so she threw a pillow at him. She didn't tell him that her mother had died two weeks earlier, or that her brother had been lurking around and saw her do it, or that she had a brother. It is possible to leave so much out of any given story.

Also, it wasn't *morbidity,* she found herself thinking on the train into the city the following afternoon. It was almost the opposite. She'd never had a clear vision of what she wanted her life to look like, she had always been directionless, but she did know that she wanted to be swept up, to be plucked from the crowd, and then when it happened, when Jonathan extended a hand and she took it, when she went in the space of a week from the mildew-plagued staff quarters of the Hotel Caiette to an enormous house in a foreign country, she was surprised by how disorienting it was, and then surprised by her surprise. She got off the train at Grand Central and let herself be absorbed into the flow of pedestrian traffic down Lexington Avenue. *How have I come to this foreign planet, so far from home?* But it wasn't just the place, it wasn't even mostly the place, it was mostly the money that made it foreign and strange. She wandered over to Fifth Avenue with no particular destination in mind, and walked until a pair of buttery yellow leather gloves in a window caught her eye. Everything in the shop was gorgeous, but the yellow gloves shone with a special light. She tried them on and bought them without looking at the price tag, because in the age of money her credit card was a magical, weightless thing.

She left the boutique with the gloves in her handbag and found her thoughts drifting a little as she walked. Her life in those days was so disorienting that she often found herself thinking about variations on reality, different permutations of events: an alternate reality where she'd quit working at the Hotel Caiette and returned to her old job at the Hotel Vancouver before Jonathan arrived, for example, or where he decided to get room service that morning instead of sitting at the bar and ordering breakfast, or where he did sit at the bar and order breakfast but he didn't like Vincent; an alternate reality where she still lived in the staff quarters of the Hotel Caiette, serving drinks to wealthy tourists all night, years passing. None of these scenarios seemed less real than the life she'd landed in, so much so that she was struck sometimes by a truly unsettling sense that there were other versions of her life being lived without her, other Vincents engaged in different events.

She'd read newspapers all her life, because she felt that she was desperately undereducated and wanted to be an informed and knowledgeable person, but in the age of money she would often read a news story and find herself uneasily distracted by its opposite: Imagining an alternate reality where there was no Iraq War, for example, or where the terrifying new swine flu in the Republic of Georgia hadn't been swiftly contained; an alternate world where the Georgia flu blossomed into an unstoppable pandemic and civilization collapsed. A variation of reality where North Korea hadn't fired test missiles, where the terrorist bombings in London hadn't happened, where the Israeli prime minister hadn't suffered a stroke. Or spin it back further: a version of history where the Korean peninsula was never divided, where the USSR had never invaded Afghanistan and al-Qaeda had never been founded, where Ariel Sharon died in combat as a young man. She could only play this game for so long before she was overcome by a kind of vertigo and had to make herself stop.

Shield

One of the first things she bought was an expensive video camera, a Canon HV10. She'd been shooting video since she was thirteen, a few days after her mother disappeared, when her grandmother Caroline arrived from Victoria to help out. That first night of her grandmother's visit, when Vincent was sitting at the table after dinner—drinking tea, which was a habit she'd picked up from her mother, and staring down the hill at the water because surely any minute now her mother would walk up the steps to the house—her grandmother brought a box to the table.

"I have something for you," she said.

Vincent opened it and found a video camera, a Panasonic. She recognized it as one of the new kind that took DV tapes, but it still had an unexpected weight. She wasn't sure what she was supposed to do with it.

"When I was younger," Caroline said, "say maybe twenty-one, twenty-two, I went through a difficult time."

"What kind of difficult time?" It was the first thing Vincent had said in some hours, maybe all day. The words were sticky in her throat.

"The details aren't very important. A friend of mine, a photographer, she gave me a camera she no longer needed. She said to me, 'Just take some pictures, take pictures every day, see if it makes you feel better.' It seemed like a dumb idea, to be honest, but I tried it, and I did feel better."

"I don't think—" Vincent said, but couldn't finish the sentence. *I don't think a camera will bring my mother back.*

"What I'm suggesting," Caroline said softly, "is that the lens can function as a shield between you and the world, when the world's just a little too much to bear. If you can't stand to look at the world directly, maybe it's possible to look at it through the viewfinder. I think your brother would laugh at me if I said something like this to him, but maybe you could just try to absorb the idea."

Vincent was quiet, considering it.

"I was going to buy you a thirty-five-millimetre film camera," Caroline said with a self-conscious little laugh, "but then I thought, it's 1994, do kids even take still photos anymore? Surely video's where it's at?"

Vincent settled quickly into a form she liked. She recorded segments of exactly five minutes each, like little portraits: five minutes of beach and sky by the pier at Caiette, and then later there were five-minute clips of the quiet street where she lived with her aunt in Vancouver's endless suburbs, five minutes from the window of the SkyTrain on her way into the city centre, five minutes of the fascinating, appalling neighbourhood where she lived with Melissa when she was seventeen—not in the film: the way she had to take off running down the street because an addict wanted her camera—and five-minute clips of the dish pit at the Hotel Vancouver that same year, the camera rigged in a plastic bag on a shelf with a timer while Vincent sprayed dishes with hot water and fed them into an industrial machine. Five-minute increments of Caiette again, and then— after she met Jonathan—five minutes of the infinity pool at the Greenwich house, the way it rippled into the lawn, precisely because she hated looking at that vanishing point and was trying to be stronger; five minutes from the window of Jonathan's private jet the first time she crossed the Atlantic, a few ships far below in the steel-grey water, no visible land. "What are you doing?" Jonathan asked, startling her. He'd been sitting in the back of the plane with Yvette Bertolli, a formidably elegant associate of his who was coming to France with them; she lived in Paris, so Jonathan was giving her a ride as far as Nice, where he had a villa. Vincent, sunk into an enormous armchair by the window, had thought she was momentarily alone.

"Kind of beautiful, don't you think?" Vincent said.

Jonathan leaned over her to peer down at the distant waves. "You're shooting video of the ocean?"

"Everyone needs a hobby."

"Just when you think you know a woman," he said, and kissed her head.

Shadows

Jonathan had a shadow. He introduced the topic a few hours after they arrived at the villa in Nice, when they were sitting together on the terrace in the late afternoon. It was only early spring but already warm here, a pleasant breeze coming in from the sea. Vincent was dazed and jet-lagged, trying to cover this with coffee and the eye drops that she'd applied in the bathroom earlier. Yvette, Jonathan's associate, had discreetly retired to a guest bedroom, so Vincent and Jonathan were alone. The view was of palm trees and then the otherworldly blue of the sea, oddly familiar after all the movies she'd seen set around the Mediterranean, most of which had involved fast cars, gamblers, and/or James Bond. Jonathan was in a contemplative mood. "This will seem an obvious statement," he said, "but success attracts a certain kind of attention."

"Positive, or negative?"

"Well, both," he said, "but I'm thinking of the negative kind."

"Are you thinking of a particular person?" A door opened behind them, and Anya appeared on the terrace with two coffee cups on a little silver tray. Vincent was startled to see her, because she hadn't realized Anya was coming to France, although it occurred to her that she hadn't seen Anya around the house in Greenwich in the last couple of days. "Thank you," Vincent said to Anya, "I desperately needed that." Anya nodded. Jonathan took his coffee from the tray without comment, because for him, coffee appearing out of thin air was so commonplace an occurrence that it didn't merit acknowledgement.

"Yes," he said. "There is a particular person. A particular obsessive."

He'd met Ella Kaspersky back in 1999, at, of all places, the Hotel Caiette. They'd had a conversation about Kaspersky's possibly investing with him, but she'd concluded—without basis, obviously—that the sheer consistency of Jonathan's returns was indicative of some kind of nefarious fraud scheme. Completely illogical and unfair, delusional even, but what could he do? People jump to their own conclusions.

"I'd think good returns would be an indication that you're good at your job," Vincent said.

"Well, exactly. I've never claimed to be a genius, but I do know what I'm doing."

"Clearly," Vincent said, with a gesture meant to encompass not just the terrace but the villa and its proximity to the Mediterranean, the private jet that had brought them here, the entirety of this remarkable life.

"I've done all right," he said. "Anyway, Kaspersky took her story to the SEC. I'm sorry, it's rude to throw obscure acronyms around. I mean the Securities and Exchange Commission. They're the people who look after my industry." Vincent knew what the SEC was, because she made an effort to follow the financial news, but she only nodded. "They investigated me thoroughly. Naturally they found nothing. There was nothing to find."

"Did you hear from her again? After the investigation?"

"Not directly. I've heard from other people whom she's spoken to."

"If she's spreading false rumours against you," Vincent said, "can't you sue her for defamation?"

"The thing you have to understand," he said, "is that in my business, credibility is everything. I can't run the risk of it becoming a news story."

"You're saying the appearance of scandal would be almost as bad as an actual scandal."

"Smart girl. But I thought about it later, when all of that insanity with the SEC had passed, and I realized what the problem was. That money she wanted to invest? It was her father's fortune. He'd died quite recently. So there was just, well, there's a lot of emotion caught up in money sometimes." Anya was moving around the periphery of the terrace, discreetly setting out candles for the evening. How much of the conversation was she hearing? Did it matter? Did Anya care? "The letter Ella

Kaspersky sent me, it was unhinged," Jonathan said, "rambling on about her father's legacy and so on. But to be fair, when I look back on it I realize she was obviously grieving, and grief can make anyone a little irrational in the moment." The unspeakable subject of Jonathan's dead wife floated between them, like a ghost; they glanced at one another but didn't say her name. Jonathan cleared his throat. "Anyway, the reason I'm telling you all this is, I just didn't want you to wonder if you ever came across anything from her online, or if we ever came across her in real life. You never saw her in Caiette, did you?"

"At the hotel? I don't really remember many of the other guests, to be honest. I was only there for six or seven months."

"Till I swept you off your feet," he said, and kissed her. His lips were cold and tasted unpleasantly of stale coffee, but Vincent smiled at him anyway.

"I think envy's understandable," she said. "Not everyone succeeds."

(Had Vincent succeeded? She felt that by any rational measure she was living an extraordinary life, but on the other hand she wasn't sure what the goal had been. Later she stood alone on the terrace, filming the Mediterranean, and thought, *Maybe this could be enough. Maybe not everyone needs to have a specific ambition. I could be the sort of person who just goes to beautiful places and owns beautiful things. Maybe I could film five-minute videos of every sea and every ocean and perhaps there would be some meaning in that project, some kind of completion.*)

The Astronaut

She met Jonathan's employees that summer, at his annual Fourth of July party, which lasted until the small hours of the morning and involved a fleet of chartered buses. There was an army of caterers and a swing band dressed in white on the lawn. The guests were all employees of Jonathan's. There were a little over a hundred employees, five in the asset management group and the rest in the brokerage company.

"Are the asset management people a little standoffish?" Vincent asked. The asset management team was standing in a tight little group at the party's edge. One of them, Oskar, was trying to juggle plastic cups while the others watched. "No, wait," Oskar was saying, "I swear I used to know how to do this . . ."

"They've always been a little insular," Jonathan said. "They work on a different floor."

When everyone was gone, the lawn seemed enormous, a twilight landscape of round tables with flickering candles on wine-stained tablecloths, plastic cups glimmering in the trampled grass. "You're so poised," Jonathan said. They were sitting by the pool with their feet in the water, while the caterers blew out candles and folded tables and packed dirty glasses into crates. *That's my job,* Vincent didn't say in return. Calling it a job seemed uncharitable, because she really did like him. It wasn't the romance of the century, but it didn't have to be; if you genuinely enjoy someone's company, she'd been thinking lately, if you enjoy your life with them and don't mind sleeping with them, isn't that enough? Do you have to actually be in love for a relationship to be real, whatever *real* means, so long as there's respect and something like friendship? She spent more time thinking about this than she would have liked, which suggested that it was an unresolved question, but she felt certain that she could go on this way for a long time, years probably. The Fourth of July was a feverish night at the peak of a heat wave.

"Well, thank you. I try." Sweat ran down her back.

"You try without *appearing* to try, though," he said. "You've no idea what a rare quality that is."

She was watching the shimmer of lights on the surface of the pool. When she looked up, one of the caterers was watching her, a young woman who was straightening deck chairs. Vincent looked away quickly. She had studied the habits of the monied with diligence. She copied their modes of dress and speech, and cultivated an air of carelessness. But she was ill at ease around the household staff and the caterers, because she feared that if anyone from her home planet were to look at her too closely, they'd see through her disguise.

Mirella

In their first winter together, they flew south to a party at a private club in Miami Beach. Jonathan seemed to belong to an extraordinary number of clubs. "It's an expensive hobby," he told Vincent, "but I've always had a weakness for places where it seems like time slows down." (Yet another clue that Vincent felt she should have picked up: Why exactly did he want time to slow down? Was there something in that statement besides a general awareness of mortality, some other inevitability that he felt was rushing toward him?) "Some of the clubs have other pleasures," he said, "golf courses and tennis courts and whatnot, but there's a certain pleasure in just drinking coffee or wine in a private lounge. Time moves differently in these places."

The Winter Formal in Miami Beach was a deadly evening of tuxedos and iridescent gowns. The women were mostly much older than Vincent. The men would have looked alike even if they weren't all dressed like penguins—the curious sameness of expensively maintained people with similar habits—and most of them had always been in this world, it was obvious, they had lived their whole lives above a safety net and were therefore of a different species from Vincent. She moved through the room in a silver gown, smiling and telling people that she was delighted to meet them, laughing convincingly at weak jokes, listening intently to dull anecdotes with the same smile she'd used on good tippers back in her bartending days. Jonathan had known most of the Miami Beach people for a decade or more. Many of the other women had been friends with Jonathan's wife, Suzanne, and they had children Vincent's age and older. Several of them had had unfortunate cosmetic procedures—puffed-out faces, immobile foreheads, swollen rubbery lips—that made her eyes widen involuntarily when they were introduced. Vincent stayed by Jonathan's side until he excused himself for a discreet conversation with a potential investor, at which point she went to the bar, where a tall woman in a blindingly fuchsia dress was ordering a gin and tonic. Vincent had noticed her earlier, as one of the very few women in the room who seemed to be about Vincent's age. They received their drinks from parallel bartenders at the same moment and nearly collided as they left the bar.

"Oh no," Vincent said. "I didn't spill any wine on your dress, did I?"

"Not a drop," the woman said. "I'm Mirella."

"I'm Vincent. Hi."

"I was just heading out to the terrace, if you'd like to join me?"

They went out to the terrace, which had Italian pretensions. There were a few women out here of their age and younger, but they all seemed to know one another and were either deep in conversation or deep in their phones. Vincent liked that she could see the ocean from here, same blue as the Mediterranean.

"Have you ever been to a more tedious party?" Vincent was normally more cautious, but Mirella had an air of boredom that set her at ease.

"Yes. The same party last year."

A man in a dark suit had followed them out. He stood some distance away, scanning the terrace.

"Is he with you?" Vincent asked.

"Always," Mirella said, and Vincent realized that the man was hired protection. Mirella lived at a high altitude.

"Is it oppressive? Having someone follow you around all the time?"

They were leaning on the balustrade, contemplating the terrace. The other women looked like a flock of tropical birds. It was Vincent's first time in Florida, and she'd noticed that people wore much brighter colours here than in New York or Connecticut.

"Funny you should ask," Mirella said. "I was just thinking about this earlier. I realized something slightly disturbing."

"Tell me."

"Sometimes I don't even see him anymore. I don't want to think of myself as a person to whom other people are invisible, but there it is."

"Has it been . . ." Vincent didn't know how to ask the question, but she was curious about how long it took for a person to become invisible. She was still aware of Jonathan Alkaitis's household staff at all times, and there was something appalling and also seductive in the idea of no longer being able to see them. "Has he been with you a long time?"

"Six years," Mirella said. "Not him personally. Different men in the same position. It was only strange for the first few months." She was looking at Vincent's left hand. "Who's your husband?"

"I don't know if you'd know him, he's not at this club very often. His name's Jonathan Alkaitis."

Mirella smiled. "I know Jonathan," she said. "My boyfriend invests with him."

Mirella was always followed by a bodyguard because her boyfriend, Faisal, was a Saudi prince. A cousin's girlfriend had been kidnapped for ransom a decade earlier, and the episode had left him a little paranoid.

"Is he going to be king someday?" Vincent asked Mirella when they met up in Manhattan the week after the party. Mirella and Faisal lived most of the year in a loft in Soho.

Mirella smiled. "Not a chance," she said. "There are something like six thousand Saudi princes."

"How many princesses?"

"No one really counts the princesses."

They met for dinner sometimes after that, Faisal and Mirella and Jonathan and Vincent. Faisal was a supremely elegant man in his forties who favoured bespoke suits and white shirts with the top two buttons undone, never a tie. He didn't work. He and Mirella had settled in New York City because he felt free here, he said. Not that he disliked Riyadh, where he was from, just that it was frankly kind of nice to live in a place that doesn't also contain hordes of your relatives. He felt he had a little more breathing room on this side of the world. That being said, he found New York winters difficult, so he'd once spent an entire February learning to play golf at the club in Miami Beach, which was where he'd met Jonathan.

Faisal had always been a disappointment in his family. He was the son who only wanted to go to jazz clubs and spend evenings at the opera and read obscure literary journals in French and English, the one who'd put half the world between himself and his family and showed no interest in marriage, let alone grandchildren. But then he invested with Alkaitis and introduced Alkaitis to several family members, whose investments performed so spectacularly that Faisal's status as the family's black sheep was at least partially reversed, and it was obvious that this mattered immensely to him.

Mirella and Faisal had lived in London for a couple of years, then briefly in Singapore, before they'd settled in New York. "My life wasn't really different in those places," Mirella said when Vincent asked. This was a month or two after they'd met. Vincent had taken Mirella to her favourite gallery at the Metropolitan Museum of Art. Vincent had no formal education in art, but she was moved by portraits, especially portraits whose subjects looked quite ordinary, like people you might see in the subway except in outmoded clothes.

"I don't think of those as similar cities," Vincent said.

"They're not, but my life was the same. It was just a change in background scenery." She glanced at Vincent. "You didn't come from money, did you?"

"No."

"Me neither. You know what I've learned about money? I was trying to figure out why my life felt more or less the same in Singapore as it did in London, and that's when I realized that money is its own country."

One of the things that Vincent tried not to think about too much: a difference between Mirella and Vincent was that Mirella was in this country of money with a man whom she truly loved. You could see it in the way she looked at Faisal, the way she brightened when he came into a room.

The Investor

If money is a country, there were other citizens whom Vincent liked much less. She and Jonathan had dinner with Lenny Xavier, a music producer from Los Angeles. Jonathan was quiet and distracted on the way to the restaurant. "He's my most important investor," he said quietly as they walked in, and then he caught sight of Lenny and Lenny's wife at the far end of the room and broke into a grin. Lenny wore an expensive-looking suit with sneakers and had hair that was messy on purpose. His wife, Tiffany, was very beautiful but didn't have much to say.

"We met at an audition, actually," she said when Vincent attempted small talk, and said almost nothing further to her. She'd been a singer but now she wasn't singing. Toward the end of the evening, Jonathan somehow drew Tiffany into conversation, and Lenny, who had had too much to drink, turned to Vincent and launched into a monologue about a girl he'd worked with years ago, another girl who'd also wanted to be a singer.

"The problem is," he told her, "some people just can't recognize opportunity."

"That's very true," Vincent said, but his statement made her uneasy. She enjoyed Jonathan's company, but it was undeniable that when he'd walked into the bar of the Hotel Caiette, she'd recognized an opportunity.

"She had real potential. Real potential. But an inability to recognize opportunity? That right there is a fatal flaw."

"Where is she now?" Vincent asked. Lenny had been talking about the girl in the past tense, which Vincent found mildly alarming.

"Annika? Who gives a fuck. I haven't seen her since 2000, maybe 2001." Lenny poured himself another glass of red. "You really want to know? She went back to Canada to play weird electronica with her friends."

("The problem is, though," Tiffany was saying to Jonathan, across the table, "when you buy jewellery online, it's really hard to tell how chunky it is.")

"You don't work with her at all anymore?"

"No, because she's a fucking idiot. Okay, so this girl, Annika, when I met her she was young. Really shockingly beautiful, okay? Just shockingly beautiful. Not a ton of talent, but enough. Great body. Her voice was just okay, but you know what? We can work with that. She writes poetry, so her lyrics are good. She plays the violin, which is a fucking useless instrument for pop music, but whatever, at least she's got a musical background. So we start working with her, we're moving toward an album, making plans for how to package her, how to roll her out. Like I said, she's beautiful, and tell you what, she's got this edge to her, this kind of rare quality, like she's really sexy but it's not *obvious*, right? Like it's not in your face, there's something a little mysterious about it."

"Mysterious?"

"Kind of remote, but not ice-queen remote, more like, I don't know, *intelligent* remote, which can be attractive in certain girls." His eyes dropped briefly to Vincent's chest. "So anyway, we're pretty far along, we're hiring a backup band and looking for a choreographer, and then she comes to us and she's like, 'I want out.' We're like, '*I'm* sorry, what?' We're pretty shocked, me and my partners. We've got her on this program, right? We're paying for vocal lessons, guitar lessons, songwriters, a personal trainer. Any musician, any recording artist would kill for an opportunity like what she's got here. We point that out and she's like, yeah, she gets it, she appreciates the effort, but we're violating her artistic integrity." Lenny paused to sip his wine. "Hilarious, right?"

Vincent smiled, unsure of what exactly she was supposed to find hilarious. ("Oh, that? That's topaz, I think," Tiffany was saying to Jonathan. "With little diamonds around it.")

"We're like, your *what*? Your *integrity*? You are twenty-one years old. You don't get to have integrity. I mean, okay, look, maybe she had integrity, you know, personally, like as a human being, but *artistic integrity*? You've got to be fucking kidding me. She's a little girl."

"So what happened?"

"Like I said, she went back to Canada. I Googled her the other day, and you know what she's doing? Touring Canada in a fucking van, playing in tiny clubs and music festivals in towns you've never heard of. You see what I mean? Couldn't recognize an opportunity. Whereas me, when I met your husband? When I figured out how his fund worked? That right there was an opportunity, and I seized it."

"Lenny," Jonathan said, cutting Tiffany off midsentence, "let's not bore our lovely wives with investment talk."

"All I'm saying is, my investment performed better than I could've imagined." Lenny raised his glass. "Anyway. Annika. It's all good, because you know what? I can predict the future." He smiled and tapped his forehead with one finger. "She'll come back to me."

"I don't doubt it," Vincent said. What was strange was that she was certain Jonathan was listening very intently to her conversation with Lenny, even though he was gazing at Tiffany and nodding at what Tiffany was saying. It seemed to her that there was something that Jonathan didn't want Lenny to reveal.

"Any year now, any *day* now, I'll hear from her again, I'd bet money on it."

"No question." If only the evening would end. Vincent's face was getting tired.

"She'll be all, like, hey, remember me, we were going to do something together, and I'll be like, yeah, we *were* going to do something together, you and me, past tense. That was five years ago, six years ago, now you're not twenty-one anymore."

Poolside

"Tell me about the place you're from," Mirella said toward the end. The age of money lasted a little under three years. During the final summer, six months before the end, Faisal went home to Riyadh to spend a few weeks with his father, who'd just received a cancer diagnosis, and during that period Mirella fell into the habit of taking a car up to Greenwich almost every afternoon. Vincent and Mirella spent languid hours swimming or lying in the shade by the pool, stunned by heat, Mirella's bodyguard reading the paper or staring at his phone on a lawn chair out of earshot.

"I grew up on a road with two dead ends," Vincent said. "That pretty much sums it up."

"Put down that camera, will you? You're making me nervous."

"I'm not filming you, I'm just filming those trees over there."

"Yeah, but they're boring trees. They're not doing anything."

"Fair point," Vincent said, and smiled and put the camera away, although it pained her to stop filming at the three-minute-twenty-seven-second mark. She was aware that the necessity of filming in precise five-minute intervals probably constituted an undiagnosed case of OCD, but this had never really struck her as a serious problem.

"How can a road have two dead ends?"

"If it's accessible only by boat or floatplane. Picture a row of houses on an inlet. Forest all around, water, nothing else."

"You had a boat?"

"Some people had their own boats. We didn't. I used to catch the mail boat to get to school in the mornings, then a bus would meet us by the pier on the other side and drive us to the nearest town. There was no television there till I was thirteen."

"What do you mean, no television?" Mirella was looking at her as if she'd just announced she was from Mars.

"I mean, there was no signal."

"So if you switched on the TV, what would happen?"

"Well, you'd just get static," Vincent said.

"On every channel?"

(A memory: thirteen years old, suspended from school for the graffiti incident, sitting by the kitchen window with a book, then looking up and seeing Dad walking up the hill from the water taxi with an unwieldy box in his arms, grinning. "Look what my mom bought for us," he said. "I got a call to come pick it up from the electronics store in Port Hardy." Grandma Caroline had departed that morning to return to her own life for a few days, but it appeared she'd left a parting gift.

A television! A tower had gone up a few months earlier in Grace Harbour, just up the inlet, which meant that for the first time in history there was a signal in Caiette, and Mom would never have allowed this but it wasn't up to her anymore, because she'd been gone for three weeks. Dad and Vincent flicked through variations of static to find a room, where two women with American accents were talking, one with long brown hair and glasses, the other with a cloud of platinum hair and tighter clothing.

"*WKRP in Cincinnati*," Dad said. "I used to watch this in the eighties."

One of the women said something funny, which made Dad laugh for the first time in three weeks. Where was Cincinnati? On television the city had a soft gleam, like the blond actress's hair. Later, Vincent pulled the atlas down from a high shelf and found it, a point in the middle of the closest country to the south. She looked up the page for southwestern British Columbia, but of course Caiette was too small to appear on the map.)

Mirella had a story about a duplex in a housing development of identical duplexes, exurban Cleveland, cornfields on one side and an expressway on the other. Her mother worked two jobs and her father was in prison. Mirella and her sister were home alone for hours every day, watching television; they walked home from the school bus stop and locked the door behind them, and then they weren't allowed to go outside again. They warmed up Hot Pockets for dinner and sometimes did their homework, sometimes didn't. "It actually wasn't that bad," she said. "I got lucky. Nothing terrible happened to me. It was just boring. You grew up with both your parents?"

"My mother drowned when I was thirteen." Vincent appreciated the way Mirella just nodded at this. Perhaps from now on she would only be friends with people who were missing at least one parent. "My dad was a tree planter, so he'd be up at these remote camps for weeks at a time during the school year, so I went to live with my aunt in Vancouver."

The conversation shifted away from points of origin, which was fine with Vincent. Everything about Caiette was either impossible to describe or too difficult to talk about, and everything after Caiette was either boring or embarrassing. Mirella was talking about how she and Faisal had met. Mirella had tried to be a model, but she hadn't made it very far. The problem, as her agent had explained it, was that Mirella was beautiful but it was an ordinary kind of beauty. There was nothing unusual about Mirella's face, except for its prettiness, and that was a moment in modelling when it wasn't enough to be beautiful, the agent said. One also had to be strange. The successful models of that moment had unusually wide-spaced eyes, or faces that were actually quite plain but had an indefinably striking quality, or ears that stuck out like jug handles. When she met Faisal, Mirella was trying to be an actor because the modelling wasn't working out, but acting wasn't going well either. She had some talent, but not enough to rise above the sea of other moderately talented beautiful young women. The night she met Faisal she was at a party in an expensive dress that she'd borrowed from her roommate, hours after a call with her agent's assistant—her agent wasn't taking her calls anymore—wherein the assistant, who'd once wanted to be an actor too, had gently broken the news that Mirella had been passed over for yet another role. Rejection is exhausting. Mirella was standing by the window, looking out at a view of downtown Los Angeles, and she realized that she was getting too tired for this life. She was thinking that maybe she should finally go to school, study something that would lead to a good job, but her sister had done that and now her sister was struggling under the weight of student loans, and Mirella wasn't sure the debt was worth it. She was standing there trying to imagine what might come next, and then Faisal appeared beside her, beautifully dressed and holding two glasses of wine, and she thought, *Why not you?*

"We met over drinks too," Vincent said, "but I was the bartender."

Mirella smiled. "I'm not surprised. You make an excellent cocktail."

"Thank you. It was a strange moment in my life. My father had just died." Mirella's eyes widened. Having one parent exit the scene was nothing unusual, but losing two was a different situation. "I had to go back to my hometown to deal with his stuff, and there was a job opening at the local hotel, so I decided to stay for a while."

"What happened to him?"

"A heart attack."

"I'm sorry."

"Thank you." Vincent didn't like to think of her parents.

"Was this the hotel Jonathan owns? I remember him talking about it."

"Yes, exactly. I thought living there would be a simpler life, but I knew it was a mistake within a month. My childhood best friend worked there, and then after a few months my brother showed up and started working there too, and, I don't know, it just started to seem a little claustrophobic, living in the same place with the same people I'd known since I was born."

"I didn't know you had a brother."

"He was never really part of my life," Vincent said. "I haven't seen him in years."

"So you went to this place in the middle of nowhere, and left because your brother was there too?"

"No, I . . . there was a strange incident," she said. "Okay, so the lobby, it had a glass wall overlooking the water. I was working one night, and there was this guest in the lobby, a man with insomnia, he was just sitting in an armchair reading or working or something, and then he made this sound and jumped out of his chair. So I looked, and someone had just written this awful message on the outside of the glass."

"What was it?"

"The message? *Why don't you swallow broken glass.*"

"Crazy," Mirella said.

"I know. And then a minute later, my brother Paul comes in from his dinner break, and it was just so obvious that he'd done it, he was all kind of shifty, couldn't even meet my eyes—"

"Why would he—?"

"I don't know. I almost asked him, but then I realized it didn't matter. There's just no scenario where writing something like that isn't horrible, is there?"

"I can't think of one." Mirella was quiet for a moment. "It's a horrible message, but I'm not sure I completely understand why it bothered you that much."

"The thing with my mother," Vincent said, "is I know she drowned, but I don't know *why* she drowned. She went canoeing all the time. She was a good swimmer."

"You think it might not have been an accident."

"I think I'll never know one way or the other." They were quiet for a while, and the buzz of the cicadas in the trees at the edge of the property was very loud. "Anyway, it wasn't just that. I was having one of those moments, where you look at your life and think, *Is this really it? I thought there'd be more.*"

"I'm familiar with those moments," Mirella said. "So you were going to leave anyway, and then Jonathan walked into the bar?"

"No more than two hours later, maybe less. It was five in the morning. I had to do two shots of espresso just to keep my eyes open."

"Here's to coffee." Mirella raised her glass.

"When I say I don't know where I'd be without it, I mean that literally," Vincent said.

A lonely man walks into a bar and sees an opportunity. An opportunity walks into a bar and meets a bartender. A lonely bartender looks up from her work and the message on the window makes her want to flee, because the bartender's mother disappeared while canoeing and she's told everyone all her life that it was an accident but there is absolutely no way of knowing whether this is true, and how could anyone who's aware of this uncertainty—as Paul definitely is—write a suggestion to commit suicide on a window with *that water* shimmering on the other side, but what's driving the bartender to despair isn't actually the graffiti, it's the fact that when she leaves this place it will only be to go to another bar, and another after that, and another, and another, and anyway that's the moment when the man, the opportunity, extends his hand.

"Would you believe I actually grew up here?" she asked Jonathan, when in the course of that first conversation he asked where she was from. She'd served him his food and they'd fallen into a surprisingly effortless conversation.

"Here as in Caiette?"

"Well, here and then Vancouver."

"Great city," he said. "I keep meaning to spend more time there."

He slipped her a folded bill as he was leaving—she thanked him without looking at it—and it turned out to be a hundred dollars, folded around a business card on which he'd scrawled a cell phone number. A hundred-dollar bill? Mortifying in retrospect, but she always appreciated the clarity of his intentions. It was always going to be a transactional arrangement. When he beckoned, she would come to him. She would always be well compensated.

Why not you?

Soho

That last summer in the kingdom of money, Vincent and Mirella met up in Soho on a subtropical afternoon, where they lingered for a while in Faisal and Mirella's loft and then went shopping, less out of need than out of boredom. Dark clouds filled the sky. In the late afternoon they wandered down Spring Street with no particular destination in mind, having spent several thousand dollars each on clothing and lingerie, and Vincent was admiring a yellow Lamborghini parked across the street when

Mirella said, "I think the rain's about to start"—and they walked faster, too late, the first thunderclap sounded and the downpour began, Mirella took her hand and they broke into a run. Vincent was laughing—she loved being caught in the rain—and Mirella didn't like what rain did to her hair, but by the time they reached the corner she was smiling too, she pulled Vincent into an espresso bar and they stood just inside for a moment, pleasantly chilled by the air conditioning, pushing wet hair away from their eyes and surveying the damage to the shopping bags. Mirella's bodyguard came in a moment later, mopping his forehead with a handkerchief.

"Well," Mirella said. "Shall we stop for a coffee?"

"Let's." Vincent had been on the East Coast of this continent for two and a half years now, but she was still startled by the violence of the summer thunderstorms, the way the sky turned green. They found a minuscule table by the window and sat there with their little coffees, wet shopping bags crowded around their legs. They'd fallen into a companionable silence, and as they watched the downpour, Vincent realized that she felt perfectly at ease, for the first time in recent memory. The truth was that in the kingdom of money, before she'd met Mirella she'd been extremely alone.

"Do you find that shopping is actually incredibly boring?" Vincent felt guilty saying this aloud. It was only possible to say it because Mirella hadn't come from money either. Ghosts of Vincent's earlier selves flocked around the table and stared at the beautiful clothes she was wearing.

"I know it's in poor taste to admit it," Mirella said, "but it's incredible how quickly the novelty wears off." There was something about the way she looked up just then, the way the light caught her face, that made Vincent think of a nursery rhyme from childhood, her favourite verse from the Mother Goose book in the elementary school library, read so many times that she had committed it to memory by the time she was five or six: *She is handsome, she is pretty, she is the girl of the golden city . . .*

"At first it felt like some kind of compensation," Vincent said. "You remember the times when you had to choose between rent and groceries, and it's like, 'Now I can afford this dress, so balance has been restored in the world,' but after a while . . ."

"After a while you find you've acquired enough dresses," Mirella said. "If Faisal knew the extent of my shopping habit, he'd probably stage an intervention."

Although of course the clothing wasn't the point, Vincent thought later, on the train back to Greenwich. It wasn't the *stuff* that kept her in this strange new life, in the kingdom of money; it wasn't the clothing and objects and handbags and shoes. It wasn't the beautiful home, the travel; it wasn't Jonathan's company, although she did genuinely like him; it wasn't even inertia. What kept her in the kingdom was the previously unimaginable condition of not having to think about money, because that's what money gives you: the freedom to stop thinking about money. If you've never been without, then you won't understand the profundity of this, how absolutely this changes your life.

When she arrived home, Jonathan was waiting in the living room. He'd been working but closed his laptop when she came in. "You poor thing," he said. "I wondered about you, out there in the deluge." She was shivering a little, her clothes damp in the chill of the air conditioning. There was a cashmere blanket on the back of the sofa, just within his reach. He put his laptop on the coffee table and held the blanket open to receive her. "Come here," he said. "Let's get you warm."

OLIVIA

On a dark afternoon in August, a painter was standing under an awning in Soho when Vincent and Mirella passed by. Across the street, a yellow Lamborghini shone in the haze of the afternoon. The car had such presence that it was almost alive, all but vibrating with possibility, like something from the future. Olivia had come to this street because behind the Lamborghini was a doorway that she'd passed through once in the late fifties, when Jonathan Alkaitis's brother was looking for models. In the summer of 2008, Olivia stood across the street under a red awning because it was obviously about to rain, eating a chocolate chip cookie even though the sugar would send her to sleep later—on a bench, in the subway, in a movie theatre, wherever she might happen to land—and allowed herself to sink into memory. In 1958 she walked briskly up to the door in her new trench coat, which she was convinced made her look like the star of her favourite French movie because it's possible to convince oneself of such things at twenty-four. When a voice crackled incoherently out of the buzzer she said, "It's me," which she'd found always worked at every building no matter which buzzer she pressed, and climbed four flights of stairs to Lucas's studio.

Lucas Alkaitis was on the run from the suburbs just like everyone else, on the run from mediocrity and Brylcreem and grey flannel suits, and Olivia had met enough fake painters by then to recognize when she was in the presence of the real thing. In 1958, Lucas was working on a series of nudes: women and men, mostly women, all sitting on a sofa the colour of the Lamborghini that would park outside his door a half century later. The sofa was much dirtier in real life than in the paintings.

The paintings were ravishing. But Lucas himself, to Olivia's amusement and disappointment, was every cliché in combination: the too-long, artfully tousled hair; the white undershirt, streaked with paint; the work boots, which he'd also allowed to become streaked with paint, presumably to advertise his painterliness to the opposite sex. He looked her over and ran his hand through his hair in a way that made her think he'd practised the motion in the mirror.

"Help you?" he asked.

"I hear you're looking for a model."

"I was hoping you'd say that." A slow, lazy smile as he appraised her. This was a profoundly self-satisfied man. "I can't pay very much."

"Actually, I have a proposition on that front."

"Oh?"

What Olivia sometimes wondered—even in the present, on the other side of the split screen in 2008, where she was still standing under the awning, had moved on to a second chocolate chip cookie, and could already feel herself coming unmoored, her blood sugar rising in a way that always made her think of a doomed hot-air balloon, an unsteady giddy motion before a precipitous fall—is if it might be possible to send out a memo to the entire population of persons below the age of thirty, no, forty, men and women alike, a memo to the effect that it is not in fact necessary to raise an eyebrow every time the word *proposition* is uttered in conversation. "I would appreciate it," she muttered aloud, in 2008, "if everyone would stop."

On the other side of the gauze, in 1958, she waited for Lucas's eyebrow to lower before she said, "Not that kind of proposition, for Christ's sake. Payment in kind."

He looked confused.

"My name's Olivia Collins." She watched as the name registered. She'd had some success, nothing earth-shattering but enough that a certain subset of the painting population south of 14th Street knew her name. She had gallery representation, which was more than most of these floppy-haired puppy dogs could say. "I'm a painter," she said, unnecessarily, "and I'm looking for models."

"Okay, yeah, so you're saying . . ."

"You paint me, I paint you," she said. "I'm working on a new portrait series."

Lucas crossed the room to a cluttered windowsill, extracted a box of cigarettes from between two paint cans that had been repurposed as vases for dying daisies, tapped the cigarette box, removed one, lit it, inhaled, exhaled while holding Olivia's gaze, all of the stalling motions that smokers perform when they're not sure what to say and have seen too many movies. If another memo could possibly be sent out, this one specific to smokers: You cannot be both an unwashed bohemian and Cary Grant. Your elegant cigarette moves are hopelessly undermined by your undershirt and your dirty hair. The combination is not particularly interesting.

"Intriguing proposition," he said, "but I don't pose."

"Well, it takes a certain boldness," Olivia said with a shrug.

In 1958, her values included a determination that no one should ever be able to tell whether she cared about any given thing or not. "Not everyone can do it." She could see that this stung, as intended. "Well, if you change your mind." She scrawled her phone number on a scrap of paper, left it on his worktable, nodded goodbye, and turned away. "Your work's good, by the way," she said from the door, as a parting shot.

In 2008, a pair of girls were approaching. Shoppers, weighted down, somewhere in their twenties, both pretty in an expensive way, a genre of girl whom fifty years ago Olivia would have both painted and seduced. They were talking about nothing, a conversation about jeans they wanted to buy, but one of them looked away and Olivia saw that she was gazing across the street at the yellow Lamborghini, brilliant in the dull pre-storm light.

"I see it too," Olivia murmured, but so quietly that neither looked her way as they passed. Perhaps she didn't say it aloud. The sky exploded in a thunderclap and they ran away into the rain.

When Lucas came to her, she wasn't alone. She'd been painting her friend Renata for days, from various angles. The problem was Renata's eyes, which were worried and doelike when Renata looked at her head-on but coolly confident when she was looking away. The effect was of two different people. Which to show?

"Okay, I've got an idea for a ghost story," Renata said. This was a game they played sometimes, when Renata was posing and starting to get bored, because they'd both loved ghost stories since childhood. "A guy gets hit by a car and dies, and then after that the intersection's haunted, but the ghost isn't the guy who gets hit by the car, the ghost is the car."

Olivia stepped back for a moment, considering the eye problem. "So it's a story about a ghost car?"

"The driver feels so guilty about the accident that his guilt manifests as a ghostly car."

"I like it."

It was cold in the studio that day and Olivia was mostly working on Renata's face and shoulders, so Renata was wearing a bathrobe that she hadn't bothered to close. Olivia heard her friend and neighbour Diego's voice in the hall, his quick knock and entry, and turned in time to see Lucas catch sight of Renata's breasts and do a double take that he tried to cover with a coughing fit.

"Fumes getting to you?"

"Those'll go straight to your head," Renata said, in that languid voice that always made her sound stoned, which often she was, but on this particular occasion she wasn't.

"I'm glad you're here," Olivia said to Lucas, which in those days was one of her signature lines. (A revelation earned only in hindsight: beauty can have a corrosive effect on character. It is possible to coast for some years on no more than a few polished lines and a dazzling smile, and those years are formative.) "We'll be done in a few minutes."

Lucas stood by the door, awkward. She sensed his taking in the work. In anticipation of his arrival, Olivia had propped seven of her best recent portraits around the room. She'd been experimenting with surrealist backgrounds: the subject painted with eighteenth-century fealty to realism—or as close as she could get to eighteenth-century fealty to realism; she was aware at all times of the limits of her technical skills—but backgrounds dissolving into a fever dream of red, of purple, of blue, interiors breaking apart into formlessness, landscapes where the light was all wrong. In her most recent completed painting, Diego was sitting on a red chair, relaxed, his arm draped over the back, but the chair lost form at its extremities and dissolved into the wall, and a red pool had formed under one of the chair's feet, as if the paint were running off.

"That chair bleeding?" Lucas asked, indicating the Diego painting with his chin.

"Take off your robe?" Olivia said to Renata, who rolled her eyes but didn't object. Her naked flesh had the desired effect of shutting up Lucas. He forgot about the bleeding chair. (Something that troubled her even years later, decades later, all the way to 2008: Was the bleeding chair even a good idea? Were any of her artistic ideas ever actually any good? Her self-doubt had been one of the few constants in her life over the past half century.) "If you want to hang out," Olivia said to Lucas, "we'll be done in a half hour."

"Twenty minutes," Renata said. "I have to pick up my kid." When she left, Lucas took her place on the chair. He hadn't spoken since the bleeding-chair comment.

"You're overdressed for the occasion," Olivia said, but it came out softer than she intended, not at all sharp. Perhaps she could be a gentler person, she thought. Her shell was so hard in those days. "Can you take off your shirt?"

Lucas shrugged and took off his denim jacket and undershirt. He was skinny and unpleasantly pale, a strictly indoor creature. He watched her as she began. She was thinking about his work, the clean lines and restraint in his portraiture. He was ridiculous in some ways, but beneath all that he was a serious person, she understood that, he was a serious person who worked very hard. She painted rapidly, not at all in her usual style, swift short strokes. She'd hoped that if she skimmed the surface of the portrait she might be able to see him better, that something might become apparent that she could use as a starting point for a deeper, more serious work, and something did: when she stepped back to look at the canvas she saw the shadows on his face, the look she'd seen before on others, the awkward way he held his arms.

"Turn your left arm toward me," she said, demonstrating.

He smiled and didn't move. But she caught a glimpse as he reached for his shirt, and added it later: she painted over his left arm so that in the final version his palm was open, shadows streaked on his inner elbow, bruised veins.

At the opening five months later, he cornered her by the door. "I could kill you," he said pleasantly, smiling so that anyone looking would think he was complimenting her work. Two or three people who weren't out of earshot moved closer, curious. "I don't mean this in the screwball-comedy sense, by the way, as in 'They just got off on the wrong foot and now they're going to fall in love.' I mean that given the chance I could actually literally kill you."

"Live by the sword, die by the sword." Olivia raised her drink.

"You think you're so cute. All those canned fucking lines. It's not even *accurate*," he said, a whine entering his voice, "you're a fucking *liar*," but in ten months he would OD behind a restaurant on Delancey Street. She went to a show of his just before the end, a group exhibition in a warehouse in Chelsea. It was an underwhelming evening. The night was freezing and the room was too cold, everyone shivering with their cups of cheap wine. A few people recognized Olivia and she saw their jealousy under their smiles, which made her feel small and hollow and like she just wanted to go home. This was the thing about her life in those years: some nights it was beautiful but some nights there was such pain, throbbing just under the surface of the evening for no discernible reason, and on nights like that she understood why Lucas and Renata did what they did, the dulling trick with the needle. She found Lucas in a far corner with three of his paintings. He'd been working on a new series without people in it, just empty streets. General streets, not specific streets. She suspected they belonged to no particular city.

"I like these," Olivia said, as a peace offering. Lucas was with a kid, a boy wearing sneakers and jeans with an untucked shirt. This was what she remembered of her first sight of Jonathan Alkaitis, years later: that his untucked shirt was somehow poignant. The kid had *suburbia* written all over him but had untucked the shirt in order to look looser, more downtown, because he wasn't quite fourteen years old and was desperate to fit in, but the shirt was deeply creased around the waist where it had been tucked into his pants before he left the house.

"Thanks so much," Lucas said flatly.

"Who's your little friend?"

"My brother. Jonathan, meet Olivia. Olivia, Jonathan."

"Pleased to meet you," Jonathan Alkaitis said. He was wide-eyed, out of his element. "Do you not like my brother's paintings?"

"I just said I liked them."

"You're a terrible actor, though," Lucas said. "Even the kid can tell you don't like them."

Olivia did not, in fact, particularly like Lucas's new paintings. They were derivative of Edward Hopper and could only have been more obvious in theme if he'd maybe painted the word *LONELINESS* across them in red.

"You're right," Olivia said to Jonathan. "I don't particularly like your brother's paintings."

Jonathan frowned. "Then why did you say you liked them?"

"Just trying to be polite," she said. "If you'll excuse me." She didn't understand what Lucas was striving for but she could see where he was going, his face more shadowed than it had been, that awful pallor, and she didn't see the profit in engaging with him seriously. (This was how she thought in her twenties: *I didn't see the profit*. She was ashamed of this later.) Death was already in him. Anyone could see that he was halfway out the door. She remembered later that she'd felt sorry for his brother, who was going to be an only child soon.

Lucas's funeral was a small, private affair near his family's house in Greenburgh. She didn't hear he'd died until at least a month after it happened. It seemed to her later that she might not even have remembered him, just another fallen sparrow in a chaotic and rapidly receding decade, except that forty years later—forty years of no money, of no sales, of embarrassing phone calls where she had to ask her sister, Monica, for rent money, forty years of temp jobs in interchangeable offices and selling jewellery at fairs for her friend Diego's silver import business, forty years in the desert—there was a retrospective exhibition of downtown artists from the fifties, Olivia among them, and in its wake there was a sudden—and vanishingly brief—resurgence of interest in her work, during which her painting *Lucas with Shadows* sold at auction for two hundred thousand dollars, which was more money than she'd ever imagined possessing at one time.

"You should invest it," Monica said. They were sitting in the backyard of Olivia's new rental house in Monticello on a summer afternoon. Not the famous Monticello in Virginia, the Monticello in upstate New York with the boarded-up main street, the giant Walmart, the army/navy/marine recruitment offices, the stores that sold prosthetic limbs, the racetrack. Olivia had rented a little house on the outskirts. The house had previously been part of a bungalow colony. It was tiny and needed a new roof, but it was a pleasure to leave the city and come here. The back-yard felt tropical in the August heat, greenery exploding in the humidity, and that particular afternoon with Monica, she'd been drifting on the edge of sleep. Her blood sugar problems wouldn't be diagnosed for another year, but she'd noticed the correlation between eating carbohydrates and difficulty staying awake an hour or two later. She'd started doing it on purpose for the pleasure of drowsing on a chaise longue in the late afternoons. On this occasion, though, she took a long draft of strong iced tea, trying to bring herself back with caffeine and ice, because Monica had told her a few years ago that she felt Olivia wasn't a good listener and that being unlistened-to made Monica feel small. Olivia remembered this only after the bagel, and felt bad for purposefully making herself sleepy.

"How does one go about . . . how does a person invest?" Money was mysterious to Olivia, but Monica had been a lawyer before she retired and had a much better grasp of the logistics of daily life.

"Well, there are different ways of going about it," Monica said, "but I recently invested some money with a guy my friend Gary met at his club."

Olivia wouldn't have described herself as an overly superstitious person, but she'd always believed in messages from the universe, and she liked to pay attention to patterns and signs. Surely it meant something that the man with whom Monica had invested her savings was Lucas's brother.

"You won't remember me," she said to Jonathan when she called him, and immediately wished she'd said something different. The trouble with that line was that it had worked when she was young because when she was young she was beautiful, also fierce in a calculated manner that she'd believed to be attractive, which had lent a certain irony to the suggestion that anyone could have possibly forgotten her—*Oh, you know, just another gorgeous magnetic fresh young talent with gallery representation*—but lately she'd found that the line sometimes elicited a tactful silence, and she'd realized that often people did not, in fact, remember her. (Idea for a ghost story: a woman gets old and falls out of time and realizes that she's become invisible.)

"We met at the gallery with Lucas," he said softly. "The night it snowed."

The night it snowed, Olivia thought, and to her amazement, her eyes filled with tears. She hadn't cried when Lucas died. She'd felt a little sad about it, obviously, she wasn't a monster, it's just that she was perpetually distracted and they'd hardly known one another. But all these decades later, the pity of it overcame her: in a version of New York so different that it might as well have been a foreign city, she'd stepped out of the cold night and into the brilliance of the gallery, which memory had transformed from a den of petty jealousies and grubby desperation into a palace of art and light, sheer brilliance in every sense of the word, walls vibrating with colour, artists vibrating with genius and youth, where Lucas—so young, so talented, so doomed—and little Jonathan—who must have been, what, twelve?—awaited her arrival.

"You have a remarkable memory," she said.

"Well, you were memorable. You were the beautiful woman who didn't like my brother's paintings."

"I wish I hadn't said so. I should've been kinder." And then, on impulse, although she'd only meant to ask for a few minutes of his time over the phone: "Would you like to meet up for lunch sometime? I've come into some money, and I could use a little investment advice."

"I would be delighted," he said.

They saw one another a few times over the years that followed. She'd stop by his office sometimes, or they'd meet up for lunch. She looked forward to these lunches immensely; he was a warm, interested person, a good conversationalist, and he always picked up the check. He liked talking about Lucas and wanted to hear everything she remembered about his mysterious life in New York. "My brother was a decade older than me," he said. "I loved him, but when you're a kid, a decade is like the space between galaxies. I never felt that I knew him very well."

"Do you know," she said, "my sister and I are only three years apart, and I've never felt I knew her very well either."

"It's always possible to fail to know the people closest to us. But I'm fairly confident you knew my brother better than I did."

"That's a sad thought," Olivia said. "I hope he had people in his life who really knew him."

"Me too. But you knew him well enough to paint him."

"We posed for each other, it's true."

"He painted you, then? I wondered about that."

"He did." In languid memory, she sat naked on his yellow sofa in the heat of a July afternoon. "Do you know, I've no idea what became of his painting of me?"

He smiled. "Really?"

"Really. He completed his painting of me in a single afternoon and sold it at some group art show a couple months later. It was pretty small, maybe a foot square, so he wouldn't have sold it for much. I don't know who bought it."

"That means you can imagine it anywhere you want," he said. "Anyone you can think of, it could be hanging in their house."

"My favourite Hollywood actor," she said, enjoying this idea. "Sure, why not?"

"Well, thank you, Jonathan, I'll enjoy the vision of that painting on display in Angelina Jolie's living room."

"I have to tell you something," he said.

"What's that?"

"I bought your painting of Lucas," he said.

She had been eating salad; she put the fork down carefully, afraid she might drop it. "You did?"

"Just last month. I tracked down the guy who bought it at auction, and he was willing to sell. It was a little painful at first," he said, "seeing how unhealthy he looked, those bruises on his arms. But I spent some time with the painting, and I realized that I love it. You captured something about him that accords with my memories. It's hanging in my Manhattan apartment."

"I'm glad you have it," Olivia said. She wouldn't have imagined that she'd be so moved.

Sometime in 2003, he arrived at lunch without a wedding ring. He'd been married to Suzanne for a long time, decades, but Olivia had never met her. Although, when had she last seen him? Over a year had passed since their last lunch, she realized.

"You're not wearing a ring," she said.

"Oh. Yes." He was quiet for a moment. "I decided it was finally time to take it off." There was something in his tone, in the way he looked at his ringless hand, and she understood that Suzanne was dead.

"I'm sorry," she said.

"Thank you." A small, pained smile, and he turned his attention to the menu. "Forgive me, but it's still difficult to talk about. Have you tried the halibut at this place?"

Three months before Jonathan Alkaitis was arrested, he invited her along on a trip on his yacht. This was September of 2008. They were sailing from New York to Charleston. It was her first time meeting Jonathan's second wife, Vincent, who turned out to be an elegant and friendly person with a talent for mixing cocktails.

"She's delightful," Olivia said to Jonathan, when they were alone on deck after dinner. Vincent had gone in to make drinks. The sunset was fading.

"Isn't she? I'm very happy."

"Where did you find her?"

"A hotel bar in British Columbia," he said. "She was the bartender."

"I suppose that explains why she's so good at mixed drinks."

"I think she'd be good at anything she set out to do."

Olivia wasn't sure what to say to this, so she only nodded, and for a moment they just listened to the waves and the engines. They were passing alongside a quiet part of North Carolina, only a few scattered lights on the shore.

"What a fortunate thing," Olivia said finally, "being good at everything." She herself had only ever been good at one thing, and possibly not even that. Few sales had followed *Lucas with Shadows*. No one seemed interested in any of the work she'd done after the fifties, and the truth was that she hadn't painted in a long time. Painting was something that had grabbed hold of her for a while, decades, but now it had let go and she had no further interest in it, or it had no further interest in her. All things end, she'd told herself, there was always going to be a last painting, but if she wasn't a painter, what was she? It was a troubling question.

"I walked into the bar and saw her," Alkaitis said, "and I thought, *She's very pretty*."

"She's gorgeous."

"Then I found I enjoyed talking with her, and I thought, *Why not?* You know, if you don't have to be alone, then maybe you shouldn't be."

Olivia, who was almost always alone, couldn't think of anything to say to this.

"It's interesting," he said, "she's got a very particular kind of gift."

"What's that?"

"She sees what a given situation requires, and she adapts herself accordingly."

"So she's an actress?" The conversation was beginning to make Olivia a little uneasy. It seemed to her that Jonathan was describing a woman who'd dissolved into his life and become what he wanted. A disappearing act, essentially.

"Not acting, exactly. More like a kind of pragmatism, driven by willpower. She decided to be a certain kind of person, and she achieved it."

"Interesting," Olivia said, to be polite, although she couldn't actually think of anything less interesting than a chameleon. Vincent was lovely but not, Olivia had decided, a serious person. Since her late teens she had been mentally dividing people into categories: either you're a serious person, she'd long ago decided, or you're not. A difficulty of her current life was that she was no longer sure which category she fell into. Vincent was returning now with another round of cocktails. The lights of the Carolinas slipped past on the shore.

PART TWO

PART TWO

6

THE COUNTERLIFE

2009

No star burns forever. Words scratched into the wall by Alkaitis's bunk, etched so delicately and in such a spidery fashion that from any distance at all they look like a smudge or a crack in the paint, at exactly the right spot so he sees them when he turns his face to the wall. He's never had much interest in earth science but of course he knows the sun is a star, everyone knows that, so is the point just that the world will eventually end, in which case, why not just write that? Alkaitis has limited patience for poetry.

"Oh, that was Roberts," his cellmate tells him. "Guy here before you." Hazelton is doing ten to fifteen for grand larceny. He talks too much. He is nervous and twitchy but seems to mean well. He's exactly half Alkaitis's age and likes to talk about how he still has his whole life ahead of him, when he gets out of here it's all going to be different, etc. Roberts has come up in conversation before. "Got transferred to the hospital," Hazelton says. "He had some kind of heart thing."

"What was he like?"

"Roberts? Old guy, maybe sixty. Sorry. No offence."

"None taken." Time moves differently in prison than in Manhattan or in the Connecticut suburbs. In prison, sixty is old.

"Reasonable guy, never had problems with anybody. We called him Professor. He wore glasses. He was always reading books."

"What kind of books?"

"The kind with Martian chicks and exploding planets on the cover."

"I see." Alkaitis tries to picture life as it was lived in this room before him: Roberts reading sci-fi, serious and bespectacled, disappearing into stories about alien planets while Hazelton chattered and cracked his knuckles and paced. "Why was he here?"

"He didn't want to talk about it. Actually, he didn't talk about anything. Real quiet guy, just sat there staring into space a lot."

This summons an unexpected memory of his mother. For three years after Lucas died, Alkaitis used to come home from school sometimes and find his mother sitting perfectly still in the living room, staring at nothing, like she was watching a film only she could see.

"Was he depressed?" Alkaitis asks.

"Bro, it's prison. Everyone's depressed."

Is Alkaitis depressed? Sure, in a manner of speaking, but his life here isn't as bad as he thought it would be, once the initial shock wears off. He was arrested in December 2008 and six months later he arrived in his new home outside the town of Florence, South Carolina, a medium-security federal correctional institute known officially as FCI Florence Medium 1, not to be confused with FCI Florence Medium 2, which is technically the same security level but considerably harsher. Medium 1 is for the shrinking violets, as Tait memorably put it. Tait is doing a fifty-year bid for child pornography and as such would probably get killed in his first week in any other prison. Medium 1 is for prisoners who are thought to be too vulnerable for the general

population: child molesters, dirty cops, the medically compro-
mised, celebrities, fragile bespectacled hackers, and spies. There's
a maximum-security prison in the same complex, also a hospital.
The hospital scares Alkaitis, because it's the place where old men
disappear.

He thinks of Roberts sometimes when he steps out into the yard.
What's striking about the yard is its terminal blandness. Green
grass criss-crossed with cement pathways, the pathways designed
for inmates to walk as efficiently as possible between buildings
during periods of movement. There's a separate recreation yard
with a jogging track, its aesthetics equally impoverished. Everyone is dressed in khaki and grey, except the guards, who wear
navy blue and black. The buildings are beige with blue accents.
Outside the fence, there's a distant tree line, all of the trees the
exact same shade as the grass. There just aren't enough colours
here, that's his first impression. It's incomprehensible that this
place exists in the same world as, say, Manhattan, so when he's
crossing the yard he sometimes pretends he's on an alien planet.

Journalists write to him sometimes. "What does it feel like to be
sentenced to 170 years?" they ask.

He doesn't reply to this, because he knows the answer will
sound insane: it feels like delirium. One morning when he was
twenty-five, Alkaitis woke up with a high fever. He was living
alone on 70th Street back then and had nothing in the apartment to treat a fever, so he had to stagger outside to the nearest
bodega. He bought Aspirin with some difficulty, too hot, the
sidewalk unsteady under his feet, made it back to his building
and up the stairs to the landing, where he found himself baffled
by the mechanics of opening his apartment door. There was a

key in his hand, and a lock on the door, and he understood in an abstract way that these two things fit together, but he couldn't figure out how to make it work, and this was how he knew he was delirious. For how long did he stand there? Five minutes, ten, a half hour. Who knows. Eventually he made it inside.

In the courtroom in Manhattan, thirty-seven years later, the judge says the number—"one hundred seventy years"—and there's a vertiginous sensation of movement, time rushing away from him toward that impossible destination, the year 2179. He understands that he'll spend the rest of his life in prison, but it's the same confusion he felt in that moment of delirium in his twenties: *the rest of his life* and *prison* are two pieces that don't fit together, the lock and the key, an incomprehensible equation.

He never noticed dandelions before he came here, but in the oppressive blankness of the yard, those little bursts of yellow on the grass are almost shocking. Likewise, the birds. They're the kind of birds that blend into the landscape on the outside, just robins and ravens and finches and such, but here there's something extraordinary about the way they alight on the grass *and then leave again,* flitting in and out of bounds. They are emissaries from another world. The prison rulebook prohibits feeding them, but some guys surreptitiously drop crumbs on the grass.

A few guys who've passed through maximum security like to proclaim that FCI Florence Medium 1 is a country club, and it isn't exactly that but it also isn't nearly as bad as Alkaitis imagined. A fair number of the men here are elderly and have limited patience for drama, and also no one wants to get sent up to maximum. No one talks about shivs or tries to kill him in the yard. The only sinister thing that happens is when a handful of white nationalist types work out together while everyone else ignores them. They know that if they're too obvious or cause trouble they'll get moved to maximum, which is what happened during a nationwide roundup of Aryan Brotherhood guys a few years back, so they mostly confine their activities to synchronized push-ups and grandiose prattle about codes of honour and tribal solidarity. Elsewhere, two brothers who collaborated in a high-profile insurance fraud hold court in their favourite corner. The brothers have employees, even in prison, guys who fetch things for them and wash their clothes in exchange for commissary goods. There are always younger guys jogging around and around, clockwise, and older guys walking on the same track. Elderly mafiosos gossip in the sun.

Alkaitis jogs in circles around the yard, lifts weights, does push-ups, and within six months he's in the best shape of his life. He isn't one of those men who keep their days as featureless and as similar as possible to make time move faster. He respects that method of survival, but he tries to do something different every day, on principle. He applies for a job even though he doesn't have to, given his age, and ends up sweeping the cafeteria. He figures out how the system works and pays another inmate $10 a month to deal with his laundry. He never had time to read on the outside, but here he joins a book club where they discuss *The Great Gatsby* and *The Beautiful and Damned* and *Tender Is the Night* with a fervent young professor who seems unaware that anyone other than F. Scott Fitzgerald has ever written a book. It's possible to rest here, in the order, in the routine, in the up-at-five count-at-five-fifteen breakfast-at-six etc., one day rolling into the next. In the outside world he used to lie awake at night worrying about being sent to prison, but he sleeps fairly well here, between head counts. There is exquisite lightness in waking each morning with the knowledge that the worst has already happened.

"There's something I can't stop wondering about," one of the journalists says. Her name is Julie Freeman. She's writing a book about him, which he finds immensely flattering. "Okay, so for a long time before your arrest, decades, you had considerable resources at your disposal."

"I did," Alkaitis says. "I had an enormous amount of money."

"And you told me a moment ago that you'd been expecting arrest for a very long time. You knew what was coming. So why didn't you just flee the country before you were arrested?"

"To be honest," he says, "it never occurred to me to flee."

Which is not to say that he doesn't have regrets. He wishes he'd had more appreciation for the people he was able to associate with, before prison. He never really had friends in his adult life, only investors, but some of them were people whom he genuinely enjoyed. He always very much liked Olivia, whose presence made him feel like his beloved lost brother wasn't so far away after all, and Faisal, who could talk at fascinating length about subjects like twentieth-century British poetry and the history of jazz. (Faisal is dead now, but no need to think about that.) He's even nostalgic for some of the investors whom he knew much less well, maybe only met once or twice. Leon Prevant, for instance, the shipping executive whom he'd had drinks with at the Hotel Caiette, the pleasure of getting into a conversation about an industry he knew nothing about, or Terrence Washington, a retired judge at the club in Miami Beach, who seemed to know everything there was to know about the history of New York City.

The people he associates with now are not people he respects, for the most part. There are a few exceptions—the mafiosos who ran terrifying criminal empires, the ex-spy who was a double agent for a decade—but for every godfather and trilingual former spy there are ten guys who are basically thugs. Alkaitis is aware that there's a hypocritical element to his snobbery, but there's a difference between (a) knowing you're a criminal just like everyone else here and (b) wanting to associate with grown men who can't read.

"It's like there's two different games, moneywise," Nemirovsky says to the table at breakfast. He's been here sixteen years for a botched bank robbery. He has a fourth-grade education and is functionally illiterate. "There's the game everyone knows, where you work your shitty job and get your paycheque and it's never enough"—nods all around the cafeteria table—"but then there's this other level, this whole other *level* of money, where it's this whole other thing, like this secret *game* or something and only some people know how to play . . ."

Nemirovsky isn't wrong, Alkaitis thinks later, while he's jogging around the recreation yard. Money is a game he knew how to play. No, money is a country and he had the keys to the kingdom.

He doesn't tell Julie Freeman this, but now that it's much too late to flee, Alkaitis finds himself thinking about flight all the time. He likes to indulge in daydreams of a parallel version of events—a counterlife, if you will—in which he fled to the United Arab Emirates. Why not? He loves the UAE and Dubai in particular, the way it's possible to live an entire life without going outdoors except to step into smooth cars, floating from beautiful interior to beautiful interior with expert drivers in between. He was last there in 2005, with Vincent. She seemed enchanted by the opulence, although in retrospect it's begun to occur to him that she may have been acting at least part of the time. She had a significant financial stake in maintaining the appearance of happiness. Anyway. In the counterlife, the hours surrounding the holiday party are very different. When Claire comes to see him in the office on the day of the holiday party, he deflects her. He pretends he doesn't know what she's talking about, maintains this air of polite bafflement until she gives up and leaves. He isn't above a little gaslighting, if that's what it takes to stay out of prison. In the counterlife, he confesses to nothing. He does not crack. That night he goes with Vincent to the holiday party, and when they leave together, they both return to the pied-à-terre. He kisses her good night as if everything were perfectly normal, revealing nothing of his plans. He stays up when she goes to sleep, drinks some coffee and makes his preparations, stares out at the dark ocean of Central Park and the lights beyond, memorizing a view that he'll never see again. He waits through the night for the window washers, who rise up the sheer wall of the tower on their suspended platform at dawn.

It's early in the morning, first light over the park, and they don't recognize him. Why would they? Over the course of the night he's given himself a buzz cut, he's wearing dark glasses and a baseball hat, and—crucially—he's dressed all in white, just like them, his gym bag slung over his shoulder. He opens the window and speaks with them. "Could I get a ride down to the street?" he asks. They refuse at first, naturally, but he has $5,000 in cash in the pied-à-terre and he gives it all to them, throws in two bottles of an exquisite Grand Cru Classé from his favourite château in Bordeaux and then Vincent's diamond bracelet and earrings—she's in the bedroom, still asleep—and persuades them: He just wants a ride down to the street. That's all. It'll be over in a few minutes. No one will know. It's a lot of money and the best wine they're ever going to drink.

Who are they? It doesn't matter. A and B. Let's say they're young guys who don't know any better, or they know better but let's say they have kids to feed. Window washing, that can't be a particularly well-paying job, unless ascending the glass curtain walls of high-rises is one of those jobs that's so terrifying no one wants to do it? Anyway, who cares, either way it's a lot of money, so let's say they take it. Alkaitis climbs out into the cold, and on the slow descent to the sidewalk, A and B are quiet and respectful, he senses that they're admiring his forethought in dressing like them—not *exactly* like them, window washers don't wear dress shirts, but enough like them that from any distance it's just three men in white on a suspended platform, an everyday sight in the glass city, and by now the rising sun is reflecting off the tower so no one can look directly at them anyway, because that's how brilliant his plan is, they descend in the glare and he climbs out and thanks them and hails a taxi to the airport. A few hours later he's on a flight to Dubai, first-class obviously, in one of those reclining seats that are actually more like a private pod with bed and television. In the counterlife, he reclines the seat flat over the Atlantic and falls into a blissful sleep.

In FCI Florence Medium 1 the lights go on, the alarm for the three a.m. count blaring, and he gets out of bed, neither awake nor asleep, putting on his slippers in an automatic movement, still halfway somewhere else, Hazelton stumbling out of bed across from him. In the counterlife, he is never arrested, let alone sentenced, let alone subject to head counts. (Guards yelling in the corridor—"get up get up get *up*"—and then one stops in the doorway with his little clicker, and after a few minutes the count is over and it's possible to go back to bed.) In the counter-life, he transfers all his money into the secret offshore accounts, out of the hands of the American government. By the time his daughter calls the FBI, he's out of reach. Dubai has no extradition treaty with the United States.

He has enough money to live in Dubai indefinitely, in tranquility, in the cool interiors and the brutal heat. Hotel, or villa? Hotel. He'll live in a hotel and order room service forever. Villas are a staffing headache. He's had enough of staff.

"I'd like to ask about your daughter," Julie Freeman says at their second meeting.

"I'm sorry," he says, "but I'd prefer not to talk about her. I think Claire deserves her privacy."

"Fair enough. In that case, I'd like to ask you about your wife."

"Do you mean Suzanne, or Vincent?"

"I thought I'd start with Vincent. Does she visit you here?"

"No. Actually, I . . ." He isn't sure it's wise to continue, but who else can he ask? His only visitors are journalists. "Would you stop taking notes, please, just for a moment?"

She sets her pen on the table.

"This is embarrassing," he says, "and I'd appreciate it if you'd keep this off the record, but do you know where she is?"

"I've been looking for her myself. I'd love to talk to her, but wherever she is, she's keeping a low profile."

Maybe the descent down the tower with the window washers is a little overdramatic. He could just as easily have kissed Vincent good night after the holiday party, told her he had to go get drinks with an investor and that she shouldn't wait up for him; he could've sent her home in a car while he fled the country. No, he would have had to go back to Greenwich for his passport. Well, if he can rewrite history so that he fled the country, surely the passport isn't an impediment. In the counterlife, maybe he's the kind of person who keeps his passport on his person at all times. He kisses Vincent good night and hails a taxi to the airport.

In the counterlife, Claire visits him in Dubai. She is happy to see him. She disapproves of his actions, but they can laugh about it. Their conversations are effortless. In the counterlife, Claire isn't the one who called the FBI.

Claire has never visited him in prison and will not take his calls.

He wrote Claire a letter his first month in prison, but she responded only with two pages of trial transcript, from the initial hearing where he had to keep saying *guilty* over and over again. He remembers standing there and repeating the word, nauseous, sweat trickling down his back. On the page it looks strange and fragmented, like bad poetry or a script.

THE COURT: How do you now plead to Count One of the information, guilty or not guilty?

THE DEFENDANT: Guilty.

THE COURT: Mr. Alkaitis, please speak up so I can hear you.

THE DEFENDANT: I'm sorry, Your Honour. I plead guilty.

THE COURT: How do you now plead to Count Two of the information, guilty or not guilty?

THE DEFENDANT: Guilty.

THE COURT: How do you now plead to Count Three of the information, guilty or not guilty?

THE DEFENDANT: Guilty.

THE COURT: How do you now plead to Count Four of the information, guilty or not guilty?

THE DEFENDANT: Guilty.

THE COURT: How do you now plead to Count Five of the information, guilty or not guilty?

THE DEFENDANT: Guilty.

THE COURT: How do you now plead to Count Six of the information, guilty or not guilty?

THE DEFENDANT: Guilty.

THE COURT: How do you now plead to Count Seven of the information, guilty or not guilty?

THE DEFENDANT: Guilty.

THE COURT: How do you now plead to Count Eight of the information, guilty or not guilty?

THE DEFENDANT: Guilty.

THE COURT: How do you now plead to Count Nine of the information, guilty or not guilty?

THE DEFENDANT: Guilty.

THE COURT: How do you now plead to Count Ten of the information, guilty or not guilty?

THE DEFENDANT: Guilty.

THE COURT: How do you now plead to Count Eleven of the information, guilty or not guilty?

THE DEFENDANT: Guilty.

THE COURT: How do you now plead to Count Twelve of the information, guilty or not guilty?

THE DEFENDANT: Guilty.

7

SEAFARER

2008–2013

The *Neptune Cumberland*

Vincent left land on a bright blue day with clouds like popcorn, in August 2013. Her first glimpse of the *Neptune Cumberland* was at Port Newark. She was escorted to the ship by port security, where she had to wait by the gangway stairs for what seemed like a long time. She was nervous and excited. There were other people around, but they were out of sight, either high overhead in the cabs of cranes or driving trucks laden with containers. She'd known where she was going, she'd studied the coursework and read the books, but the scale of this world was still astonishing to her. The hull of the *Neptune Cumberland* was a sheer wall of steel. The cranes were the size of Manhattan towers. She knew that the containers could weigh as much as sixty-seven thousand pounds, but the cranes plucked them from the flatbed trucks as if they were nothing, and there was an improbable grace in that illusion of weightlessness. She stood in a landscape of unadulterated industry and enormous machines, a port where humans had no place, feeling smaller and smaller, until her escorts appeared, two men descending the white steel steps from the deck. It took them a long time to reach her. They introduced themselves as they stepped down onto land: Geoffrey Bell and Felix Mendoza, third mate and steward, her colleague and her boss respectively.

"Welcome aboard," Mendoza said.

"Yes, welcome," said Bell. They shook her hand, and the port security guy got back in his car and drove off. Mendoza led the way and Bell followed with her suitcase, although she could easily have managed it herself.

"I'm glad you're here," Mendoza said. He kept up a running monologue all the way up the stairs. He'd specifically requested an assistant cook with experience in more than one restaurant, he said, because he'd been at sea for too long and frankly could use some new menu ideas. He hoped Vincent didn't mind starting tonight. (She didn't.) He was glad she was Canadian because several of his favourite colleagues over the years had been Canadian too. She let him talk, because all she wanted was to absorb this place, the deck high above the port, and she kept thinking, *I'm here, I'm actually here,* while Mendoza led the way into the accommodations house and down a narrow industrial corridor that reminded her of the interiors of the ferries that run from Vancouver to Vancouver Island.

"Take a little time to unpack," Mendoza said, "and I'll come back for you in a couple hours." Bell, who hadn't said anything since offering to take the suitcase, set it inside the threshold of the room with surprising gentleness and smiled as he closed the door.

The room was more or less what Vincent had expected, small and blandly utilitarian, all imitation-wood cabinetry and white walls. There was a narrow bed, a closet, a desk, a sofa, everything either built into a wall or bolted to the floor. She had her own small bathroom. There was a window, but she kept the curtain closed, because she wanted the ocean to be the first thing she saw through it. From outside there was a constant clanging and grinding and creaking, cranes lowering containers into the holds and stacking them high on the lashing bridges. She unpacked her possessions—clothes, a few books, her camera—and found as she did so that she was thinking of Bell. She'd never believed in love at first sight but she did believe in *recognition* at first sight, she believed in understanding upon meeting someone for the first time that they were going to be important in her life, a sensation like recognizing a familiar face in an old photograph: in a sea of faces that mean nothing, one comes into focus. *You.*

She zipped up the empty suitcase, stowed it in the closet, and turned to the stack of sheets and blankets and the well-used pillow on the bed. She made the bed and then sat on it for a while, acclimatizing herself to the room. It was impossible not to think in that moment of the master bedroom suite in Jonathan's house in Greenwich, the wasteful acres of carpeting and empty space. Luxury is a weakness.

It had taken so much to come here, all the training and studying and certifications and hassle, and when Mendoza came to collect her, when she was shown the galley where she'd spend her working life, it seemed improbable that she was actually here, on board, that she'd successfully left land, and it was all she could do to refrain from grinning like an idiot while he kept up a running monologue about his meal plans—French fries with almost every meal as a matter of policy, say four dinners out of five, because the guys liked them and potatoes were cheap so it helped keep the budget under control; rice biryani twice a week for the same reason—and the first shift was such a blur of information and French fries that she didn't realize the ship had left

Newark until later that night, after the cleanup, when she stumbled grimy and exhausted out onto the deck, a constellation of tiny burns stinging on her forearms from the deep-fat fryer, and found that the air had changed, the humidity broken by a cool breeze that carried no scent of land. They were travelling south toward Charleston, the East Coast of the United States marked by a string of lights on the starboard horizon. She walked to the other side of the ship to look out at the Atlantic, its darkness broken only by the far lights of a distant ship and by airplanes beginning their descents into the eastern cities, and her thought at that moment was that she never wanted to live on land again.

"Why did you want to go to sea?" Geoffrey Bell asked her, the first time they talked. She'd been at sea for a week by then, give or take. The ship had just left the Bahamas and had begun the long Atlantic crossing, toward Port Elizabeth in South Africa. Geoffrey had come to the galley at the end of her shift and had asked if she might like to go for a walk with him. He'd taken her to his favourite place on the ship, a corner of the deck on C level that he liked because it was out of sight of the security cameras, "which I realize sounds sinister," he said, "now that I'm actually saying it aloud, but the trouble with being on a ship is the lack of privacy, don't you find?"

"I don't disagree," Vincent said. "Is that a barbecue?" There was a strange tubular contraption with four legs chained to a railing.

"Oh, it is," he said, "but I haven't seen it used in years." Onboard barbecues were dismal, he explained. Picture twenty men standing around on a steel deck, trying to make conversation in the wind while they eat hot dogs and chicken, a wall of containers rising up behind them. No, he's not explaining it right. Not twenty men, twenty *co-workers*, twenty colleagues who've been stuck at sea together for months and are fairly sick of one another's company, and not a single solitary beer for lubrication, because of the no-alcohol rule. Still, he liked this deck, he said.

Vincent liked it too. It was quiet, except for the ever-present hum of the engines. She leaned over the railing to look down at the ocean.

"It's a pleasure to be out of sight of land," she said. The horizons were uninterrupted on all sides.

"I notice you didn't answer my question."

"Right, you asked why I went to sea."

"It's not my best conversational opener," he said. "Maybe even kind of overly obvious, since here we are, standing on a ship. But one has to start somewhere."

"It's a strange story," Vincent said.

"Thank god. I haven't heard a decent story in months."

"Well," Vincent said. "I was with a man for a while. It ended in a complicated way."

"I see," he said. "I don't mean to pry, if it's something you'd prefer not to talk about."

She could see that he perceived the outlines of a story, lurking under the surface like an iceberg, and two possibilities opened before her, two variations: she could tell him that she'd been affiliated with a criminal and risk his contempt, or she could be one of those exhaustingly mysterious people whom no one wants to talk to because they can't open their mouths without hinting at dark secrets that they can't quite bring themselves to reveal. "No, it's fine. Actually, it wasn't quite . . . I didn't leave land because of what he did, specifically," she said. "I left land because I kept running into the wrong people."

"That's the trouble with land," Geoffrey said. "It's got too many people on it."

Last Evenings on Land

At first, it seemed there would be a way to withstand the collapse of the kingdom of money, to remain in the city that she loved and find a new life there. The morning after Jonathan's last holiday party, she'd woken alone and shivering in the pied-à-terre in Manhattan. The duvet had slipped to the floor. She rose, showered, made some coffee, and spent a few minutes looking out at the view of Central Park. She knew by then that Jonathan was going to be arrested, and knew this was the last time she'd admire this view. Jonathan had left a beautiful little duffel bag in the pied-à-terre, creamy white with brown leather accents. Her side of the closet held two gowns, which she thought might have some resale value, and there were also five thousand dollars in cash and some jewellery in the safe. She put the cash and the jewellery in the bag and in her jacket, rolled the dresses carefully into the duffel bag along with a couple of changes of clothes.

She brought her coffee to the bathroom, where she reached for the lacquered box where she kept her makeup here, and then stopped. In all of her time with Jonathan, she had never failed to put on makeup. She thought her face looked strange without it, but now, on this particular morning, with her pretend husband either on the verge of arrest or in police custody, there was some appeal in the thought of not looking like herself. Vincent studied her face in the mirror while she drank her coffee. She saw that at some point in the near past she had slipped over a border, into the era of her life where when she was tired she looked not just tired but slightly older. She was almost twenty-eight years old.

She found a pair of nail scissors in a drawer and began method-ically cutting off her hair. Her head felt immediately lighter, and a little cold. A half hour later, when she left the building for the last time, the concierge in the lobby did a double take before his smile snapped into place. She got her hair recut at the first salon she passed—"Did your kid cut your hair while you were sleeping?" the stylist asked, concerned—and then stopped into a drugstore, where she bought a pair of minimum-strength read-ing glasses, although her eyes were fine. Vincent examined her-self in a drugstore mirror. In glasses, without makeup, her hair cut short, she thought she looked like a very different person.

Within a week she'd found a place to live in a satellite town a few stops up the Hudson Line from Grand Central, an au pair's suite that was really just a room above a garage, with a bathroom carved out of one corner and a kitchenette in another. She slept on a mattress on the floor and had a dresser that she'd purchased from Goodwill for $40, a card table that her landlord had given her, and a single chair that she'd found on the street on garbage day. It was enough. Within three weeks of Jonathan's arrest, she'd found a job bartending in Chelsea. The hours weren't enough, so she was also a kitchen trainee at a restaurant on the Lower East Side. She preferred the kitchen, because bartending is a perfor-mance. The public streams through your workplace and watches your every move. Every time she looked up and saw a new face at the bar, there was a moment of terror when she thought it was going to be an investor.

She saw Mirella again, just once, a year and a half later. In the spring of 2010, Vincent was tending bar in Chelsea when Mirella came in with a group of people, six or seven of them.

Mirella's hair was teased into a magnificent Afro. Her lipstick was fire-engine red. She was dressed in one of those outfits that look casual at first glance but are in fact composed entirely of coded signals—the sweatshirt that cost $700, the jeans whose rips were carefully executed by artisans in Detroit, the scuffed boots that retailed for a thousand dollars, etc. She looked spectacular.

"Regulars," Ned said, following the direction of Vincent's gaze. He was her best friend at work, a mild sort of person who was pursuing an MFA in poetry that he didn't want to talk about. They were both working the bar that night, although the place wasn't crowded enough to justify both of them.

"Really? I've never seen them here." The hostess was leading Mirella's group to a booth in the back corner.

"Only because you never work Thursdays."

A man in a shiny blue blazer had his arm draped over Mirella's shoulders. Vincent's desire to be seen by her was matched only by her desire to hide. She had tried to call Mirella three times: once the day after Jonathan was arrested, then twice when she learned that Faisal had died. All three calls went to voicemail.

"You okay?" Ned asked.

"Not at all," Vincent said. "You mind if I take five?"

"No, go ahead."

Vincent slipped out through the kitchen door and walked down the block a little. Cherry blossoms had appeared almost overnight on the trees across the street, and the flowers looked like an explosion, like fireworks suspended in the dark. The cigarette couldn't last forever, and when she came back in, Mirella and one of her friends had left the group at the table and moved to the bar. Whatever Mirella had to say, whatever accusations and condemnations she'd been rehearsing these past two years, she could say them now, and Vincent could tell her that words couldn't express how sorry she was, and that if she'd known— if she'd even suspected—then of course she would have said something, she would have told Mirella immediately, she would have called the FBI herself. *I didn't know,* Vincent wanted to tell her, *I didn't know anything, but I am so sorry.* Then they could go their separate ways with nominally lighter burdens, or something like that.

"Hello," Mirella said, smiling politely at Vincent, "do you have any bar snacks?"

"Oh, that's the best idea ever," her friend said. She was about Vincent and Mirella's age, at some indeterminate point in her thirties, with aggressively bleached hair cut in a squared-off bob like a 1920s flapper.

"Bar snacks," Vincent repeated. "Um, yes, mixed nuts or pretzels?"

"Mixed nuts!" the flapper said. "God yes, that's exactly what I need. This martini's super-sweet."

"Actually," Mirella said, holding Vincent's gaze, "could we possibly have both?"

"Of course. Mixed nuts and pretzels, coming right up." This was a dream, wasn't it?

"I haven't had mixed nuts in like a million years," the flapper said to Mirella.

"I'd say you've been missing out," Mirella said.

Vincent felt strangely outside of herself. She observed her hands as she poured mixed nuts and pretzels into little steel bowls. *I dreamed you came into my bar and didn't know me.* She set the bowls gently on the bar before her former best friend, who said thanks without looking at Vincent and returned to her conversation. "The thing with New York," Mirella's friend was saying as Vincent turned away, "is everybody leaves. I really thought I'd be the exception."

"Everyone thinks they're the exception."

"You're probably right. It's just, my friends started taking off ten years ago, going to Atlanta or Minneapolis or wherever, and I guess I thought I'd be the one to stay and make a go of it."

"But it's a better job in Milwaukee, isn't it?"

"I could afford a huge apartment there," the flapper said. "Probably actually a whole house. I don't know, it just seems like such a cliché, living in New York City for your twenties and then leaving."

"Yeah, but people do that for a reason," Mirella said. "Don't you ever get the impression that it's easier to live pretty much everywhere else?" *Look at me,* Vincent thought, *notice me, say my name,* but Mirella ignored Vincent as completely as if she were a stranger.

"Hey, excuse me," Mirella said.

Vincent took off her glasses before she turned to face her.

"Mirella," she said.

"Could I get another martini?" As though she hadn't heard her name.

"Of course. What's that you were drinking, Mirella, a Sunday Morning?"

"No, just a plain old Cosmo."

"I thought you didn't like Cosmos," Vincent said.

"Oh, I'll take another Midnight in Saigon, please," the flapper said.

"Coming right up," Vincent said. Was it possible that she was actually unrecognizable to someone who'd once been her dearest friend? A more likely possibility was that this was Mirella's revenge, pretending not to know Vincent, or perhaps she was playing the same game Vincent was, living in disguise, except that Mirella's disguise was more comprehensive and included pointedly not recognizing anyone from her previous life, or alternatively, possibly Vincent was losing her mind and maybe none of her memories were real.

"One Cosmopolitan, one Midnight in Saigon." Vincent set the drinks on the bar.

"Thanks so much," Mirella said, and Vincent heard the glasses clink as she turned away. She emptied the tip jar on the counter.

"Little early to count out, isn't it?" Ned was looking at her curiously. There was no one at the bar now except Mirella and her friend, deep in conversation.

"Ned, I'm sorry about this, but you're going to have to close up on your own tonight." Vincent divided the tip money into two piles and pocketed one of them.

"What's going on? Are you sick?"

"No, I'm walking off the job. I apologize."

"Vincent, you can't just—"

"I can, though," Vincent said, and left him there. She was much more ruthless after Alkaitis than before. She exited via the kitchen door. Mirella didn't look at her as she left. She wouldn't have imagined that Mirella could be so cold, but what were they if not actors? *You didn't come from money,* Mirella had said to Vincent once, in a different, unimaginable life. If they were plausible in the age of money because they could disguise their origins, why should it be surprising that Mirella was capable of pretending they'd never met? Pretending was their area of mutual expertise.

That night she walked down to lower Manhattan, to the Russian Café, a place she'd frequented during her years with Alkaitis, although if anyone recognized her from that time, they never let on. Her favourite manager was working that night, a woman in her thirties named Ilieva who spoke with a slight Russian accent and had once let slip that she'd acquired her green card in exchange for testimony in a criminal case.

"You have no coat?" Ilieva asked when she came to Vincent's table. "You'll freeze to death."

"I just quit my job," Vincent said. "I forgot my coat in the break room."

"You just walked off the job?"

"I did."

"Glass of red on the house?"

"Thank you," Vincent said, although the wine here was terrible. The point of this place wasn't the wine, the point was the atmosphere. Here in the warmth and dim lighting, with scents of coffee and cheesecake in the air, Nina Simone on the sound system, the gripped feeling in her chest was beginning to subside. This place was the one constant between the kingdom of money and her current life.

"So," Ilieva said when she came back with the wine, "what next? Another bartending job?"

"No, I have my second job, in the other place," Vincent said. "I'm going to try to get more hours."

"It's a kitchen job, isn't it? What, you want to be a chef, open your own restaurant?"

"No," Vincent said. "I think I'd like to go to sea."

Vincent's mother went to sea in her early twenties. Vincent had always pressed her for stories from when she was young, because while the contours of Vincent's father's life were fairly straightforward—an undramatic childhood in the Seattle suburbs, a brief stint studying philosophy before he dropped out and found work as a tree planter—Vincent's mother's past held a certain mystery. Vincent's mother had survived a miserable childhood in a small town in the Prairies—there were aunts, an uncle, and even a set of grandparents whom Vincent had been given to understand she would never meet—and gone east when she was seventeen, to Nova Scotia, where she worked as a waitress and wrote poetry, then at nineteen she got a job as a steward on a Canadian Coast Guard vessel that maintained navigational aids in the shipping lanes. She loved it and hated it in equal measure. She saw the northern lights and sailed past icebergs, but also she was always cold and thought she might actually die of claustrophobia, so she quit after two rotations and drove across the country with a new boyfriend. She was a restless person. Within a year the boyfriend was going to medical school in Vancouver and Vincent's mother was living precariously in Caiette, writing poetry that was sometimes accepted for publication in obscure literary journals, commuting back and forth on the mail boat and hitchhiking into Port Hardy for a job cleaning houses, until she fell in love with a married man down the road—Vincent's father—and got pregnant with Vincent. She was still only twenty-three years old.

Vincent's mother would not talk about her family. "They're not nice people," she'd say. "They're not worth talking about, sweetie, so please don't ask." But of the stories she was willing to tell, what Vincent most wanted to hear about was the time on the coast guard vessel, and she pressed her mother for those stories so many times that they began to seem like Vincent's own memories: she'd never been to that coast but held mental images of the northern lights shifting over a winter sky, the silent towers of icebergs in a dark grey sea. And then after her mother was gone, Vincent started trying to place her mother in the picture—her mother gazing at the iceberg, her mother's face tilted toward the aurora borealis—but who was her mother at twenty, at twenty-one? It's so difficult to picture your parents in the time before you existed. In memory her mother was stranded forever at thirty-six, the age she'd been when she came into thirteen-year-old Vincent's bedroom, kissed her on the top of the head—Vincent barely looked up from her book—and said, "I'm just taking the canoe out for a bit, sweetie, I'll see you later"—before she descended the stairs for the last time.

The day after she saw Mirella, Vincent took the train back into the city and then boarded a southbound subway and rode it to its terminal point, to stand for a while on a white-sand beach at the edge of the city, filming the waves. A cold, grey day, but the cold was bracing. A containership was passing on the far horizon. She was thinking of her mother, and then, watching the ship, she found herself thinking of one of her last nights at the Hotel Caiette, a day or two after she first met Jonathan. He'd been eating dinner at the bar that night, and she'd been talking to him, when another guest arrived, a man staying in the hotel with his wife. She couldn't remember his name, but she remembered a detail of the conversation: "I'm in shipping," he'd said to Jonathan when the subject of work came up, and this was memorable because he was someone who clearly loved his job, she could see that immediately, the way he lit up when the topic was introduced. Years later, standing by the ocean on a cold spring day, she lowered her camera to watch the passing ship. How difficult would it be to get a job at sea?

Geoffrey

"Thailand," Geoffrey Bell repeated, aboard the *Neptune Cumberland* in the fall of 2013. "Why are you going to Thailand when your leave comes up?"

"Because I've never been," Vincent said.

"Seems like a solid reason. It's just that most people use their shore leave to go home."

"Where would that be, though? I don't mean this in any kind of tragic sense," Vincent said, "but I don't feel that I really have a home on land at this point."

"Don't tell me you think of the *Neptune Cumberland* as home," Geoffrey said. "You've been at sea for, what, two months?"

"Three."

Three months of rising in her cabin for a middle-of-the-night shower before breakfast prep, long hours of cooking in a windowless room that moved in rough weather, walks on the deck in rain and in sunlight, sleeping with Geoffrey, overtime hours, three months of hard labour and dreamless sleep while the ship moved on a sixty-eight-day cycle from Newark down to Baltimore and Charleston, from Charleston over to Freeport in the Bahamas, from Freeport to Port Elizabeth in South Africa, up to Rotterdam in the Netherlands and Bremerhaven in Germany, then back across the Atlantic to Newark again. Most of the men on board—she was the only woman—worked for six months straight and then took three months off, and she'd decided to do the same.

Geoffrey smiled but didn't look up. He was folding a tiny origami swan. She'd told him his cabin was bleak and he'd agreed with her, so they were making little swans and hanging them from his curtain rod. "I had such romantic visions of going to sea," he said, "as a boy, I mean. You know, *see the world,* that kind of thing. Turns out most of the world looks very much like a series of interchangeable container ports."

"And yet you're still here."

"I'm still here. One gets sucked in. Did you read that book

I gave you for your birthday?" He held up a swan, turning it between his fingers, and passed it to Vincent.

"I'm almost halfway done. I love it." Vincent pierced the swan with her needle—the commissary sold sewing kits—and drew the fishing line through.

"I thought you would. If you're halfway through, then you've got to the part where they go fishing for birds, haven't you?"

"Yes. I loved that image." The book he'd given her was a collection of narratives written by the captain and crew of the *Columbia Rediviva*, an American trading ship that circled the globe in the last decade of the eighteenth century, and it contained an image that would never leave her: On the last day of 1790, two hundred miles off the coast of Argentina, the air filled with albatrosses. The crew gathered on deck and cast fishing hooks baited with salt pork into the ocean, to pull in the birds diving out of the sky.

"I loved it too. I read the book when I was sixteen, and after that, going to sea was a fixation of mine." He was having trouble with his latest origami swan: he frowned at it, smoothed out the paper, and started again. "Would you like to hear something mildly devastating?"

"Sure."

"My father once told me that he'd dreamed of being a pilot. Why, you may ask, might one find this devastating?"

"Because you told me he was a coal miner." Vincent was standing on his chair to hang swans from the curtain rod, which was otherwise unused, because Geoffrey's window was always blocked by the container stacks. "God, you're right, Geoffrey, that's ghastly. You dream of flying, but instead . . ."

"I didn't want to regret not going to sea."

"That makes perfect sense."

"Do you like it?" He was holding up another swan, an orange one, a little lopsided.

"Do I like what, your swan?"

"No, all of this. Being at sea. Your life."

"Yes." She realized the truth of this as she spoke. "I like all of it. I love all of it. I've never been so happy."

8

THE COUNTERLIFE

2015

In the counterlife, Alkaitis moves through a nameless hotel. Outside, the view keeps changing, because he keeps changing his mind about which hotel he's in. He can't remember the names of these places, but they come with distinct sets of details and impressions. Let's say it's the hotel with the massive white staircase by the reception desk, the suite with the hot tub sunk into the floor by the full-length windows. In that case the view is of a shadowless pale blue sea, meeting the white sky at the blinding horizon.

"These morons think they're warrior monks or something," Churchwell says, inclining his head toward the five younger white guys doing calisthenics in unison at the far end of the recreation yard. "All these dumb ideas about codes of honour."

"Well, you've got to have a code of some kind, I suppose," Alkaitis says, a little resentful at being jolted out of the counterlife.

"I get the need for structure," Churchwell says. "Sense of belonging, familial feeling, sure, I get it. All I'm saying is, don't talk to me about your code of honour when you're doing a fifty-year bid for child pornography."

———

The child pornographer, Tait, had no tattoos when he came to Florence—upon arrival he was a pale, soft person with glasses and unmarked skin—but now he has a little swastika inked on his back. "Some people have families from the beginning," he says. "Other people have to look a little harder." This is in the cafeteria. Alkaitis, who expends a great deal of effort trying not to think about his family, lets himself drift. One of the things he likes about the counterlife is that Tait isn't there. Say it's the other hotel, not the one on the mainland with the view of the horizon but the one on that island, that man-made island whose name he can't remember that's shaped like a palm tree. In that case, the view is of the stagnant trapped water between the palm fronds, as it were, a gaudy row of McMansions shimmering in the heat on the opposite shore. He liked that suite. It was enormous. Vincent spent a lot of time in the hot tub.

But no, that's memory, not the counterlife. Vincent isn't in the counterlife. He feels it's important to keep the two separate, memory vs. counterlife, but he's been finding the separation increasingly difficult. It's a permeable border. In memory, the air conditioning was so aggressive that she had trouble keeping warm, which was why she was always in the hot tub, whereas in the counterlife she's not there at all.

In the counterlife he turns away from the view of McMansions and leaves the room, walks out into the wide corridor with its elaborately patterned strip of carpeting, into the elevator made of dark mirrored surfaces, which opens unexpectedly into the lobby of the Hotel Caiette, where Vincent sits with Walter, the night manager, on leather armchairs. This is a memory: they came back here a year before he was arrested. He woke up alone in the bed, he remembers, he woke at five a.m. and went looking for her, found her here in the lobby with Walter.

The memory stays with him because when she looked up, her

mask slipped just a little, and for just a flash he saw something like disappointment on her face. She wasn't happy to see him. But here memory and the counterlife diverge, because while in real life he got involved in one of those painfully superficial conversations about jet lag, in the counterlife his gaze has shifted to the window, where outside it seems much too bright for five in the morning in British Columbia, a different quality of sunlight altogether, because once again he's in Dubai, on the palm-tree island, looking out at houses across the narrow bay, and now the lobby is empty.

Do all of the other men have counterlives too? Alkaitis searches their faces for clues. He's never been curious about other people before. He doesn't know how to ask. But he sees them gazing into the distance and wonders where they are.

"You ever think about alternate universes?" he asks Churchwell, sometime in early 2015. He came across the idea at some point in his free life and dismissed it, because it sounded frankly ridiculous, but now it holds increasing appeal. Churchwell isn't a friend, exactly, but they often eat at the same table because they're part of the same loose-knit club of people who are never going to be free again, also part of a different loose-knit club of New Yorkers. These clubs are called cars, which Alkaitis likes. *We're all together in the same car,* he finds himself thinking sometimes, with a little flicker of camaraderie, when he's with Churchwell or one of the other lifers, although of course he'd never voice this aloud and also it's depressing if you think about it too much. (*We're all together in the same car that's stalled and will never go anywhere ever again.*) Churchwell can be counted on to have heard of multiverse theory or anything else anyone mentions, because all he ever does is read books and write letters. Churchwell was an honest-to-god double agent, CIA/KGB, who's using his life sentence as an opportunity to get some reading done.

"Who doesn't? In an alternate universe, I got away with it and I've got a sweet pad in Moscow," Churchwell says.

"I'd live in Dubai. I liked it there."

"I've thought this through. I'd've married an oligarch's daughter, maybe a supermodel? Two or three kids, golden retriever, summer house in a warm country with no extradition treaty."

"I'd live in Dubai." He catches Churchwell's glance and realizes that he already said this.

"Mr. Alkaitis, how are you this afternoon?" The doctor looks too young to be a doctor.

"I've been having some trouble with memory and concentration." He doesn't add *hallucinations,* because he doesn't want to end up on hard-core antipsychotics, and men who go into the hospital often don't come back. Anyway *hallucinations* is the wrong word, it's more like a creeping sense of unreality, a sense of collapsing borders, reality seeping into the counterlife and the counterlife seeping into memory. But maybe there's something to be done, some medication that won't turn him into a shuffling zombie but that might stop or at least slow the deterioration, if deterioration is what he's facing. He's trying to be clear-eyed about it.

"Okay. I'm just going to ask you a series of simple questions, and that should give us a better idea of where we're at. Can you tell me what year it is?"

"Seriously? I'm not that far gone, I hope."

"I'm not saying you are. Just the first in a series of standard questions to screen you for potential memory problems. What's the year?"

"Two thousand fifteen," Alkaitis says. Has he been here for six years already? It seems impossible. Maybe he shouldn't discount the view from the palm-tree-island hotel, actually. The thing with white-sand beaches, blue sea to the horizon under a cloudless sky: that's a view with two colours, just blue and white, tranquil but you could die of boredom. But the palm-tree-island hotel looked over an inlet to the enormous houses on the other side, and there's life in that. One of the mansions was pink, memorable because he and Vincent had laughed at it. It wasn't a tasteful muted pink, it was pink like Pepto-Bismol.

"What month is it?"

"December," Alkaitis says. "We were in the Emirates for Christmas."

The doctor's face is carefully blank as he makes a note, and Alkaitis realizes his mistake. "I'm sorry, I was thinking of something else. It's June. June 2015."

"Good. Do you know today's date?"

"Sure, it's the seventeenth. July seventeenth."

"I'm going to give you a name and address," the doctor says, "and I'll ask you to repeat it back to me in a few minutes. Ready?"

"Yes."

"Mr. Jones, twenty-three Cecil Court, London."

"Okay. Got it."

"What time is it to the nearest hour?"

Alkaitis glances around but sees no clock in the room.

"To the nearest hour," the doctor repeats. "Your best guess."

"Well, our appointment was at ten and you kept me waiting, so I'll go with eleven."

"Count backwards from twenty to one."

He counts backwards from twenty to one. The details of that weird palm-tree-shaped island are a little hazy. Is it one island, or a collection of islands that taken together form a palm tree? Anyway, that was the hotel where he and Suzanne stayed on his first visit to the UAE, where they held hands over a table in a restaurant that featured a giant aquarium with a shark in it. This was in the last year before her diagnosis, which means that there in that beautiful memory Suzanne is already secretly, invisibly sick, malignant cells proliferating silently on liver and pancreas. God, she was stunning. Much older than Vincent, obviously, but frankly there's something to be said for having a companion who isn't young enough to be your daughter, also something to be said for a companion from whom you don't have to hide. He remembered holding hands with her and discussing the investors. "If you think Lenny Xavier doesn't know what he's doing," she said, "I've got a bridge to sell you."

"Say the months of the year in reverse order." The doctor, intruding.

"December, November, October, September, August, June, July . . . May, April, March. February. January." Thinking of the thrill of that moment in the hotel, the delight in having a co-conspirator. "You think we can keep it going?" he asked her. Dessert was just arriving: chocolate cake with ice cream for Alkaitis, a dish of fresh fruit for Suzanne.

"Tell me the name and address I gave you earlier," the doctor says.

"I'm sorry?"

"The address?"

"It was Palm Jumeirah." Alkaitis smiles, pleased to have remembered the name. "Definitely Palm Jumeirah, in Dubai. I don't remember if there was a street number."

He leaves the doctor's office with a sense of unease. He knows he messed up that last answer, but is it his fault that his life here is so boring that it sometimes takes him a minute or two to snap out of the counterlife and back to reality, if that's what this is? "I'm distracted, not demented," he mutters to himself, loudly enough that the guard escorting him back to the cell block glances at him. It isn't his fault that his days are so similar that he keeps sliding into memories, or into the counterlife, although it is troubling that his memories and the counterlife have started blurring together.

An unsettling thought while standing in line for the commissary: when he dies in prison, will he die in the counterlife too?

When he's not in the counterlife, he has dreams in which nothing happens except a mounting sense of dread. In the dream, he knows that someone is approaching, and then one evening he's reading the paper in the cell after dinner—awake, not dreaming—and he hears a voice say, quite distinctly, "I'm here."

He looks up. Hazelton has been pacing for a solid hour, but it wasn't Hazelton who spoke. Alkaitis is quiet for a long time before he can bring himself to say anything.

"You believe in ghosts?" Alkaitis asks as casually as possible.

Hazelton grins, apparently delighted by the question. Hazelton is an understimulated person who longs for conversation. "I don't know, bro, I always *wanted* to believe in ghosts, I think it'd be cool if they were floating around, but I'm not so sure they're real."

"You ever met anyone who saw one?" What he doesn't tell Hazelton is that Faisal is standing in a corner of the cell. Alkaitis has been trying to convince himself that he's hallucinating. Faisal cannot possibly be in this room, because (a) it's a prison cell and (b) Faisal is dead. Nonetheless, Faisal looks alarmingly real. He's wearing his favourite gold velvet slippers. He's standing under the cell window, craning his neck to look at the moon.

"I knew a guy who swore he'd seen one. But the ghost he'd seen, it was a guy he killed by accident in a robbery."

"Did you believe him?"

"Nah. Well, kind of. I mean, I don't think it was an actual ghost, I think it was just his guilty conscience."

Faisal flickers slightly, like a faulty hologram, then blinks out.

9

A FAIRY TALE

2008

The Boat

In the last September Vincent and Alkaitis spent together, they "went sailing," as he called it, which seemed an odd way to describe a few days of lounging around on an enormous boat with no sails. He invited his friend Olivia, who Vincent gathered had known Jonathan's brother, and at night the three of them had dinner and then drank together in the breeze on deck. Vincent, who always tried to stay sharp, could make a single cocktail last for hours, but she liked making drinks for other people.

"We were just talking about you," Olivia said when Vincent returned to the deck with a fresh round that she'd mixed inside.

"I hope you made up some interesting rumours, at least," Vincent said.

"We didn't have to," Jonathan said. "You're an interesting person." He accepted his drink from Vincent with a little nod and passed the other glass to Olivia.

"You remind me so much of myself at your age," Olivia said with an obvious air of bestowing a compliment.

"Oh," Vincent said. "I'm flattered." She glanced at Jonathan, who was suppressing a smile. Olivia sipped her drink and gazed out at the ocean.

"This is delicious," Olivia said. "Thank you."

"I'm so glad you like it." Vincent was charmed by Olivia, as she knew Jonathan was, but something about Olivia made Vincent a little sad. Olivia's dress was too formal, her lipstick was too bright, her hair was freshly trimmed, she was slightly too attentive in the way she looked at Jonathan, and the combined effect was overeager. *You're showing your hand,* Vincent wanted to tell her, *you can't let anyone see how hard you're trying,* but of course there was no way to give advice to a woman two or three times her age.

"Do you ever go to the Brooklyn Academy of Music?" Olivia asked after a while. "My sister was just telling me the other day about a show she'd seen there, and it occurred to me, I haven't gone in years."

"You know I try not to cross that river if I can help it," Jonathan said.

"Snob," Olivia said.

"Guilty as charged. Although, I was just thinking about Brooklyn the other day. I was looking at a real estate listing, this loft a friend of mine was thinking about buying, and I'm looking at all this luxury, some four-thousand-square-foot place in this gorgeous neighbourhood by the Manhattan Bridge, and I'm thinking, *Whatever this place is now, it has nothing to do with the Brooklyn I used to know.* Seemed like a different city."

"And then there's BAM," Olivia said. "My sister Monica was telling me about this show she'd seen, and I realized, when was the last time I've been? Two thousand four? Two thousand five?"

"We should all go together," said Vincent, without much intention, but a month later, back on land, at home with a head cold on a hazy October afternoon, she found herself wondering if she should propose some sort of unexpected evening activity to Jonathan for the weekend, perhaps surprise him with theatre tickets or something, and her thoughts drifted back to the conversation. She looked up the Brooklyn Academy of Music online, and found her brother.

Melissa in the Water

It seemed that Paul, against all odds, had attained some success as a composer and performer. In early December he had a three-night series of performances at the Brooklyn Academy of Music. The program was called *Distant Northern Land: Soundtracks for Experimental Film.* She hadn't seen him in three years, since the last shift they'd worked together at the Hotel Caiette. In the image on the BAM website, he looked possessed: he was on a stage surrounded by equipment that she didn't understand, keyboards and inscrutable boxes with dials and knobs, hands blurred with motion, and above him, projected on a screen, was a picture that she thought she recognized as the shoreline of Caiette, a rocky beach with dark evergreens under a cloudy sky.

> *In* Distant Northern Land, *the emerging composer Paul James Smith presents a series of mysterious home videos, each with a running time of exactly five minutes, all filmed by the composer during his childhood in rural western Canada, presented here as part of an arresting composition that blurs the lines between musical genres and interrogates our preconceived notions of home movies, of wilderness, of—*

Vincent closed her eyes. She'd never been very careful with her videos. She'd made them and recorded over them, or made them and then left them in boxes in her childhood room. How often had Paul visited their father without her, in the years after she left Caiette? Often enough, she supposed. There was nothing stopping him from plundering her belongings. She found herself sitting outside by the pool, staring at the water, although she didn't specifically remember leaving the house.

On a late-summer afternoon in distant childhood, she and her mother had accompanied Paul as far as the Port Hardy airport, where he boarded a propeller plane to Vancouver to catch a connecting flight to Toronto. Vincent would have been ten or so. Paul had been awful all day, laughing at her whenever she said anything, then at the airport he turned away from them with a cursory wave and got into the security line without looking back, and afterward, on the way home with her mother, Vincent was quiet and a little sad.

"The thing with Paul," her mother said, while they were waiting for the water taxi on the pier at Grace Harbour, "is he's always seemed to think that you owe him something." Vincent remembered looking up at her mother, startled by the idea. "You don't," her mother said. "Nothing that happened to him is your fault."

In 2008, by the pool, Vincent heard footsteps and looked up. Anya was approaching with a blanket. "I thought you might need this," Anya said. "It's cold out here."

"Thank you," Vincent said.

Anya frowned. "Are you crying?"

It was difficult to uphold her contract with Jonathan in the two months that followed, difficult to maintain an air of lightness, but he seemed not to notice. In the last months of 2008, he was working all the time. He was always at the office, or in the study with his door closed. She heard his voice on the phone when she walked by in the hallway but could never quite make out the words. When he was with her, he seemed tired and distracted.

In early December she boarded a series of trains that brought her eventually to the steps of the Brooklyn Academy of Music. She'd worried about how to explain a Thursday night absence to Jonathan, but he'd texted to say he was working late and spending the night at the pied-à-terre. She arrived early and lingered outside for a while as a cross-section of affluent Brooklyn assembled on the sidewalk in their uniforms: flat-heeled boots and complicated arrangements of scarves for the women, beards and unflatteringly tight jeans on the men. It was a pleasure to watch them meet one another and pair off, streaming past her in twos and threes and fours, latecomers hurrying around the corner in a fluster of apologies and complaints about the subway. At last Vincent allowed herself to be pulled into the theatre with the last of the crowd, found her seat in the front row, and set about the usual preshow business of blowing her nose, unwrapping a cough drop just in case, turning off her phone, anything to not think about what she was about to see.

"Do you know the artist?" the woman beside her whispered. She looked to be in her eighties, white hair arranged into spikes. She was elegantly dressed, but she looked ill; she was emaciated and her hands trembled.

"No." Vincent felt that this was technically true. She'd *known* her brother, past tense. The lights were dimming around them.

"I was here last night too," the woman said. "I just think he's brilliant."

"Oh," Vincent said. "I'm looking forward to seeing him, then."

"Do you know the artist?" the woman asked again, after a moment, and Vincent felt a stab of pity.

"Yes," Vincent said. Applause rose around them, and when she looked up, her brother was walking out onto the stage. Paul was thinner and noticeably older, and she couldn't tell if his black suit and thin dark tie were meant to be ironic. He looked like an undertaker. He nodded to the audience, smiled at the applause with what seemed to Vincent to be genuine pleasure, and took his place behind a keyboard, then the stage lights dimmed too, until he was barely illuminated. The screen above his head lit up, a field of white with a black title, "Melissa in the Water," and then the white resolved into a shoreline. Vincent recognized the beach by the pier at Caiette, grainy and oversaturated, the water and sky too blue, the islands in the inlet an unnatural green. Paul's music sounded at first like white noise, a radio caught between stations. He played a sequence of notes on a keyboard, the notes emerging a few seconds later as cello music, to which he added a quietly meandering piano, moving between the keyboard and a laptop perched on a stand, pressing buttons and tapping pedals to create loops and distortions, a one-man band. The static had taken on a pulsating quality, a steady beat. Onstage, the screen burst into life as a group of children dashed across the frame. Vincent could see from their faces that they were shouting and laughing, but the film had no sound. She remembered this video. This was the first summer without her mother. She'd been living in Vancouver for ten or eleven months—long hours alone in her aunt's basement with the television, long commutes by bus to school—but she'd come home to visit Dad for the summer. She'd stood on the beach filming the swimmers, a.k.a. the entire underage population of Caiette circa 1995: a little girl whose name she'd forgotten—Amy? Anna?—who stopped at the water's edge, giggling but afraid to go in; the twins, Carl and Gary, a little older, splashing around in a corner of the frame;

Vincent's friend Melissa, who would have been fourteen but was small for her age and looked closer to twelve. Melissa's pale hair and the yellow swimsuit and the graininess and oversaturation of the film lent her an air of radiance. She was doing somersaults in the water, laughing when she surfaced. In three years she would move to Vancouver to go to the University of British Columbia and live with Vincent in that ghastly basement apartment on the Downtown Eastside; she would go dancing with Vincent and Paul on the last night of the twentieth century; at nineteen she would develop a drug problem, drop out of school, return to Caiette to live with her parents while she pulled herself together; a year after that she would be hired as a chauffeur and gardening assistant at the Hotel Caiette; but in the video all of this was in the unimaginable future and she was just a kid twisting around in the water like a fish. The music had a shifting, unstable quality that Vincent found unpleasant, like a soundtrack for one of those nightmares where you try to run but your feet won't move, and now there were voices in the static, overlapping.

On the stage below the projection screen, Paul was in motion, making adjustments to dials, following the projection on his laptop, playing the keyboard at intervals. Vincent sensed movement to her right, and when she looked, the woman had fallen asleep, her head on her chest. Vincent rose and slipped out into the lobby, where the lights and the solid reality of marble and benches made her want to weep with relief, and fled outside into the winter air. She walked over the Manhattan Bridge and all the way up to Grand Central Terminal, trying to steady her thoughts. The idea came to her that she could sue him, but with what proof? He'd been in Caiette every summer and every second Christmas of her childhood. There was no way of proving that he hadn't filmed the videos himself. And any legal action would be difficult or impossible to hide from Jonathan, for whom she was supposed to be a calm harbour, no drama, no friction. On the train back to Greenwich, she caught sight of her reflection in the window and closed her eyes. She'd started paying her own rent at seventeen. How had she become so dependent on another person? Of course the answer was depressingly obvious: she had slipped into dependency because dependency was easier.

A Nightmare

In the week that followed, Jonathan worked such long hours that she hardly saw him—small mercy—so she only had to feign lightness for brief periods. She read the news to distract herself, but the news was a litany of economic collapse. She thought of going back to Brooklyn and waiting outside the stage door, but the thought of seeing Paul again was repulsive.

On the following Wednesday, Vincent was awakened by a nightmare for the third time in three nights. She'd been sleeping poorly for longer than that, weeks, but the nightmare was a new and unsettling problem. She was certain that it was the same dream, repeated, but she retained only a vague impression of falling, a sense of catastrophe that persisted in daylight. She stared at the ceiling for a while, Jonathan asleep beside her, before she finally rose and fumbled for her workout clothes— she kept them folded on a chair by the bed—and laced her running shoes in darkness, collected her keys from the hook by the kitchen door. She liked to make a game of leaving the house without turning on any lights. There's an inherent pleasure in being unseen.

In the kingdom of money it was important to be thin, but she would have run anyway. She loved the suburbs at this hour, when there was still some mystery here. It was early December but the weather had been well above freezing all week. She walked quickly down the long driveway that led past Gil and Anya's cottage—no lights in the windows—to the cul-de-sac, where the equally excessive houses of two neighbours glimmered through the trees, and then broke into a light jog when she reached the first real street, the first street that went somewhere. She liked the stillness of the predawn neighbourhood, the secrecy of a street where everyone else was sleeping, their windows unlit. Jonathan wouldn't have liked her to be out alone in the dark, but these streets had never struck her as dangerous, and she carried mace on her key chain. By the time she returned to the house, it was four o'clock and still dark. She left a note for Jonathan, who wouldn't wake till five-thirty, then showered and dressed and called a taxi to take her to the five a.m. train.

The others on the train at that hour were mostly financial-industry maniacs, eyes bright in the shine of their little screens, sending and receiving messages from other continents. Vincent had a row of seats to herself. After a while the night gave way to shadows and a murky dawn, the towns shifting from collections of lights to silhouettes of rooftops. How could Paul do it, she found herself thinking, how could he steal from her like that, but she was too tired to maintain the line of thought and drifted into a twilight state that wasn't sleep and wasn't consciousness, towns reappearing and blinking out between intervals of trees. She woke with a start as the train pulled into Grand Central.

That was the last morning in the kingdom of money. She ate breakfast in a hotel restaurant near Grand Central. There was an hour in a bookstore, time spent in various shops, an interval of newspapers and coffee in an espresso bar in Chelsea. A strange moment: she stepped out of the espresso bar and into a tour group, a pack of tourists following a leader who held a red umbrella up in the air, and just for a moment, she saw her mother in the crowd. Only a flash, but it was unmistakable—the long brown braid down her back, the red cardigan she'd been wearing when she drowned—and then the crowd shifted and her mother was gone. Vincent stood for a long time on the sidewalk, watching the group walk away. Was she hallucinating? She was alert for signs of madness as she walked uptown through the grey city but saw nothing else that seemed obviously unreal. Central Park was monochromatic, dark trees dripping under a colourless sky.

She was on the steps of the Met when Jonathan called.

"Christmas party tonight," he said. "You want to come by the office around seven-thirty, and we'll walk over together?"

"Seven-thirty's perfect," Vincent said. "I'm looking forward to it." She had in fact entirely forgotten about the holiday party. The dress she'd planned to wear was hanging in the bedroom closet in Greenwich, and there was nothing suitable in the pied-à-terre. But the age of money wouldn't end for a few more hours, so this didn't constitute an emergency, and she was free to linger for a while with her favourite painting. She had fallen in love with Thomas Eakins's *The Thinker*, a massive image of a man in a dark suit, perhaps in his thirties, hands in his pockets, lost in pensive thought. She'd come back to this gallery several times in the past few weeks and stood before this painting, unaccountably moved by it. Her mother would have liked it, she thought.

When she turned to leave, she saw a man she recognized. He'd been looking at the same painting, standing back a little.

"Oskar," she said. "You work with my husband, don't you?"

"In the asset management unit." They shook hands. "Nice to see you again."

"I don't mean this as a pickup line," Vincent said, "but do you come here often?"

"Not as often as I'd like. I took a couple art history classes in college," he added, as if he had to justify his presence here. They parted ways after a brief volley of small talk—"I hope you're coming to the party tonight?"—and it might have been unmemorable except that that was the first time she found herself dwelling on the limitations of her arrangement with Jonathan. She enjoyed being with Jonathan, for the most part, she didn't mind it, but lately she'd found herself thinking that it might be nice to fall in love, or failing that, at least to sleep with someone she was actually attracted to and to whom she owed nothing. She hailed a taxi and travelled to Saks, where she spent some time under dazzling lights and emerged an hour later with a blue velvet dress and black patent leather shoes. There were still so many hours left in the day. Don't think of Paul, probably in a studio somewhere composing new music to accompany her plundered work. She hailed another taxi and went downtown to the financial district, to linger for a while in a café that she'd always especially liked. She stayed in the Russian Café for two hours, drinking cappuccinos and reading the *International Herald Tribune*.

By five o'clock she was restless, so she gathered her things and stepped out into the rain. She would find another café, she decided. She'd go up to Midtown and stake out a position near Jonathan's office, so as to arrive perfectly on time. But halfway down the stairs to Bowling Green station, she was overcome by the certainty that if she went into the subway, she would die. She knew it as clearly as she knew her own name. Vincent turned around and half stumbled, half ran back up the stairs, pushing through a sea of commuters coming the other way, desperate to reach a bench before she fainted. She'd never fainted before but surely this was what it felt like, this terrible lightheadedness, the awareness of being just at the edge of an abyss. *I should ask my mother,* she thought, and the equally irrational thought that followed was *My mother's waiting for me in the subway.*

Vincent made it to the nearest bench, gasping, and a few minutes passed before she had the presence of mind to unfurl her umbrella. She sat there for what seemed like a long time, holding the umbrella low enough to hide her face from passersby, trying to catch her breath, trying to stop crying. If she'd started having panic attacks—she'd never had one before, but surely that moment just now on the steps would qualify—then she'd slipped further than she'd thought, no longer quite as cohesive as she had been, her systems failing. She sat very still until her breathing slowed, listening to the rain on the umbrella and watching the feet of passing pedestrians.

Her phone vibrated in her pocket, and she saw Jonathan's receptionist's number on the call display. "Oh, I'm great, thank you," she said in response to a question, "and how are you?"

"So listen," the receptionist said, instead of answering, "Mr. Alkaitis was wondering if you could come up to the office a little early. He tells me it's urgent."

"Of course." Jonathan's idea of urgent was needing Vincent's advice on which tie to wear for the holiday party. "Please tell him I'm on my way."

A car is the worst possible way to travel during rush hour in Manhattan, but attempting the descent into Bowling Green station again was a risk that Vincent couldn't afford, so she hailed a taxi that crept uptown in dense traffic, dark streets passing in slow motion, until a mile from the office she got out and walked.

It's just that you're very tired, she told herself. *There is nothing seriously wrong with you. Anyone could have a panic attack after three nights of not sleeping. Anyone would be a little shaky after what Paul did.* In the mirrored elevator of the Gradia Building she quickly pulled back her wet hair and tried to avoid looking too closely at the dark circles under her eyes. The doors opened to the corporate splendour of the eighteenth floor.

"Ms. Alkaitis, good afternoon. You can go on in," Jonathan's receptionist said. Her name was Simone. In several months' time, she would be a key witness for the prosecution.

When Vincent entered the office she found Jonathan at his desk, hands clasped before him, and she was struck immediately by his stillness. He looked like a statue of himself, cast in wax. They weren't alone. His daughter, Claire, was slumped on the sofa with her head in her hands, and at the other end of the sofa sat a man in his late fifties or early sixties, soft around the middle, with an expensive suit and silvering hair.

"Hello," Vincent said. The man's name escaped her.

"Mrs. Alkaitis." His voice was flat. "I'm Harvey Alexander. I work with your husband."

"Oh yes, of course, we've met." Vincent shook his hand. What was wrong with everyone? Harvey wore the expression of a man at a funeral. Jonathan's hands were still clasped, and Vincent saw now that his knuckles were white. Vincent and Claire didn't like one another, per se, but they'd always managed a veneer of politeness, and Claire had never before failed to look up or say hello when Vincent entered a room.

"Is someone going to tell me what's going on?" Vincent asked. Keeping her tone as light as possible, because she understood lightness to be part of her job.

"Please close the door," Jonathan said. Vincent did as he asked, but he said nothing further, and no one in the room seemed quite able to look at her, so she took temporary refuge in a series of small tasks. She placed the Saks bag by the coat stand, took off her coat and hung it, removed her gloves and draped them over the Saks bag, and finally, having run out of things to do, sat in one of the visitors' chairs, crossed her legs, and waited. They all sat there in silence. It was like being in a play where no one knew the next line.

"Someone has to tell her," Claire said, and Vincent was shocked to realize that Claire was crying.

"Tell me what?"

"Vincent," Jonathan said, but words seemed to fail him, and he briefly pressed the palms of his hands to his eyes. Was he crying too? Vincent tightened her grip on the armrests of the chair.

"Tell me," she said.

"Vincent, listen, my business, not the whole thing, not the brokerage company, where Claire works, but the asset management unit, it's all . . ." He seemed unable to continue.

"Are you bankrupt?" Vincent had been following the news carefully. These were the last few weeks of 2008, the age of faltering stock prices and collapsing banks.

"Oh, it's so much worse than that!" Claire's voice held an edge of hysteria. "Really so much fucking worse."

"I think we should all bear in mind," Harvey said, "that there's a pretty good chance anything we say in this room today will eventually be repeated in a courtroom." He spoke very calmly, staring at a painting of Jonathan's yacht on the opposite wall. He seemed curiously detached from the scene.

"Just tell her," Claire said.

"Careful, now," Harvey said in that same tone of disinterest.

After a pained interval of silence, Jonathan settled on a question. "Vincent," he said, "do you know what a Ponzi scheme is?"

PART THREE

THE OFFICE CHORUS

December 2008

1

We had crossed a line, that much was obvious, but it was difficult to say later exactly where that line had been. Or perhaps we'd all had different lines, or crossed the same line at different times. Simone, the new receptionist, didn't even know the line was there until the day before Alkaitis was arrested, which is to say the day of the 2008 holiday party, when Enrico came around to our desks in the late morning and told us that Alkaitis wanted us assembled in the seventeenth-floor conference room at one o'clock. This had never happened before. The Arrangement was something we did, not something we talked about.

Alkaitis came in at one-fifteen, sat at the head of the table without making eye contact with anyone, and said, "We have liquidity problems."

There was no air in the room.

"I've arranged for a loan from the brokerage company," he said. "We'll route it through London and record the wire transfers as income from European trading."

"Will the loan be enough?" Enrico asked quietly.

"For the moment."

A knock on the door just then, and Simone came in with the coffee. No one was sure where to look. Simone had only been on the job for three weeks and wasn't party to the Arrangement, but it was immediately obvious to her that something was amiss. There was a charged quality to the room's internal atmosphere, like the air just before an electrical storm. She was certain that someone had said something terrible just before she walked in. Only Ron returned her smile. Joelle stared blankly at her. Oskar was looking very fixedly at the legal pad on the table before him, and it seemed to Simone that there were tears in his eyes. Enrico and Harvey were staring into space. Alkaitis nodded when she came in and watched her until she left. Simone finished pouring the coffee and let herself out, closed the door, and waited in the corridor instead of walking away. It seemed to her that no one spoke for an unnaturally long time.

"Look," Alkaitis said finally, "we all know what we do here."

Later, some of us would pretend that we didn't hear this, but Simone's testimony would echo the accounts of several of us who *did* hear it. Some of us who pretended not to hear it would also pretend not to know there was a line—"I'm as much a victim as Mr. Alkaitis's investors," Joelle told a judge, who disagreed and sentenced her to twelve years—but then at the far opposite end of the spectrum was Harvey Alexander, who would agree wholeheartedly with Simone's testimony and go on to confess to things he hadn't even been accused of in a kind of ecstasy of guilt, weepily admitting to padding his expenses and stealing office supplies, while puzzled investigators took notes and tried to gently steer the conversation back to the crime.

But for those of us who did hear what Alkaitis said in that meeting—those of us who admitted to hearing it—that statement represented the final crossing, or perhaps more accurately, the moment when it was no longer possible to ignore the topography and pretend that the border hadn't already been crossed. Of course we all knew what we did there. We weren't idiots, except for Ron. We shuffled our papers, or stared fixedly at our notes, or stared into space and imagined leaving the country (Oskar), or looked out the window and made firm, actionable plans to leave the country (Enrico), or looked out the window and decided fatalistically that it was too late to go anywhere (Harvey), or indulged in the fantastical notion that somehow everything would work itself out (Joelle).

Ron glanced around, confused. He often seemed confused, the rest of us had noticed that about him, and it seemed he actually didn't know what we did here, which was baffling in retrospect: what did he think we were doing, if not running a Ponzi scheme? When we talked among ourselves about the Arrangement, as we'd come to refer to it, what exactly did he think we were discussing? Still, there it was. He looked around in the silence, cleared his throat, and said, "Well, we have so much trading activity with the London office already, though."

The silence that followed this remark was, if possible, even worse than the silence that had preceded it. No trade had ever been executed through the London office, because the London office comprised a single employee with five email addresses whose job consisted primarily of wiring funds to New York to give the appearance of European trading activity.

"That's an excellent point, Ron," Harvey said. He spoke kindly and with a certain sadness.

The meeting ended a few minutes later. Alkaitis had offices on the seventeenth and eighteenth floors of the Gradia Building, and after the meeting he left us in our dismal little office suite on Seventeen and went back upstairs to Eighteen, which was a different world. Alkaitis had the entire floor up there, and it gleamed. The people on Eighteen were doing what their clients thought they were doing, which was recommending and trading stocks and other securities. A hundred people worked on Eighteen, in a broker-dealer firm whose activities, the FBI eventually concluded, were entirely above board. On Seventeen we were running a criminal enterprise in lieu of investing our clients' money, and this fundamental disorder was reflected in our office space. Whereas Eighteen was a sea of glass desks aligned in symmetrical perfection on deep silvery carpets, Seventeen had a thirty-year-old carpet of indeterminate colour, peeling paint, secondhand furniture, and towers of file boxes.

When Jonathan Alkaitis stepped out of the elevator on Eighteen, he found Simone chatting with an investor. Most investors weren't allowed to drop by unannounced, especially investors like Olivia Collins who'd invested less than a million dollars, but Alkaitis had always been fond of her. She'd known his brother Lucas, long dead. When Alkaitis saw Olivia now, seventy-four years old and dressed all in black except for an enormous turquoise scarf, it seemed to Simone that he visibly winced in the instant before a smile appeared on his face.

"Hello, my dear." Alkaitis double-kissed her cheeks in the French style.

"I was in the neighbourhood," Olivia said.

"Then I'm glad you dropped by. Coffee?"

"Wouldn't say no."

Simone made coffee and brought it into Alkaitis's office, where Olivia was describing an art exhibition of some kind, Simone told investigators later, or at least that's what it sounded like. Simone liked to stave off terminal boredom by playing games with herself: when she had to fetch coffee, she sometimes pretended that she was involved in some kind of arcane coffee ceremony with mysteriously high stakes, a ritual in which the precision of her movements somehow mattered immensely. She was engaged in this with Alkaitis's and Olivia's coffee, laying the tray in the precise centre of the table, placing china cups in the precise centre of the coasters, etc., and then—this had never happened before—Alkaitis raised a finger to interrupt Olivia's monologue and addressed Simone directly: "Simone—Olivia, I'm terribly sorry to interrupt, this is fascinating and I want to hear the rest of it—Simone, can you stay late tonight, to help out with a project?"

"Of course," Simone said, but felt defeated on the walk back to her desk, because she was fairly confident that as a salaried employee she wasn't entitled to any kind of overtime, which meant that anything beyond the limits of nine a.m. to five p.m. was unpaid labour. Olivia left a few minutes later with a hurt expression—she was used to occupying Jonathan's time by the hour—and his office door closed behind her.

Only a half hour had elapsed since the end of the meeting, but downstairs on Seventeen, all of us had been busy. Harvey went to the stockroom for a fresh legal pad, took it to his desk, and began writing a full confession; Joelle stepped out for a brisk walk around the block that did nothing to alleviate her panic; Enrico went to his computer, purchased a one-way ticket to Mexico City, printed his boarding pass, and then walked out for the last time without looking at anyone; Ron returned to his desk and spent some time watching cat videos and clicking Like on other people's Facebook posts, confused and trying to shake a pervasive sense of dread. Oskar spent a full ninety minutes looking up real estate prices in Warsaw, then seven minutes researching which countries had extradition treaties with the United States, then another twenty-three minutes looking up real estate prices in Kazakhstan, where he had a couple of cousins, before finally logging out and leaving the office, with the thought of spending a few hours somewhere else—anywhere else—before the party. It was only midafternoon, but he thought that he wouldn't mind being fired.

As he walked toward the subway, he even thought about how he'd spin it: "I realized there was fraud going on," he imagined telling an admiring future employer, "and that was the day I walked out. I never would have imagined walking off a job like that, but sometimes you just have to draw the line." Although the line, for Oskar, had been crossed eleven years earlier, when he'd first been asked to backdate a transaction. "It's possible to both know and not know something," he said later, under cross-examination, and the state tore him to pieces over this but he spoke for several of us, actually, several of us who'd been thinking a great deal about that doubleness, that knowing and not knowing, being honourable and not being honourable, knowing you're not a good person but trying to be a good person regardless around the margins of the bad. We'd all die for the truth in our secret lives, or if not die exactly, then at least maybe make a couple of confidential phone calls and try to feign surprise when the authorities arrived, but in our actual lives we were being paid an exorbitant amount of money to keep our mouths shut, and you don't have to be an entirely terrible person, we told ourselves later, to turn a blind eye to certain things—even actively participate in certain other things—when it's not just you, because who among us is fully alone in the world? There are always other people in the picture. Our salaries and bonuses covered roofs over heads, crackers shaped like goldfish, tuition, retirement home expenses, the mortgage on Oskar's mother's apartment in Warsaw, etc.

And then there's the part of the equation that could somehow never be mentioned at trial but that seemed extremely relevant, which is that when you've worked with a given group of people for a while, calling the authorities means destroying the lives of your friends. Our lawyers asked us not to bring this up on the stand, but it's a real thing, this aversion to sending your colleagues to prison. We'd worked together for a very long time.

But the day of that meeting was also the day when it was too late to avoid arrest, the trap closing quite rapidly now for everyone except Enrico, solely because he was willing to do the obvious thing and leave before the police arrived, and Simone, who was blameless and should have known nothing but by nightfall was shredding documents in an eighteenth-floor conference room. Alkaitis had come to her five minutes after Olivia left, and asked her to go out and buy some paper shredders.

"How many?"

"Three."

"I'll order those right away," she said.

"No, we need them immediately. Could you make a run to the office supply store?"

"I'd be happy to, but I don't think I can carry three paper shredders by myself. Can I bring someone with me?"

He hesitated. "I'll come with you," he said. "I could use some air."

It was awkward, standing in the elevator and walking out into the street with her boss. She was less than half his age; they had different concerns and lived in fundamentally different New York Cities; they had nothing to say to one another. She wondered if she should be trying to make conversation and was just formulating a casual remark about the weather when he pulled out his cell phone, frowning at the screen and scrolling through contacts without breaking stride. "Joelle," he said, "bring all of the Xavier file boxes up to the small conference room on Eighteen, will you? Yeah, Conference Room B. You can get Oskar and Ron to help. Yeah, statements, correspondence, memos, the works. Just bring up any box with his name on it. Thanks." He put the phone back in his pocket, and a few minutes later they were in the office supply store, blinking under the glare of fluorescent lights.

It seemed to Simone that Alkaitis didn't look well, although in fairness no one looked well in this lighting. The air was stale. Tired office workers walked slowly between high steel shelves. Alkaitis seemed oddly helpless, looking around as if he'd never before considered where the pens on his desk came from, as if he hadn't quite imagined that such vast depositories of sticky notes and file folders existed on this earth. Simone led him to the paper shredders, where he stared at the selection.

"This one seems good," Simone said at last, pointing to a model in the middle of the pricing spread.

"Okay," he said. "Yes."

"Three of these?"

"Let's get four," he said, snapping back into focus. They carried the shredders to the counter, where Alkaitis paid for them with cash, and stepped out into the rain. Alkaitis walked quickly, Simone struggling to keep up. She'd worn heels an inch taller than usual, because of the holiday party that evening, and she was starting to regret this. In the elevator, they stood side by side in silence.

"Thanks for staying late tonight," he said when they reached the eighteenth floor. "You can leave early on Friday."

"Okay, thanks."

Simone followed him into the conference room, where someone—presumably Joelle—had left a stack of file boxes, all labelled XAVIER. Alkaitis hung his damp overcoat on the back of the door and left her there with one of the paper shredders, returned a few minutes later with a box of recycling bags. By then she'd plugged in the machine and was opening boxes. "Here are some bags you can use for the shredded paper," he said. "Just leave the bags in here when you're done, and the cleaners will get them. Thanks again for staying." And he was gone.

A few minutes later, Claire Alkaitis appeared in the doorway. Simone hadn't yet spoken with Claire, and had actually only found out who Claire was the day before, when she'd finally asked someone about the woman who was always swanning in and out of Alkaitis's office without an appointment and without looking at Simone.

"Hello, Simone," Claire said. Simone was surprised that she knew her name. "Someone told me I could find my father in here . . . ?"

"He was here just a moment ago," Simone said. "His coat's still on the door, so I assume he's coming back." Claire was frowning at the paper shredder and the XAVIER boxes.

"Can I ask what you're doing?"

"A project for Mr. Alkaitis. He's trying to clear some space in the filing cabinets."

"Jesus," Claire muttered under her breath, and for a moment Simone thought this was an insult, but whatever concerned Claire, it seemed it had nothing to do with Simone, because Claire turned away and left without saying anything further. Eighteen had the kind of carpeting that silenced all footsteps, but it seemed to Simone she was moving very quickly. Simone looked at the piece of paper in her hand. A memo from Alkaitis to Joelle: *"Re: L. Xavier account: I need a long-term capital gain of $561,000 on an investment of $241,000 for a sale proceed of $802,000,"* the memo said. Simone stared at it for a moment, folded it, and put it in her pocket.

Claire found her father back in his office, sitting very still at his desk with his head in his hands. Harvey was on the sofa, hands clasped, looking at the floor with a strange little smile. Harvey felt almost giddy at this point, he said later. It had been a momentous day. He knew investors were pulling out. He knew that the withdrawal requests exceeded the balance in the accounts. Obviously the end was near. He kept tearing up, yet there were moments of almost manic joy. His written confession-in-progress was stowed under a file in the top left drawer of his desk, and for the first time in decades, he felt free. He felt—he apologized in the courtroom for using such a clichéd term, but perhaps we can agree, ladies and gentlemen of the jury, that some clichés exist for a reason—like a weight had been lifted.

They both looked up as Claire entered.

"Jonathan," she said, "why is your receptionist shredding documents in the conference room?"

"Just clearing some space in the filing cabinets," Alkaitis said.

Harvey made an odd sound in his throat, as if he'd tried to laugh but had choked instead.

"Okay," Claire said, clinging to normalcy like it was a life preserver. "Anyway. I wanted to ask you about those transfers that went through yesterday. The loans from the brokerage company to the asset management side."

He was silent.

"Four loans," she continued, to jog his memory, but the silence only persisted. "Look," she said, "to be clear, I'm not *suggesting* anything here. It's just that these were the eighth, ninth, tenth, and eleventh loans this quarter, with no repayments, and it's the kind of thing that . . . look, please understand, I'm not suggesting anything other than the *appearance* of impropriety."

"These transfers are fairly routine, Claire. We're expanding the London operation."

"Why would you do that?"

"I'm not sure I understand the question."

"Everything's contracting," she said. "I heard you speaking with Enrico last week, and you said you were losing investors, not gaining them."

"You look tired, Claire."

"Because I couldn't sleep last night, thinking about this."

"Claire, honey, I know what I'm doing."

"No, I know, I'm just saying, the optics of the thing, the timing of it—"

"Right," he said. "The optics." He blinked.

"Dad." She hadn't called him that in over a decade.

"I can't keep it going," he said quietly. "I thought I could cover the losses."

"What do you mean, *cover the losses?*"

2

Why was Simone shredding documents? Why would Alkaitis leave his receptionist alone in a conference room with several file boxes of incriminating evidence? In his deposition, Alkaitis claimed not to understand the question. Harvey, in his own deposition, offered the opinion that Alkaitis, who in most matters had an impressive capacity for self-delusion, understood finally that it was too late to avoid arrest but possibly hoped to shield Lenny Xavier, his most important investor, who'd understood that it was a Ponzi from the beginning and had provided the occasional infusion of cash. Perhaps Simone was shredding documents precisely *because* she was only a receptionist, and Alkaitis didn't think she would understand anything she saw. He was an intelligent man, but he suffered from the tendency of certain long-term senior executives to think of receptionists as office fixtures, not quite on the level of the filing cabinets but close. Perhaps, because Simone was not just new to the office but new to the world—polished in that young-in-Midtown way, but after all only twenty-three years old—Alkaitis was counting on her naïveté, thinking that perhaps she wasn't someone who would necessarily know that being asked to stay late and help her boss "clear some space in the file cabinets" was a probable indicator of a cover-up. Or perhaps the paper shredding was something of a token effort and we'd already reached the point where it didn't really matter who saw what.

After some incalculable amount of time had passed, Alkaitis returned to Conference Room B. His demeanour had changed considerably since Simone had seen him last. Were there tears in his eyes? He had the look of a man on a precipice.

"Simone," he said, "I'd like you to call my wife, please. Tell her it's an urgent matter and I'd like her to meet me here as soon as possible."

"Okay," she said, "right away," and by the time she reached her desk he was already back in his office, the door firmly closed. She called Vincent, relayed the message, and returned to Conference Room B and the paper shredder.

Simone was surprised when Harvey came in with pizza. This was around seven-thirty. She smelled the pizza before he entered the room.

"Look at you!" he said brightly. "Still at it."

"I thought you'd left."

"I was stuck in a long meeting," he said. "Then I went out for a quick walk and came back with pizza."

"To supervise me?"

"To take over. You've been here for hours and you're not getting overtime, which obviously isn't right, and more importantly, the holiday party starts in a half hour." He set the pizza on the conference table. "Are you hungry? I'm assuming there'll be food at the party, but you can't count on passed hors d'oeuvres as a dinner substitute."

She was hungry. Simone had been at work for nearly eleven hours and was worn through, her eyes burning a little from the dry tower air. The conference room had an L-shaped arrangement of two sofas in a corner, with a lamp on a little table between them. At some point she'd turned off the fluorescents and switched on the lamp, which cast the room in a much gentler light and made her feel slightly better. If there was ever a time when she had some control over her working life, she'd decided, she wouldn't work under fluorescent lights. Was there some way she could work outside? She didn't see how—she had an indoor skill set—but the thought was appealing.

"Have as much as you want," Harvey said, "and then you might as well head over to the party. I'll stay and finish this."

"Aren't you going to the party?"

"I like to make a late arrival."

"Why are we shredding all these files?" She was midway through her first slice. It was ham and pineapple, the pineapple cloyingly sweet.

"That's a perfectly reasonable question," Harvey said. She watched him, but he seemed to have nothing further to say. He wiped his fingers on a napkin, considered a moment, then took a second slice.

"Are you going to answer it?"

"No," he said. "Nothing personal."

"Okay."

"I'm going to offer some pizza to the others." He left the room with two of the pizza boxes, and Simone finished her slice and left too, gathered her coat and bag at the reception desk and walked out. What was strange was that the day had been so long and so tedious and she'd longed for this moment, but now that she'd been released, she wanted to go back in. She felt certain that something was about to happen. She was increasingly curious about the nature of the time bomb in the office, and she wanted to be there when it exploded.

3

The door to Alkaitis's office was still closed when everyone else on Eighteen left for the party. On Seventeen, we lingered and procrastinated, except Enrico, who was waiting to board an Aeromexico flight at JFK, and Oskar, who was presently in a nearby bar, looking at Astana real estate on his phone. Harvey was in Conference Room B, looking through the Xavier files. Ron was trying to get a spot of soup off his tie in the bathroom. Joelle was drifting through Facebook. But eventually we were all gathered in a restaurant a few blocks away, clustered by the chocolate fondue station. If it were just us, just the asset management unit, we wouldn't have had holiday parties, or so we told ourselves later—we weren't *completely* depraved—but it wasn't just us, we were only one corrupted branch of an otherwise perfectly above-board operation, and the holiday party was a large affair, both the asset management group and the brokerage company, the hundred or so people who worked on Eighteen and didn't quite know who we were.

Later, we all remembered the party differently, either because of the open bar or because, of course, memories are always bent in retrospect to fit individual narratives. We were gossiping and drinking when Alkaitis and his wife arrived, all of us except Ron aware of our impending doom, trying to distract ourselves with banal comments about the food circulating on little trays and by surreptitiously examining our colleagues' spouses, who seemed shiningly exotic by virtue of not being people whom we saw every day. Ron's wife, Sheila, had large startled-looking eyes, like a deer. Joelle's husband, Gareth, was a slow-moving, lethargic person in a too-big suit, with a face so bland you almost couldn't see him. ("He's like a sort of black hole," Oskar said to Harvey, almost admiringly. "He'd make a good secret agent.") Harvey's wife, Elaine, was a pretty woman who radiated silent resentment and left after forty minutes, ostensibly because she had a headache. And then Alkaitis arrived with Vincent, who always automatically outshone every spouse in the room. We watched them enter together, two hours late; Alkaitis in his sixties, his wife maybe in her late twenties, early thirties tops, a full-on trophy wife, absurdly gorgeous in a blue dress. There were tasteless jokes to be made but no one made them, although Oskar came close: "Where do you think those two fall on the May-December Gap Measure?" He was two drinks ahead of the rest of us.

"The what now?" Gareth asked.

"It's Oskar's personal formula," Joelle said. "He thinks a relationship can reasonably be classified as creepy if the age difference exceeds the age of the younger party." There were dark circles under her eyes.

"So if he were, say, sixty-three," Oskar said, "and she were let's say twenty-seven—"

"Oh, let's not," Harvey said, at his breeziest and most deflective. His written confession was up to eight pages.

"Anyway, she seems nice," Oskar said, feeling a little guilty. "I talked to her for a while at the barbecue last summer."

"She always seemed a little hard-edged to me," Joelle said, which Oskar recognized as Joelle-speak for "paid by the hour," which was crazy, unless it wasn't?

"Enrico's not here," Oskar said, obviously hoping to change the subject. Enrico's absence was one of the few things that everyone would agree on later. At that moment, he was on a southbound plane.

Later, Ron told investigators that Jonathan Alkaitis seemed perfectly normal: warm, listening attentively, talking easily with his staff, working the room. But Oskar recalled seeing Alkaitis sitting alone at the bar for several minutes with a look of devastation; later Oskar described it as "kind of a blank expression," but that description didn't do it justice; it was more as though death had entered Alkaitis, Oskar thought at the time, as though death had entered him and gazed out through his eyes. Some of us remembered that Alkaitis left the party early. "I think they only stayed about an hour," Joelle said in her first FBI interview. "It wasn't a happy night." She herself left not long afterward, as did Harvey, pleading an unexpected emergency at the office. They would've enlisted Oskar—there were after all four paper shredders on hand—but Oskar was nowhere to be found.

Oskar was standing by the door when Jonathan and Vincent Alkaitis walked out. He saw the way Vincent flinched when her husband touched her lower back, and there was such intimacy in this that it seemed wrong to mention it to anyone later, even when he was being grilled for the second or third time about that miserable party. He certainly told no one that he slipped out just behind them, partly out of curiosity and partly because he was desperate to escape. When he stepped out of the elevator in the lobby, Alkaitis and his wife were just walking out onto the sidewalk. A black car waited at the curb. Alkaitis opened the car door for his wife. She shook her head. Oskar watched them, unnoticed, just out of earshot. She wouldn't get in the car. He heard Alkaitis say, with infinite weariness, "Just at least call me when you get there, *please*," at which Vincent only laughed. She turned away from him, walking north into a cold wind. Alkaitis stared after her for a moment before he climbed into the car and left.

Oskar hesitated for only a moment before he began walking north too, following Vincent.

4

Back at the office, Harvey carried the paper shredder and then the Xavier files from the conference room to Alkaitis's office. Alkaitis wouldn't be needing his office anymore, and he felt someone might as well enjoy this room in these last few hours before the end. Harvey loved Alkaitis's office. It was all dark wood cabinetry and expensive fixtures, thick carpet and ornate little lamps. Tonight the room shone like an oasis, a pool of warm light in the chaos, and by nine-thirty Joelle had hauled a paper shredder and a few boxes of folders upstairs to join him. Harvey took the desk chair, Joelle sat on the sofa, and they shredded evidence together. It was almost pleasant.

"What did you tell your husband?" Harvey asked, after they'd been at it for a little while. He'd exchanged a series of increasingly terse text messages with his wife.

"About staying so late, you mean? Emergency at work." Joelle had been crying earlier, but now she seemed detached, almost dreamy. Harvey wondered if she'd taken something for her nerves.

"Seems pretty general," Harvey said. He was shredding documents in a steady rhythm, but he'd positioned himself in such a way that Joelle couldn't see that he was rescuing every third or fourth page. He'd decided to save the most damning pages, because earlier he'd been struck by a thought that was no less horrific for being completely irrational: What if he confessed and no one believed him? What if they thought he was crazy?

"What do you mean?" Joelle asked.

"I mean, that's kind of a vague excuse."

"But that's where people get tripped up with their excuses," Joelle said. "They get nervous and throw in all these excessive details, and that's how you know they're lying." Was Joelle saving documents too? Harvey couldn't tell. She stopped sometimes to look at one document or another, but she seemed to be shredding everything, unless she'd left certain key files down on Seventeen.

"My husband never asks for details anyway," Joelle said. Harvey concluded from this statement that Joelle's husband was likely having an affair but decided not to share this insight. Harvey was shuffling papers around in a complicated way, winnowing out the most incriminating documents with a casual glance, letting these slip into the open garbage bag behind Alkaitis's desk instead of putting them through the shredder.

"My wife will want details," Harvey said after a while. "I'll get home, she'll be like, 'What kind of emergency forced you back to the office after a holiday party?'" He was quiet for a moment, fixing a paper jam. "Would you like a drink?"

"Does Alkaitis keep alcohol in this office?"

"He does," Harvey said, rising with some difficulty. His knees were bothering him. Alkaitis's workspace arrangement involved a lot of discreet cabinetry, so it took him some time to locate the Scotch. Harvey poured a tumbler for Joelle and used Alkaitis's coffee mug for himself. The nice thing about the coffee mug was its opacity. Joelle couldn't see how little Harvey had poured for himself, so he could stay more or less sober while he saved the evidence of their crimes.

5

At that moment, Oskar was standing by the window of Alkaitis's pied-à-terre in a high tower on Columbus Circle, drinking wine with Vincent. He'd waited until Alkaitis was gone before he went after her. Vincent had been walking slowly, hands deep in the pockets of her coat, staring at the sidewalk.

"Excuse me," Oskar had said.

She looked at him.

"Oskar." She managed a smile. "What happened to your coat?"

He'd left it at the party. "I misplaced it. Can I walk with you?"

"Yes." They walked in silence for a while. The rain had subsided to a drizzle that made the sidewalk sparkle and left a glittering mist on Vincent's coat, her hair, on Oskar's folded arms when he looked down at himself. He walked alongside her and willed his mind to go blank. *There is only this moment,* he told himself. *Don't think of anything else, prison for example, just walk up the street with this beautiful woman. It doesn't matter that she isn't yours.*

"Where are you headed?" he asked finally.

"Columbus Circle," she said. "We have—Jonathan has a pied-à-terre by the park. Would you like to come up for a drink?"

"I'd love to." Columbus Circle was still a half mile away, a half mile as measured by ten uptown Manhattan blocks, ten blocks of night and cold drizzle and headlights, traffic signals and shop-windows and the blank shutters of small businesses closed for the night, steam rising from a plastic chimney in the street, that steam turned luminous by streetlights. At Columbus Circle, two dark glass towers rose over a crescent-shaped shopping mall, facing the darkness of the park. Vincent stopped just outside the entrance to the mall, staring into the heart of the traffic circle, the ring of illuminated benches around the statue of Columbus.

"Everything okay?" He wanted to get upstairs before she changed her mind.

"Do you see a woman sitting there?" She was pointing, and just for a second he did think he saw someone, an impression of movement, but it was a trick of the light, a passing shadow between the beams of headlights as cars pulled in and out of the traffic circle. The benches were empty.

"I thought I saw someone for a second," he said, "but I think it was maybe just some kind of reflection or something."

"I keep thinking I see my mother," Vincent said.

"Oh," he said, at a loss for the appropriate response to this. Did her mother live in New York? Did she have a habit of trailing Vincent around the city? The moment passed. Vincent was expressionless in the white light of the shopping concourse, but she seemed to him to be someone who was enduring something, and he didn't want to ask but of course she knew, she had to, why else would she have been in Alkaitis's office for so long before the party, why else would she have refused to get in the car, don't think about it, don't think about it. *We all know what we do here.* They were ascending on the escalator to the mezzanine level, a more rarefied elevation where the shops were even more expensive, Vincent's gaze fixed on some indeterminate point in the middle distance.

"This way," Vincent said, and Oskar thought he understood some of the appeal of this place; if you were a person with an enormous amount of money who craved privacy, and if you came in here during normal shopping hours, it would be possible to mingle with the crowds right up until the moment when you slipped through the discreet door that led to the upper lobby, this tastefully lit room with sound-muffling carpets, two doormen, and a concierge, who nodded to Oskar and said good evening to Vincent.

"Good evening," she said. Did she have a slight accent? He'd never noticed before. She didn't sound like she was from New York. In the elevator, Oskar glanced at her—the silence between them was becoming a third presence, like another person who'd elbowed in between them and was taking up space—and saw that her gaze was fixed on the camera above the elevator buttons.

"Is it always this quiet?" Oskar asked when they stepped out onto the thirty-seventh floor. They were in a silent corridor of heavy grey doors and low lighting.

"Always." She'd stopped before one of the doors and was searching in her wallet. She produced a key card, and the door unlocked with a soft beep. "The building's mostly empty. People buy these places for investment purposes and then show up once or twice a year, if that."

"Why did you and your husband buy here?"

She was leading him into an aggressively modern apartment, all clean lines and sharp angles, with a gleaming kitchen in which he suspected no one had ever cooked anything. A floor-to-ceiling window looked out over Central Park.

"He's not my husband." She took off her shoes and padded into the kitchen in her stockings. "But to answer your question, to be perfectly honest, I have no idea why he bought this apartment or anything else."

"Because he could," Oskar suggested. He was trying to understand the first thing she'd said, in light of the wedding ring on her finger. She saw him looking at it, twisted it off, and calmly dropped it into the kitchen garbage.

"Probably. Yes, that was probably the reason." There was a certain flatness in her voice. "All we have to drink is wine. Red, or white?"

"Red. Thank you." He was standing by the window with his back to her when she appeared at his side with two glasses, but he'd been watching her reflection as she approached.

"Cheers," she said. "Here's to making it to the end of the day."

"Was your day as bad as mine?"

"Probably worse."

"I doubt that."

She smiled. "Today Jonathan told me he's a criminal. What was your day like?"

"It was . . . it was, uh . . ." It was what? *We all know what we do here.* Today I realized that I'm going to prison, he wanted to tell her, but of course there was no reason to believe she wasn't working with the FBI. Maybe Oskar could go work for the FBI, if only so he could stop wondering if everyone around him was working for the FBI, this exhausting paranoia, but of course that would entail confessing and accepting his punishment, and what if there was still a chance, what if he could somehow get lost in the shuffle, maybe the investigators would swoop down on Alkaitis and his top guys, Enrico and Harvey, and leave the rest of us—"You know what," he said, "how about we talk about anything other than today."

She smiled. "That's not the worst idea I've heard this evening. This wine's not great, is it?"

"I thought it was just me," he said. "I don't know that much about wine."

"I know too much about wine, but I can't say I've ever found it all that interesting." She set her glass on the coffee table. "So. Here we are."

"Here we are." He felt a touch of vertigo. She was standing very close, and her perfume was going to his head.

6

"In theory," Harvey said, after a long period of shredding evidence and not speaking, "couldn't a person flee the country and take their kids?"

"Uproot them from everyone they know, somehow get your spouse on board so you don't get charged with abduction, and then drag them where, exactly?" Joelle stopped shredding documents for a moment, to take a sip of Scotch.

"Somewhere nice," Harvey said. "If you're going to flee the country, you're headed for a tropical paradise, right?"

"I don't know," Joelle said. "What kind of an upbringing would that be?"

"An interesting one. 'Where did you grow up?' 'Oh, I was on the lam with my parents in a tropical paradise.' You could do a lot worse, childhood-wise."

"Maybe we could stop talking about children," Joelle said.

"Listen," Harvey said, trying to save her from visions of prison visitation rooms, "I think there's a very good chance we'll get off with probation. At worst, maybe an electronic monitoring bracelet, a few months of house arrest."

"It's a bit like an out-of-body experience," Joelle said later, "isn't it?"

"I've never had an out-of-body experience," Harvey said. He knew what she meant, though. The moment didn't seem quite real.

"I have," she said. "I was shredding paper for hours, and getting drunker and drunker, and then the next thing I knew I'd literally died of boredom and I was floating above the scene, looking down at my hair from above . . ."

Sometime around eleven-thirty, Joelle fed a final page into her paper shredder, dusted off her hands with theatrical flair, and rose carefully. "I'm going down to my office for a minute," she said, then turned and walked slowly in the direction of the elevators. Harvey found her in her office on Seventeen, curled up under her desk. She was snoring softly. He covered her with her overcoat and returned to Alkaitis's office. Harvey wasn't drunk at all, but after all these hours, several regions of his brain seemed to have shut down, and he was having a harder and harder time determining which documents to keep and which to put through the shredder. The words on the pages held less and less meaning, letters and numbers squiggling away from him.

At midnight in the winter city, Harvey was alone in his office with ten file boxes of incriminating evidence. He'd numbered them. Later he'd go through them all to make sure of what he had, he decided, and maybe make footnotes in his confession: *See staff memo in box #1, Relevant correspondence in box #2,* etc. Although how much time would that take, all that cross-indexing? Probably too much time. Probably more time than he had. He was tired but he felt so light. Maybe he could ask Simone to help. Harvey was thinking about this as he left the building. Simone was a poor idea, he decided, since she was so new and had no firm loyalties. He couldn't count on her not to call the police before the indexing was done. He hailed a taxi and watched the streets slip past, the lights and the late-night dog walkers, the sheer walls of towers, the delivery people on bicycles with hot food swinging in bags from the handlebars, the young people in packs or paired off and holding hands. He felt such love for this city tonight, for its grandeur and indifference. He woke with a start, the cabdriver peering through the partition, "Wake up buddy, wake up, you're home."

At two in the morning:

Harvey was pacing the rooms of his house, trying to memorize every detail. He loved his home, and when he went away to prison he wanted to be able to return here, to walk from one room to another in his mind.

Simone was drinking wine with her roommates in Brooklyn. There were three of them sharing a two-bedroom, so they had no living room and gathered around the table in the kitchen when they wanted to socialize. They were up late because the youngest, Linette, had been groped by a chef at the restaurant where she waited tables and had come home in tears, and then the conversation had shifted to other jobs and Simone had been getting some mileage out of the shadow hanging over Alkaitis's office. "Sounds shady as hell," Linette was saying. "You're sure that's exactly what you heard?" "'We all know what we do here,'" Simone quoted again, pouring wine for the others. "But I'm telling you, it wasn't just those words, it was also the *atmosphere*, like everyone was upset about something that had happened just before I walked in . . ."

In the Gradia Building, Joelle was sleeping under her desk.

Oskar was sleeping too, but naked and lying next to Vincent.

Enrico was on a southbound plane. He was staring at a movie but neither saw nor heard it. He'd been trying to imagine the life he was flying into, but he kept thinking of Lucia, his girlfriend abandoned in New York. He wished he'd realized he loved her before he left.

Jonathan Alkaitis was at his desk in his home office, writing a letter to his daughter. *Dear Claire,* the letter began, but he wasn't sure how to continue and had been staring into space for some time.

7

At three in the morning, Oskar woke in Alkaitis's pied-à-terre. He was desperate for a glass of water. Vincent was asleep beside him, breathing quietly, and her hair was like a pool of ink in the room's dim light.

He wasn't sure what to do. The thought of stealing away in the darkness made him feel sleazy, but on the other hand, what would the morning be like if he stayed? He'd read somewhere that the FBI liked to arrest people in the early hours of the morning, four or five a.m., on the theory that suspects are at their least dangerous when they're sleep-addled and in disarray. He had every reason to believe that the Arrangement was collapsing, in which case he might be arrested within hours, and surely it would be less embarrassing for everyone if he wasn't arrested at Alkaitis's apartment. He rose and dressed as quietly as possible.

When Oskar stepped out into the living room, he was momentarily blinded. Oskar and Vincent had left all the lights on in their hurry to get to the bedroom, and the apartment was too bright, a nightmare of track lighting and reflective surfaces. He stood with his hands over his eyes for a moment, adjusting, and when he finally looked at the room, the first thing he saw was the painting. He hadn't really noticed it before, but it was large, maybe five feet by six feet, a portrait of a young man, mounted with its own lighting fixture on the wall by the kitchen. The man sat on a red chair, wearing only jeans and combat boots. He looked too pale and too thin. There was something unsettling about the portrait, but it took Oskar a moment to register the faint streaks of bruises on his left arm, the shadows running along his veins. Oskar drew near, to see if he could decipher the signature in the lower right corner of the painting, and found that he could: *Olivia Collins*.

He recognized the name. Harvey had told him to give her a higher-than-normal rate of return, because Alkaitis liked her, and this was something he'd carefully avoided thinking about until this moment. Some of the investors were institutions. Some of them were sovereign wealth funds. There were charities and retirement funds, unions and schools. There were individuals who lived at a level of wealth that Oskar could barely imagine, even after all these years in the city, even standing here in an apartment in the sky in one of the most expensive neighbou: hoods in the world. But there were also people like Olivia Collins, people who'd come into a little money or had been able to save over a lifetime. Of course Jonathan Alkaitis would have one of Olivia Collins's paintings in his pied-à-terre. She was an old friend, in Oskar's understanding. It wasn't that she was about to lose everything, it was that she'd already lost everything and just didn't know it yet. Oskar fled the apartment with tears in his eyes.

8

At four a.m., Joelle woke under her desk. The room was dark. *I've been abandoned*, she thought, and she knew she was still drunk because this thought flooded her with purest grief. But then she realized that someone had pulled her overcoat over her, and she was so moved by this that she had to blink away tears. It was warm under the desk, under the overcoat, so she closed her eyes and drifted back to sleep.

9

At four-thirty in the morning, Alkaitis was jolted from sleep by a ringing doorbell.

10

Oskar was home by then, lying awake in his own bed, staring at a complicated pattern of shadow and light cast through a window of glass bricks on his bedroom wall. He was thinking of the beginning, a conversation with Harvey that he could replay in memory like a film. Not the *beginning* beginning, the job interview where he'd sat there trying to explain why Alkaitis should hire him even though he'd just dropped out of college and didn't have especially good grades or much of an employment history. The other beginning, the moment when he'd understood his job. Over a decade had passed since Harvey walked into his office and asked him to backdate a trade.

"Backdate it," Oskar said. "As in, falsify an account statement?"

"He's our biggest investor," Harvey said, as though that explained the request.

"I know," Oskar said in a tone that made it clear that the explanation fell short. The investor, Lenny Xavier, had three billion dollars in his Alkaitis accounts.

"And he's requested no losses on his accounts going forward." Harvey sounded so calm, but he must have been sweating. "You're an intelligent guy, Oskar. You've seen some things by now."

"I . . ." Yes, he'd seen some things. There were things that didn't make sense and other things he was ignoring, because he was being absurdly overpaid and he had his own office.

"I almost forgot," Harvey said, "here's your Christmas bonus."

Could the buy-off have been any more obvious? Oskar was embarrassed for both of them. The envelope Harvey passed across the desk contained a cheque that made Oskar gasp involuntarily.

"You've entered into a higher degree of trust," Harvey said, "and that means that the bonus payments increase accordingly. Look at Xavier's account statements for the past month, read through the correspondence, then backdate the trade and go buy yourself a boat or something."

"A boat," Oskar said absently, still looking at the cheque.

"Or a vacation. You look like you could use some sun." Harvey rose with some effort. There was a heaviness about him even then, so long before the end. Oskar watched him leave the room and then turned to Lenny Xavier's file.

The account statements: $2.92 billion dollars.

The correspondence: a letter from Xavier to Alkaitis, requesting a withdrawal of $200 million. A letter from Alkaitis confirming a withdrawal of $126 million. A second letter from Xavier, confirming receipt of the same.

A confirmation, of sorts, of something Oskar had been wondering for a while. There were only two explanations: Either Xavier and Alkaitis had had some unrecorded conversation, come to an understanding that Xavier had changed his mind and only wanted $126 million after all, and proceeded accordingly. Or Alkaitis had shorted him, *because there wasn't enough money in the accounts to pay Xavier the full $200 million*, and in return for Xavier's generosity in remaining silent, from now on Xavier's accounts would show no losses, hence the backdated trade, oh god oh god oh god.

In a ghost version of his life, a version of himself that he'd been thinking about more and more lately, Oskar closed the door to his office and called the FBI.

But in real life, he called no one. He left the office in a daze, but by the time he reached the corner he realized that he couldn't pretend to be shocked, and he knew he was going to deposit the cheque, because he was already complicit, he was already on the inside and had been for some time. "You already knew this," he heard himself murmuring, speaking aloud. "There are no surprises here. You know what you are."

II

WINTER

1

The day after the last holiday party, time moved unevenly in the Gradia Building.

For Oskar, the hours of the day crashed into one another so rapidly that he felt himself in constant motion, vertiginous at his desk. To stay or flee? There might still be time to leave the country, but every passing hour cemented his position. The coffee wasn't working as well as Oskar had hoped, and later, the day came back to him in disconnected flashes. In the early afternoon he passed by Harvey's office and saw him scribbling something on a legal pad. Oskar saw a solid thicket of handwriting, no space between lines.

"What are you writing there?"

"Oh," Harvey said, glancing at the writing as if he'd only just noticed it. *This old thing?* "Nothing much." He went back to writing, and Oskar went to use the photocopier, but he found Joelle there by the machine, standing perfectly still, staring at nothing. Oskar turned away silently and went to use the photocopier on the eighteenth floor. Eighteen was bustling, as always. It was a brighter world up there. They would be fine, wouldn't they, all of the people up here? If the brokerage company was legitimate, which had always been his general understanding, he saw no reason why they wouldn't be. If he were a better person, he thought, he'd be happy for them instead of resentful. The scale of the Arrangement took Oskar's breath away when he thought of it. He'd always secretly loved the intrigue of Seventeen, the feeling of being in an inner circle, of operating outside of the edges of society, perhaps even outside of the edges of reality itself—was there any difference, actually, in the grand universal scheme of things, between a trade that had actually occurred and a trade that *appeared* to have occurred on Oskar's impeccably formatted account statements?—but up here on this higher level were people who worked in utter innocence, people whose idea of a transgression was charging dinner with friends to the corporate Amex, and he felt such longing to be one of them.

When he passed by Alkaitis's office, the door was open, but Alkaitis wasn't there. Two men in dark suits were looking at something on his desk, their coats thrown carelessly over the back of one of the visitors' chairs. One of the men was on his cell phone, speaking too quietly for Oskar to hear. Simone sat at her desk outside his office door, watching them.

"Who are these guys?" Oskar asked.

She beckoned him close. "Alkaitis was arrested this morning," she whispered. He smelled the cool mint gum on her breath.

He gripped the edge of her desk. "For what?" he made himself ask.

"They said securities fraud. Did you know," she said, "he had me shredding documents?"

"What kind of . . . ?" Oskar was having trouble breathing, but she seemed not to have noticed.

"Account statements," she said. "Memos. Letters. It makes

sense now that the cops are here. Hold on," she said. Her phone was ringing. "Jonathan Alkaitis's office." She listened, frowning. "No, of course not, I had no idea." She drew in her breath sharply and held the phone away from her face. A new call was coming in, then another, the lines lighting up. "He called me a cunt and then hung up," she said to Oskar, and took the next call, which freed up the first phone line, which immediately began to ring. "Jonathan Alkaitis's office," she said, and then, "I know as much as you do. We—I literally just found out. I know. I—" She flinched, and placed the phone softly in the cradle. All six lines were lit up now, a cacophony of overlapping ringtones.

"Don't answer any more," Oskar said. "You don't deserve this."

"I guess it must be all over the news." Simone reached behind the phone and pulled out the cord, and they looked at one another in the silence.

"I have to go," Oskar said. He returned to Seventeen for only long enough to grab his jacket. He was too agitated to stand and wait for the elevator so he opted for the stairs. He was moving quickly, not quite running but a little faster than a walk, and he almost tripped over Joelle, who was sitting on the twelfth-floor landing with her legs extended before her. Joelle's eyes were closed.

"Are you dead?" Oskar asked.

"Maybe." Joelle's voice was leaden.

"Are you okay?"

"Is that a serious question?"

"What I'm asking is did you just sit down for a minute," Oskar said, "or are you having a heart attack or something."

"I don't think I'm having a heart attack."

"If I leave you here and keep walking, are you going to throw yourself off a bridge?"

"He's been *arrested*," Joelle said.

"Yeah."

"My husband's going to see it, if he hasn't already, and then he'll say to me, 'Oh my god, can you believe it?' and I'll either have to lie to his face, which isn't going to be plausible because he isn't actually a moron, or I'll have to say 'Well yes, honey, actually I can.'"

Oskar was silent.

"You ever think about why we were chosen?" Joelle asked. "For the seventeenth floor?" She still hadn't opened her eyes. It occurred to Oskar that perhaps the FBI had already gotten to her, that maybe she was recording this conversation. What wouldn't a mother with a young family do to avoid prison?

"I mean, here's the question," Joelle said, "and I'd be genuinely interested to hear your thoughts: How did he know we'd do it? Would *anyone* do something like this, given enough money, or is there something special about us? Did he look at me one day and just think, *That woman seems conveniently lacking in a moral centre, that person seems well suited to participate in a—*"

"I should go," Oskar said. "I'm actually not feeling that well." He stepped over Joelle's legs and fled, jogging down flight after flight. There's something a little nightmarish about tower stairwells, the repetitive downward spiral of doors and landings. When he emerged from a side door into the lobby, Oskar found himself in the midst of a small crowd, at least two dozen people trying to talk their way in. Something twisted in his stomach. These were Alkaitis's investors. Several of them were openly weeping. Others were arguing with security guards, who had formed a small crowd of their own and looked confused and distressed.

"Look," a guard was explaining, "I sympathize, but we can't just let anyone—"

"You." A woman had caught sight of Oskar. "What company do you work for?"

"Cantor Fitzgerald," Oskar said. It was just the first company that came to mind.

"I didn't know Cantor Fitzgerald had offices here," someone said, but Oskar was already out on the sidewalk, where a separate crowd was assembling: news vans were parking on the curb and blocking traffic, men carried TV cameras with shockingly brilliant lights, journalists were moving in on everyone exiting the building.

"Did you work with Jonathan Alkaitis?" someone asked.

"Who?" Oskar said. "God no, of course not."

2

Oskar walked by Olivia Collins as he left, but because she'd never been to the seventeenth floor—Alkaitis conducted his meetings on Eighteen—she didn't recognize him. She was standing in the lobby with the other investors, trying to make sense of the altered world. She'd been here for some time, and the scene—the weeping investors, the camera people, the news vans pulling up outside—had the quality of a bad dream.

A few hours earlier, she'd been awakened from a nap by a ringing phone. "I'm sorry, Monica," she said, after a moment of confusion, "I was sleeping just now, and I'm not sure I quite . . ." She went quiet, frowning, trying to understand what her sister was saying. "Monica," she said, "are you crying?" She'd been sitting on the edge of the bed, looking at her beloved tiny apartment, this place that she rented mostly with the proceeds of her investment with Alkaitis, but what Monica seemed to be telling her was that there had never been any investments at all, and in some fundamental way the situation didn't compute. Olivia stood slowly—rising too quickly made her dizzy sometimes—

and fumbled around in the mess of the closet for her waterproof boots, the handbag that she always meant to hang on a hook but never did, her winter coat. "Monica," she'd said, interrupting her sister midsentence, "I'm going to go down to his office and see if I can find anything out. I'll call you later."

In the taxi, she applied bright lipstick and tied a silk scarf over her hair for added fortitude. She'd hoped to get into Jonathan's offices, to talk to someone—anyone—but she was far from the first to have this idea. A crowd was gathering in the lobby of the Gradia Building. "It's my life savings," a man was shouting to one of the security guards, "you have to let me at least talk to someone, this is my entire life—" but the guards, four of them, were arrayed along the turnstiles and seemingly had no intention of letting anyone through. Olivia stood by the doors, unsettled by the crowd's fury.

"Do you not understand?" A man was speaking to a guard who seemed to Olivia to be very young, although in fairness most people looked young to her these days. "All of my money has been stolen."

"I understand, sir, but—"

"You have to calm down," a guard was saying to a woman who was talking very close to his face.

"I will not calm down," the woman said, "I will not be told to be calm."

"Ma'am, I sympathize, but—"

"But *what*? But *what*?"

"What am I supposed to do, ma'am? Let a crowd of angry people storm the eighteenth floor?" The guard was sweating. "I'm just doing my job. I am doing my job. Step away from me, please."

Olivia stepped forward as the other woman retreated. "I'm a personal friend of Mr. Alkaitis's," she said.

"Then call up there and get someone to come down and get you," the guard said.

She called Alkaitis's number, again and again, but no one picked up. The cowardice of it. She pictured them hiding up there behind locked doors, listening to ringing phones, doing nothing. She knew no one else's extension. She stayed in the lobby for a long time, milling around with the others, falling in and out of conversations, and at first there was some solace in being with people who'd also been robbed, who were also in shock, but after a while the miasma of sadness and fury was too much to bear, so she hailed a taxi—the last taxi she'd take for a while, she realized, watching the numbers tick up on the meter—and went back to her little apartment uptown.

After the pandemonium in the lobby of the Gradia Building, her home was very quiet and still. Olivia closed the door behind her and stood for a moment in the silence. She set her keys on the kitchen table and sat for a while, drinking a glass of water and trying to adjust to the world at hand. After a concentrated search, she found her most recent bank statement and studied it carefully. Until today, she'd had two sources of income: Alkaitis's investment fund and Social Security. If she was very careful, she decided, looking at the numbers, she could afford to stay in her home for two more months.

3

Darkness had fallen in New York, but it was still only three in the afternoon in Las Vegas, where Leon Prevant, the shipping executive who had once had the colossal misfortune of meeting Alkaitis at the bar of the Hotel Caiette, was trapped in a meeting that had outlived its natural lifespan but refused to die. His phone vibrated in his pocket. "Forgive me," Leon said to the other attendees, "this is urgent," even though it probably wasn't. He realized his mistake as he left the room. Leon had been coming to this conference for fifteen years and his lanyard still carried the company name, but he was here as a consultant, and his current contract ended next month. His boss had been told to put a freeze on consulting contracts, "until the landscape looks a little brighter," but when would that be? He had been laid off two years ago in the wake of a merger, and now, in late 2008, ships were moving across oceans at half capacity or less and could be chartered for a third of last year's cost. The landscape— the seascape—was clouded and dim. In other words, it wasn't an optimal moment to run out of meetings, even zombie meetings that should have ended twenty minutes ago. It was his accountant calling. Whatever she was calling about, surely it could wait, so he let the call go to voicemail, counted slowly to five, and re-entered the room with an apology for leaving.

"Everything all right?" His boss, D'Ambrosio, was still frowning at the report that Leon had given him.

"Perfectly, thank you. If you've all had a chance to digest the numbers—" He'd been hoping everyone would take a quick look at the numbers and agree to discuss them later, but the meeting was apparently immortal.

"We have, unfortunately," D'Ambrosio said. "Bit of a blood-bath, isn't it?"

"Well. As you can see, we're facing a significant overcapacity problem."

"Understatement of the goddamn century," someone said.

"Obviously, we're not alone. I had an interesting conversation this morning with a friend over at CMA. They've got ships at anchor off the coast of Malaysia."

"Just sitting there?" Miranda had been Leon's junior colleague in Toronto and then in the New York office, in the years before he'd been restructured into consultant status. Now she had Leon's former title, office, and telephone extension, though not his former salary.

"For the moment, yes. Just waiting it out."

"It's an interesting idea," D'Ambrosio said. "By 'interesting,' I mean 'possibly the best of several bad options.'"

"We'd be creating this weird kind of ghost fleet." This was Daniel Park, who'd worked alongside Leon in the Toronto office and was now director of operations for Asia. "Are we sure we don't want to just scrap a few of our older vessels?"

"That strikes me as a permanent solution to a temporary problem," Miranda said.

"But this downturn," Park said, "this chaos, whatever you want to call it—"

"'This period of sustained uncertainty,'" one of the Europeans interjected in ironic tones, quoting the morning's keynote speaker. He was German and relatively new. Leon couldn't remember his name.

"Right, yes, whatever euphemism we're going with here, this thing could last years. Are we prepared to commit to potentially several years of staffing a fleet of unused ships off the coast of Malaysia?"

"The staffing would be light," Leon said. "Skeleton crew, just enough men on board to keep it afloat."

"If we do it, maybe we set a time limit," the German said. Wilhelm, Leon remembered now, his name was Wilhelm, but what was the surname? It was troubling that he didn't know. He'd known everyone in senior management once. "Maybe we put the ships out to anchor now, then commit to revisiting the question in a year, two years, and if we still don't need them, we scrap the excess."

"Seems like a reasonable course of action to me," D'Ambrosio said. "Thoughts, objections?"

"There's the question of the new Panamax vessels," Miranda said. There was a collective sigh. The company had commissioned two new ships back in the lost paradise of 2005, when the demand had seemed endless and they were struggling to keep up, and the ships—under contract, paid for, two and a half years into the building process, and now extravagantly unnecessary—would be delivered from the South Korean shipyards in six months.

"I say we send them straight to the ghost fleet." D'Ambrosio glanced at his watch. "Gentlemen, Miranda, I'm afraid we're out of time. Let's pick this up tomorrow. Wilhelm, if you could get us an analysis . . ."

The meeting finally unwound, the room breaking into small groups or rushing away to get to a conference session that had already started. Leon walked out alongside Daniel. "Are you going to the economic outlook panel?" Daniel asked.

"Skipping it, I think. I've been up to my neck in economic outlooks for the past four months."

"Haven't we all." The corridor was several degrees colder than the conference room, the wintry chill of Las Vegas air conditioning. Two young hotel employees were clearing dirty mugs from the coffee and pastry stations. "I'm going to go call my wife," Daniel said. "Catch up with you at dinner?"

"Looking forward to it."

It was a pleasure to be away from other people for a moment, with no one making obvious proclamations about economic collapse or pulling him into hysterical conversations about the chartering horizon. Leon poured himself a hazelnut coffee and stepped out into the atrium.

Miranda had left the meeting ahead of him and was sitting

some distance away on an industrial sofa, writing something in her legal pad. No, not writing, sketching: the pad was angled away from him, but he watched the movements of her wrist with some interest as he approached. She'd started out at the company as his administrative assistant, which all these years later seemed like a faintly unbelievable rumour. He cleared his throat, and she flipped a page over as she set the pad on the marble coffee table, so that he couldn't see whatever she'd been working on. He'd seen her perform this motion a hundred times, at least, and as always, he made a point of not asking. Leon held strong opinions about privacy.

"You're skipping the economic outlook session too," she said.

"This entire conference is an economic outlook session. I decided coffee was more important."

"I like your priorities. That's an interesting idea, by the way, parking ships off the coast of Malaysia."

"Do you mind if we talk about literally anything other than the economic downturn?" he asked.

"Not at all. I'm thinking about making an excuse and leaving early tomorrow."

"What, you're not enjoying the atmosphere of barely suppressed panic?"

"There's something almost tedious about disaster," Miranda said. "Don't you find? I mean, at first it's all dramatic, 'Oh my god, the economy's collapsing, there was a run on my bank so my bank ceased to exist over the weekend and got swallowed up by JPMorgan Chase,' but then that keeps happening, it just keeps collapsing, week after week, and at a certain point . . ."

"I know what you mean," Leon said. "It's the *surprise* that bothers me, personally, the way everyone I talk to seems shocked by the downturn in the industry."

"Yeah, so, true story, one of our colleagues pulled me aside today, I'm not naming names, and he said, 'I just can't believe what's happening to our industry, can you?' And I'm trying to be patient with these people, I really am, but I had to ask him, which part is surprising to you? Let's break this down. What is it you can't believe, exactly? That people don't want to buy goods when the economy collapses, or that people don't want to ship goods that nobody's buying?"

"Predictable outcomes, and all that." Leon remembered at that moment that his accountant had called earlier and absently checked his phone. She'd called again, ten minutes ago. "Sorry," he said, "I think I have to call this person."

"If you don't see me at dinner, it means I successfully escaped."

"I'll be silently cheering you on from the sidelines," he said as he rose, and wandered away from her, toward the glass atrium wall, toward the phone call that would split his life neatly into a before and an after.

"I'm going to assume you haven't heard the news," his accountant said, "or you would've called me already."

"What news? What's going on?"

"You didn't hear?"

"Obviously not." He'd never liked her. *Bit of a robot*, he remembered Miranda telling him when he'd asked if she could recommend a good accountant, *but the best I've ever worked with. She sees all the angles.* Although what was the point of hiring the best accountant you've ever worked with if you're going to ignore her advice and park all your retirement savings in a single investment fund?

"Leon"—and she didn't sound like a robot at all, she sounded human and deeply shaken; she was conveying information, he realized just before she told him, that she very much didn't want to convey—"Alkaitis was arrested this morning."

"What?" He sank gracelessly into the nearest sofa, staring at an embankment on the other side of the glass, red gravel dotted with cacti under a garishly blue sky. "I'm sorry, did you say— *what*?"

"It's all over the news," she said. "He was a con man. The whole thing was a fraud."

"The whole . . . what?"

"It was a con," the accountant said.

"What do you mean? All the money I invested, you're saying . . . ?"

"Leon," she said, "I'm so sorry, but your money wasn't invested."

"That isn't possible. The returns have been excellent, we've been living off of them, we—"

"Leon."

"I don't understand," he said. "I just don't understand what you're telling me."

"What I'm telling you is that Alkaitis was running a Ponzi scheme," she said. "The money you gave him, he didn't invest it. He stole it. Your account statements were fictional."

"What does this mean?" he asked, but he knew what it meant.

"Your money's gone," she said softly.

"All of it?"

"Leon, it wasn't real. None of it was real. Those returns . . ." She didn't add *that I told you seemed almost too good to be true*, because she didn't have to. They both remembered the conversation. How could he have been so stupid? He was staring at the sky, inexplicably out of breath. He didn't remember hanging up on the accountant, but he must have, because now he was no longer speaking with her, now he was reading a news story on his phone about the arrest of Jonathan Alkaitis at his home in Greenwich that morning, about a Ponzi scheme's collapsing when one too many investors pulled out, more arrests expected, the SEC and FBI investigating, and somewhere in that morass was Leon's retirement savings, or rather the ghost of his retirement savings, the savings themselves having been spirited away.

"This isn't a disaster," he whispered to himself. Time had skipped again; he was no longer looking at his phone; he was standing by the wall of glass. The economic outlook panel had apparently just broken up, his colleagues spilling out into the corridor and mobbing the coffee stations, a rising tide of overlapping voices. He had to get out. He crossed the plains of grey carpet and floated down the escalator, through the lower atrium and past the casino, out into the thin air of the winter desert. The sidewalk was crowded and the tourists walked in slow motion. Why was a shipping conference being held in a desert city? Because Las Vegas hotel rooms are cheap. Because the desert is a sea. *It isn't a disaster,* he told himself, *we will not be destitute.* He could say he was robbed and that wouldn't be inaccurate, but on the other hand, these were the facts of the case: he'd met Alkaitis at a hotel bar, Alkaitis had explained the investment strategy, *Leon hadn't understood,* and he'd given Alkaitis his retirement savings anyway. He didn't insist on a detailed explanation. One of our signature flaws as a species: we will risk almost anything to avoid looking stupid. The strategy had seemed to adhere to a certain logic, even if the precise mechanics—puts, calls, options, holds, conversions—swam just outside of his grasp. "Look," Alkaitis had said, at his warmest and most accommodating, "I could break it all down for you, but I think you understand the gist of it, and at the end of the day, the returns speak for themselves." It was true, Leon could see it for himself, a steadiness in that column of numbers that appealed to his deepest longing for order in the universe.

A pair of showgirls walked by, eighteen or nineteen years old in matching outfits, holding heavy headdresses of plumed feathers in their hands, their faces set hard with exhaustion and makeup. Not real showgirls, just girls who collected tips for posing with tourists on the sidewalk. He kept passing middle-aged men and women in red T-shirts that read GIRLS TO YOUR ROOM IN 20 MINUTES, handing out flyers that presumably said the same. The people passing out flyers had thousand-yard stares and were worn down in a manner suggestive of a difficult life, or was Leon imagining this? He didn't think he was imagining it. He stepped into a hotel lobby, he hardly noticed which one, just to get off the sidewalk. He was thinking about the girls: if they could be in your room in twenty minutes, then probably they were already here somewhere, on the Strip, waiting. Picture the hotel suite where the girls are waiting, the air thick with cigarette smoke and perfume, girls staring at their phones, doing lines in the bathroom, talking about whatever it is that twenty-minute girls discuss, waiting, counting hours, counting money, hoping the next date isn't a psychopath. The vision made him profoundly sad. He could live without retirement savings. No one in this country actually starves to death. It's just one future slipping away and being replaced by another. He had his health. They could sell the house. He found a padded bench away from other people, near the entrance to the hotel casino, and called his wife.

"I saw the news," she said before Leon could say hello. The fear in her voice was unbearable. "How bad is it, L?"

"It's a disaster, Marie." He realized that he was crying, for the first time in well over a decade. "I'm so sorry, sweetheart, I am just so sorry, it's an absolute disaster."

4

Ella Kaspersky was on CNN that night. Olivia and Leon were both watching, Olivia at her sister's apartment in New York and Leon in a hotel room in Las Vegas. "Well, of course it occurred to me that the returns *could* be legitimate, Mark," she said to the interviewer, "but it's just that that would make it the first legitimate fund in history whose returns could be graphed on a nearly perfect forty-five-degree angle, so you'll understand my skepticism."

Oskar and Joelle were watching too, at a bar in Midtown. They'd comforted themselves over the years by telling themselves that Kaspersky was a marginal figure, but on the other hand, of course she'd always been perfectly correct about the nature of Alkaitis's asset management unit, and Oskar had read her furious and disconcertingly accurate blog posts.

"There's no pleasure in having been right," she said now, elegant and impeccable in a CNN studio. She was telling her story—approached by Alkaitis in a hotel lobby; did her research and concluded that the returns were impossible; contacted the SEC, who bungled the investigation to such an egregious degree that there was talk now of congressional inquiries; tried for years to get the story out and was written off as a crank—and even though Oskar knew all of this to be correct and knew Kaspersky was in the right, he still wanted to throw his shoe at the screen. Why are the righteous so often irritating?

"She couldn't be happier," Joelle said. "She *loves* that she was right."

5

In the morning, the investors were back at the Gradia Building. Harvey, who had turned off his phone and spoken to no one, was surprised that people were already in position at seven-thirty, a dozen of them in an anguished knot on the far side of the sidewalk, where they'd apparently been banished by building security. He tried to waft by without making eye contact, but a woman reached out and touched his arm.

"Harvey."

"Olivia." He'd met Olivia a few times over the years, in Alkaitis's office. She wore a white coat and yellow scarf, and in the unrelenting grey of Manhattan in December, she looked like a daffodil.

"You work with him, right?" Another investor was interrupting his vision, a red-faced man with terror in his eyes. "With Alkaitis?"

Harvey stared at Olivia, who stared at Harvey. He wished he could be alone with her, so that he could confess everything without these extraneous people crowding in.

"Harvey," she said, "is it true? Did you know?"

Another investor had joined them, no, two more, the scene becoming angrier and more crowded, Olivia radiant in her white coat and the others in their New York winter monochromes, black and grey, standing too close with their fear and their coffee breath. Harvey was afraid for his life. They would be entirely justified, he felt, in picking him up and throwing him in front of a passing car. They looked like they wanted to. He was a big man, but they could do it, six of them together. The street was right there.

"I have to go upstairs and see what's going on," he said.

"Oh, you're not going anywhere," one of them said, "not until you tell us—"

But the last thing they'd expected was for him to bolt like a startled horse, so no one was able to catch him before he darted away. When had he last run? It had been years. He hadn't realized how fast he could be. He was already across the lobby. He swiped his card and got through the turnstiles while they stood dumbfounded on the sidewalk, staring. He was in terrible shape, though, so now he couldn't breathe. He'd done something to his ankle—no, both ankles. In prison, Harvey decided, he was going to be one of those men who work out all the time, push-ups in his cell, weights and jogging in the yard. When he arrived on Seventeen, he found that the door to the office suite had been propped open. A police officer was standing by the door. The people in the suite registered, at first, as a mass of undifferentiated shadow: dark suits, dark jackets with FBI or ENFORCEMENT on the back.

There are moments in life that require some courage. Harvey didn't turn around and walk back to the elevators and take a cab to JFK and leave the country, although at that point he still had possession of his passport. Instead, he walked into the heart of the swarm and introduced himself.

Harvey's office was populated this morning by agents of both the FBI and the SEC, several of whom were very interested in speaking with him, why don't you just take a minute to gather yourself and we'll all take a seat in the conference room.

"I just need to get something out of my desk," Harvey said.

They offered to get it for him, possibly fearing a hitherto-unnoticed handgun.

"If you look in the top left drawer," Harvey said, "under the files, you'll find a legal pad with my handwriting on it. Several pages of writing. I think it'll be of interest to you." He floated ahead of them to the conference room.

Oskar passed him on the way in. "What is all this?" he asked, white around the mouth.

"You know what this is," Harvey said. Oskar looked like he wanted to be sick, but the odd thing was, Harvey didn't actually feel that bad. None of this felt real to him. Oskar texted Joelle, so she didn't come in at all. She drove to her kids' school and signed them out midmorning, took them to F. A. O. Schwarz and told them they could have anything, smiling all the while, but the youngest burst into tears because if they could have anything then obviously something was drastically wrong. Later the children remembered this as a long, uneasy day of trooping around Manhattan in the cold, in and out of toy stores and hot chocolate dispensaries and the Children's Museum while their mother kept saying "Isn't this fun?" but also kept tearing up, alternately lavishing them with attention and disappearing into her phone.

"We'll remember this day always, don't you think?" she said in the car on their way home to Scarsdale. They were moving very slowly in the late-afternoon traffic. "Yes," her children said, but later their memories were destabilized by Joelle's letters from prison: how much fun we had that last day, she wrote, that toy store, that giant stuffed giraffe, those cups of hot chocolate, I am so glad we had that day together, do you remember that wonderful display in the museum, and they wondered if they were misremembering, because what they mostly remembered was the cold, their wet feet, the feeling of wrongness, the grey of Manhattan in the winter rain, the way the giraffe dragged in a puddle on the way back to the car.

By the time Joelle's children acquired the giraffe, Ron had already left. He slipped out at noon to meet with a lawyer, who advised him not to come back. Harvey was still being interviewed in the conference room. Oskar was playing Solitaire on his computer, which had been backed up and disconnected from both the internet and the internal network, while investigators went through his filing cabinets. Enrico was at his aunt's house in Mexico City. He'd spent some hours digging through drawers in search of his dead cousin's old passport, and now that he had it he was sitting with her on the patio, the two of them smoking cigarette after cigarette in silence, Enrico glancing at his phone from time to time, following the news of Alkaitis's arrest, reflecting on how strange it was that he'd never felt less free in his life.

Oskar was the last to leave that night. He'd spent the day acting as confused as possible, directing investigators to the locations of various files while asking what this was all about, trying to convey the illusion of helpfulness without actually giving anything away. It had been an exhausting performance. The elevator doors opened to reveal Simone, on her way down from Eighteen with a file box in her arms.

"Crazy day," Oskar said as he stepped in beside her.

She nodded.

"What's in the box?"

"A few personal effects from Claire Alkaitis's desk. She asked me to get them for her."

He saw a crystal figurine, a framed photo of Claire and her family, a few books. The kids in the photo looked young, no older than six or seven. Oskar looked away. In the ghost version of his life, the parallel-universe version in which he'd gone to the FBI eleven or twelve years ago, those children were spared all of this; in that life, Claire Alkaitis would have been in her teens when her father was arrested, obviously terribly traumatic but not the same thing as being implicated, not at all like being a VP in one of her father's companies and having her name dragged through the press; in that ghost life, he realized, Claire Alkaitis and her children were probably fine.

"Do you want to grab a quick drink or something?" he asked Simone.

"No," Simone said.

"Are you sure?"

"You're pretty much the last person I'd want to get a drink with."

"Okay, got it. You could just say no."

"I did." The doors opened on the lobby and she walked away. The crowd of investors had dwindled to six or seven on the sidewalk, no longer weeping but still in shock, staring at the Gradia Building, staring at everyone coming out. Simone walked by without looking at them and disappeared into a black SUV that idled at the curb.

Claire Alkaitis was where Simone had left her, in the backseat. "Thank you," she said, "I appreciate this." Her voice was barely above a whisper. She took the box from Simone, studied the photograph—an artifact of a civilization that had recently ended—and looked at the books as if she'd never seen them before. She lowered the window slightly, in order to push the crystal figurine through the crack. It made a pleasant tinkling sound as it shattered on the pavement. "Gift from my father," she said. The driver carefully avoided making eye contact with her in the rear-view mirror. "Where do you live, Simone?"

"East Williamsburg."

"Okay. Aaron, can you take us to East Williamsburg?"

"Sure, you got an address for me?"

Simone gave it to him. "Don't you have to get home?" she asked Claire, who had closed her eyes again.

"Home's actually the last place I want to be just at the moment."

An interlude of quiet, then, while the car moved south toward the Williamsburg Bridge. Outside, it was beginning to snow. Simone had been in New York City for six months by now, and she thought that she was starting to understand how a person could become very tired here. She'd seen them on the subway, the tired people, the people who'd worked too long and too hard, caught up in the machine, eyes closed on the evening trains. Simone had always thought of them as citizens of a separate city, but the gap between their city and hers was beginning to close.

"How many people knew about it?" Simone asked eventually. They were passing through the East Village.

"I assume everyone in the asset management unit. Everyone who worked on the seventeenth floor." Claire didn't open her eyes. Simone was beginning to wonder if Claire was sedated.

"All of them? Oskar, Enrico, Harvey . . . ?"

"It turns out that's literally all they were doing on that floor, running a fraudulent scheme."

"Did anyone else know? Up on Eighteen?"

"I don't know. I don't think so. The companies were always kept completely separate. Everything's still so unclear." The car was rattling over the Williamsburg Bridge, and now the snow was falling in a frenzied way that Simone found hypnotic. "You're so lucky," Claire said.

"I don't feel lucky."

"You know what you are?"

"Unemployed?"

"That's a temporary condition. You know what's permanent? You're a person with a really excellent cocktail story. Ten, twenty years from now, at a cocktail party, you'll be holding a martini in a circle of people, and you'll be like, 'Did I ever tell you about the time I worked for Jonathan Alkaitis?'" Claire's voice cracked when she spoke her father's name. "You get to walk away untarnished."

Simone didn't know what to say.

"One seventy Graham Avenue," the driver said.

"Okay," Simone said, "this is me. Are you going to be all right?"

"No," Claire said dreamily.

Simone glanced at the driver, who shrugged.

"Okay, well, thanks for the ride." She left Claire in the SUV and let herself in through the iron gate, then the front door, into the shadowy and never-cleaned foyer. The light over the stairs buzzed unpleasantly. Her roommate Yasmin was in the kitchen, eating ramen noodles and reading something on her laptop.

"How'd it go?" Yasmin asked.

"I just took the most awkward car ride ever with Claire Alkaitis."

"She's the wife?"

"Daughter."

"What was she like?"

"Like she'd taken three Ambien," Simone said. "Also kind of hostile. She was like, 'You get to walk out of this with a story for cocktail parties. In twenty years, you'll be telling this story to people over martinis.'"

"Yeah, but she's right," Yasmin said. "I mean objectively. Twenty years from now, you'll literally be telling the story at cocktail parties."

Oskar walked out of the Gradia Building and into the beginning of the snowstorm, the first light flakes drifting down. He didn't notice the detectives until they were almost upon him, a block from the office. There were two of them, a man and a woman, flashing their badges as they got out of an unmarked car that had pulled to a smooth stop in front of a fire hydrant.

"Oskar Novak?"

In a parallel version of events he might have run, and in his ghost life, his honourable life, his non-Ponzi life, he was never here at all. But in this world Oskar stopped in his tracks, and standing there on the sidewalk in the first snow of that winter, seconds away from his first pair of handcuffs, he was surprised to realize that what he felt was relief.

"FBI," the woman said. "I'm Detective Davis, and this is Detective Ihara." In a distant way he realized that they'd been merciful; they must have been tracking him since he walked out of the Gradia Building, but they'd waited until he was out of sight of the investors and the reporters gathered outside.

"You're under arrest," Detective Ihara said calmly. The few people passing on the sidewalk eyed him surreptitiously or openly stared, but all of them gave him a wide berth. The detectives were reciting their lines—*You have the right to remain silent, anything you say can and will be used against you in a court of law, you have the right to an attorney*—and Oskar stood still, accepted the handcuffs without protest, snow falling on his face, while here and there, in the city and in the suburbs, the rest of us were being arrested too.

6

At the sentencing hearing six months later, Alkaitis's lawyer appealed to the judge on compassionate grounds. "If we are to be honest with ourselves," the lawyer said, "who among us has never made a mistake?" But this was an error, Olivia saw that immediately. The judge was giving the lawyer an incredulous look, because sure, yes, everyone makes mistakes, but those mistakes are typically more on the order of forgetting to pay a phone bill, or leaving the oven on for a couple hours after dinner, or entering the wrong number into a spreadsheet. Perpetuating a multibillion-dollar fraud over a period of decades is something entirely different.

Could the lawyer see the error too? Impossible to tell. Veer

Sethi was a sleek, expensively dressed person with silvery hair and a sense of performance. The man sitting next to Olivia—a fellow investor, a retired dentist who all but quivered with rage when he talked about the fraud—had told her that Alkaitis's lawyer was one of the most expensive criminal defence attorneys in the city, but Sethi didn't strike Olivia as a particularly formidable person. He'd made a mistake but he pressed on with the story, like a boy following a dwindling trail into the woods at nightfall: Once upon a time there was a family, Jonathan and Suzanne and then a daughter, Claire. (Speaking of which, where was Claire? Olivia had attended three hearings without seeing her.) They lived in a small house in an unfashionable suburb, then a slightly larger house, Jonathan working long hours and Suzanne working a little too, brief and inexpensive summer vacations in places that could be reached by car, Christmases with her family in Virginia or with his family in Westchester County, the inevitable struggles of starting a business, the business's ever-increasing success, Claire goes to Columbia and then takes a job in her father's brokerage company—the legitimate company, Sethi wished to stress to the courtroom, the company that had absolutely nothing to do with the crime—and then Suzanne is diagnosed with an aggressive cancer.

"I don't suggest that anything in this excuses my client's actions," the lawyer said. "But I've been married to my wife for thirty-five years, and as a husband, I can only imagine what those days must have been like for that family." Vincent had shown up, which Olivia thought must have required a certain courage. She was a few rows up and on the other side of the courtroom, sitting very still in a grey suit.

"And while no measure of grief can excuse his actions, it was during that period," the lawyer continued, "that the fraud began." He seemed to be trying to convey the impression that the Ponzi was something that *happened*, the way weather happens, as opposed to a premeditated crime coldly perpetuated and covered up with the assistance of a dedicated staff. (If only the staff were here! Olivia would have liked to personally kill them. She would start with Harvey Alexander. He would beg. She would be merciless.) The judge was writing something. Sethi was going on about hospitals and surgeries and rounds of chemotherapy, Alkaitis's vanishing from the office for weeks at a time, distracted and not paying as much attention as he should have been. He'd been heavily invested in several dot-com companies and had been caught flat-footed when they imploded. There'd been signs that the tech bubble was ending, but he'd been distracted by his wife's illness and death, and he hadn't read the signals correctly.

"And this was the moment," the lawyer said, "when my client made his fatal mistake." How many times could he drop the word *mistake* into a single address? Was his strategy as transparent to the judge as it was to Olivia? She couldn't tell. The judge was impassive. "My client took a loss, and he thought, *You know what, I can cover this*. He made a terrible, terrible error in judgment, a terrible mistake. He decided to cover his losses with income from new investors. He was embarrassed. He thought he could make up for the shortfall over a month or two, and no one would know. Why would he do such a thing? Why would he make a mistake like that?" Here, a pause for dramatic effect. Veer Sethi had been handed an impossible task. He was performing to the best of his abilities.

"What I believe, Your Honour, is that it comes down to a question of fear. Every life contains a measure of terrifying moments. My client had lost his wife. He was desolate. All he had left was his work, his job. And the fraud started, this terrible mistake of his, because he could not bear to lose his work, which at that moment was the last thing he had." Which wasn't particularly flattering to Claire, Olivia thought. Perhaps she should have followed her sister, Monica, to law school. She felt she could do a better job than this guy was doing. The courtroom was too warm. Olivia let herself drift for just a moment, back to a particular afternoon in the studio in Soho, sitting on the sofa with Renata during one of those violent August rainstorms, taking a break from painting, listening to the rain, drinking wine, Renata saying, "I couldn't join the working world even if I wanted to," but in a way that sounded like she was trying to convince herself, which Olivia suspected was why the moment had stayed with her. Renata had made it to 1972 before she succumbed to her habit. 1973? No, definitely '72, because Olivia remembered watching reports of Watergate and wondering what Renata would have thought about it, if Renata were still alive, Renata who'd left her politician father and secretly alcoholic mother in the Maryland suburbs to come here, Renata who claimed not to care at all about that world but who carefully followed politics all her life.

Back in the courtroom, Veer Sethi was still talking. "When you look at my client," he said, "you are not looking at an evil man. You are looking at a deeply flawed man, a man who, at the moment when it mattered, at the moment when he realized that he had losses he couldn't cover, did not find his courage. You are looking at a decent man who made a mistake."

It was impossible not to notice, as Sethi thanked the judge for his consideration and resumed his seat at the table, that the lawyers for the state were smirking and shaking their heads. Alkaitis was making careful notes in a legal pad. Sethi and his two junior sidekick lawyers were conferring and shuffling papers in order to avoid looking at anyone, especially not at the state. The state was rising from the prosecution table, the state was buttoning its suit jacket, the state was beginning, with barely disguised contempt, to rip holes in the timeline that the defence had laid out. It was curious, the state noted, that the Ponzi scheme was supposed to have begun around the time of the dot-com crash, when one of Alkaitis's employees—a Harvey Alexander—had confessed to participating in a scheme that had begun in the late seventies. Olivia's mind wandered. She hadn't been sleeping well. She'd given up her apartment and moved in with Monica, and the bed in Monica's guest room was uncomfortable. Was there any point, actually, in staying to listen to more of this?

But Olivia stayed till the end. The sentence, when it came, was like something from a fairy tale: there once was a man locked away in a castle for one hundred and seventy years.

The intake of breath in the courtroom was audible. *A hundred and seventy years,* someone repeated nearby. A soft whistle. Some muted cheers. Olivia sat very still and felt absolutely nothing.

She'd set out before dawn with a sense of embarking on a mission, but after the verdict came down, she almost wished she'd stayed home. She couldn't have hoped for a longer sentence, and yet there was a curious sense of anticlimax. She was slow leaving the courthouse and went unnoticed when she finally straggled out. She didn't mind her cloak of invisibility, in this instance. She wasn't feeling very well. There'd been a time when a New York City heat wave wouldn't have bothered her, but that time had passed. The media were clustered around other investors. "Look, it's just, it changes nothing," she heard the dentist say. He was right, she supposed. Jonathan was going to prison forever, but

Olivia still lived in her sister's guest bedroom. She made her way uptown through the furnace of the subway system and observed the way the life of the city continued around her, indifferent and uninterrupted. When she'd boarded the downtown train that morning she'd had the thought that she was witnessing history, but would history remember Jonathan Alkaitis? Just another empty suit in a time of collapse and dissipation, architect of an embarrassingly unsophisticated scheme that had run for a while and then imploded. The heat was too much. The subway was crowded. When she finally emerged into the Upper East Side, a few blocks from her sister's apartment, she had to walk very slowly so as not to faint. A man walking in the opposite direction almost walked into her; he frowned as he stepped out of the way at the last minute, as if she were entirely at fault.

"This is academic," the judge had said, "but I'm required for technical reasons to impose a period of supervised release following your sentence." Idea for a ghost story: there once was a man who remained under supervised release for three years following the end of his 170-year prison term. Idea for a ghost story: there once was a woman who drifted unseen through the city of New York until she faded into the crowds and the heat.

12

THE COUNTERLIFE

There's a morning in FCI Florence Medium 1 when Alkaitis steps out into the yard and sees a flash of colour in the crowd. It's red, but that's impossible. Red isn't allowed here. Not just red, but a red power suit, of the kind he hasn't seen on a woman since the early nineties, mid-nineties at the latest, fire-engine red with extremely padded shoulders. The woman wearing it seems to move too quickly; in a few steps she has somehow crossed the yard and is standing near him, staring.

"Madame Bertolli," he says quietly, trying to steady his voice.

"You say something?" a nearby guy asks.

"No, nothing." Yvette Bertolli obviously isn't here, because that would be impossible and no one else seems to have noticed her. Nonetheless, here she is. She begins a slow circle of the yard, sometimes flickering slightly. She looks much younger than she was the last time he saw her. This may actually be the same suit she was wearing when he met her for the first time, which would've been, what, 1986, '87? A lunch in Paris. She'd just started her own investment advisory business and she had a few high-net-worth French and Italian clients for him. On the morning of Alkaitis's arrest, her clients had a combined total of

$320 million of their money in the Ponzi. Yvette Bertolli died of a heart attack that afternoon.

Now she circles the yard, glancing every so often at Alkaitis. He closes his eyes, pinches himself, every trick he can think of, but she's still there when he goes inside an hour later, conferring with Faisal under a tree.

"I'd like to ask about your employees," the journalist Julie Freeman says on one of her visits.

"They were good people," he says. "Loyal."

"It's interesting that you think of them as good people, when they were involved in the crime."

"No, I did all of that on my own." He has decided to stick with this story until the end of his life, even though three of his five asset management staffers have been convicted. He detects a flicker of irritation as she makes a note.

"I assume you heard that Lenny Xavier lost his appeal," she says. "Guilty on nine counts, all involving the Ponzi."

"I'd prefer not to talk about him," Alkaitis says.

"Let's switch tracks, then. I'd like to ask you about something one of your staffers said on the stand," she says. "When Oskar Novak was cross-examined, he was asked about the search history on his computer, and he said, and I quote, 'It's possible to both know and not know something.'"

"Why, what was his search history?" Alkaitis hasn't actually spent much time thinking about Oskar or any of the others. He carried them for years. They could've quit at any time.

"He spent a combined total of nine and a half hours researching residency requirements for countries that don't have extradition treaties with the United States," Freeman says.

"Ouch. Poor kid." In his mind, Oskar is still the nineteen-year-old college dropout in a too-big suit at his job interview. "That can't have gone well for him."

"It didn't." She waits a beat or two, but he doesn't ask. The truth is, he doesn't really care what happened to Oskar, which prison he ended up at, or the length of his sentence. "Anyway," she says, "I was curious about whether that idea has any relevance for you, that notion that a person can know and not know something at the same time."

"It's an interesting idea, Julie. I'll think about it."

There's something in it, he decides later, standing in line for dinner. It's possible to know you're a criminal, a liar, a man of weak moral character, and yet *not* know it, in the sense of feeling that your punishment is somehow undeserved, that despite the cold facts you're deserving of warmth and some kind of special treatment. You can know that you're guilty of an enormous crime, that you stole an immense amount of money from multiple people, and that this caused destitution for some of them and suicide for others, you can know all of this and yet still somehow feel you've been wronged when your judgment arrives.

Between Freeman's visits, Alkaitis finds himself dwelling on Oskar's search history. It's kind of poignant, actually, thinking of the kid running internet searches on countries without extradition treaties, research for a project he lacks the guts to carry out. Not like Enrico, who remains at large.

He's in line for the commissary when he sees Olivia. She's wandering around, touching various items on the shelves, not looking at him. She's wearing a blue dress that he remembers from that last summer before he went to prison; she wore this dress on the yacht. He backs away and leaves without buying anything, deeply shaken. He goes back to his cell and lies down with an arm over his eyes. Hazelton is somewhere else, thank god. He's desperate to be alone, but the problem is that now he can no longer be sure of whether he's alone in any given room. Certain borders are dissolving.

"Can I ask you to look someone up for me?" he asks Julie Freeman on her next visit. Two days have passed since he saw Olivia in the commissary. "One of the investors was an old friend of mine, a painter who'd also known my brother. Her name was Olivia Collins. I wondered if you could just do a search and see what became of her."

When he sees Freeman again, two weeks later, he knows what she's going to say before she says it. "I have some bad news," she tells him when she sits down. "That woman you asked me to look up, Olivia Collins. She died last month."

"Oh," he says. But he already knew this, he realizes. He's seen Olivia twice now, once in the commissary and once in the yard, where she was engaged in conversation with Yvette Bertolli.

"I'm sorry," Freeman says, and launches into her questions.

"Can I ask you something?" he asks a little later, interrupting a line of tedious questioning about account statements.

"Go ahead."

"Why do you want to write about all this?"

"I've always had an interest in mass delusion," she says. "My senior thesis was about a cult in Texas."

"I'm not sure I follow."

"Well, look at it this way. I believe we're in agreement that it should have been obvious to any sophisticated investor that you were running a fraudulent scheme."

"I've always maintained that," Alkaitis says.

"So in order for your scheme to succeed for as long as it did, a great many people had to believe in a story that didn't actually make sense. But everyone was making money, so no one cared, except Ella Kaspersky."

"People believe in all kinds of things," he said. "Just because it's a delusion doesn't mean it can't make real money for people. You want to talk about mass delusions, I know a lot of guys who got rich off of subprime mortgages."

"Is it fair to call you the embodiment of the era, do you think?"

"That seems a little harsh, Julie. I didn't cause a global economic meltdown. I was as much a victim of the economic collapse as anyone. By the time Lehman Brothers folded, I knew I couldn't keep it going much longer."

"I'd like to ask you about Ella Kaspersky," Freeman says.

"Not my favourite person in the world."

"Do you remember your first meeting with her?"

He met Kaspersky in 1999, at the Hotel Caiette. The trip was ill-starred from the beginning. Suzanne was sick by then and had stayed home in New York, and by the time he arrived at the hotel he was already regretting going out there and thinking about cutting the trip short. But he needed investors, so he'd been spending a week of every month away from New York City, trawling club drawing rooms and hotel bars. He liked the Hotel Caiette in particular, because the fact that he owned the property lent instant credibility: *Look, here we are having a conversation under a roof that I own.* Not that he played any role whatsoever in the management of the place, but that wasn't important.

On that visit to the Hotel Caiette he came downstairs on his second evening and there was Ella Kaspersky, an elegant woman in early middle age, drinking whisky in an armchair and gazing out at the twilight luminescence of the inlet, the reflection of the lobby rising to the surface of the glass. Alkaitis positioned himself nearby, nodded when she glanced at him. What did they talk about? Italy, if he remembers correctly. She was an art collector. She didn't work. She travelled, she studied languages, she went to auctions and art fairs. She'd just spent three months studying Italian in Rome, and so they went off together on an extended tangent about the pleasures of Italy before the conversation turned to what he did for a living. She was interested. It emerged quite naturally that she had money to invest; her father, who'd died only a few months earlier, had bequeathed most of his fortune to their family's charitable foundation, and Ella was involved in the foundation's investment decisions.

"Tell me about your investment strategy," she said.

He went into it in some detail. He told her he was using the split-strike conversion strategy, which involved buying a collection of stocks along with option contracts to sell those stocks at a set price later, thus minimizing risk. He timed these purchases according to fluctuations in the market, he told her, sometimes pulling out of the market altogether to invest his clients' money in government-backed securities, U.S. Treasury bills and such, re-entering the market when the time seemed right. She gave the impression of listening intently, but she was at least three drinks in by then and he wouldn't have guessed that she'd retained everything he'd said, until a letter arrived at his New York office a few weeks later. She'd done some research on his trading strategy and methods. She'd analyzed the performance of a fund that he managed. She'd spoken with two experts on the investment strategy he claimed to be using, neither of whom could explain to her how Alkaitis's returns were so high and so smooth; she was aware of two mutual funds that employed the same strategy, but their returns were much more volatile than his. She was puzzled by his ability to trade stocks in such quantities without affecting the stock prices. His returns would seem to require an almost psychic knowledge of when the market was going to fall. "I don't wish to imply," she wrote, "that I'm entirely closed to the possibility of mystery in the universe, or that I'm unprepared to accept the existence of unusual talent, even outright genius, when it comes to predicting the movement of markets, and yet one can't help but note that your trading strategy, as practised at the scale at which you seem to practise it, would require more OEX put options than actually exist on the Chicago Board Options Exchange." On a personal note, perhaps he could understand her horror when she made inquiries and discovered that her family's private foundation—which, she wasn't sure if she'd mentioned this in Caiette, had been founded for the purpose of funding research into colon cancer, which had killed her mother a decade ago—was already heavily invested in Alkaitis's fund. "Naturally," she wrote, "I took the matter to the foundation's director, who shared my alarm and immediately sent you a withdrawal request. Thus disaster was averted, but it is personally appalling to me to consider how close my family's foundation came to being wiped out. How terrible to think of my parents' legacy having been so imperilled." She'd taken the liberty of forwarding a copy of her letter to the SEC.

Alkaitis called Enrico into his office. It was interesting to observe Enrico as he read Kaspersky's letter; his face didn't change, but his hands shook a little. He sighed as he handed it back.

"She can't prove any of this," Enrico said. "It's innuendo and speculation."

"She sent this to the SEC. They could walk in at any minute."

"We'll jump off that bridge when we come to it, boss." Something that occurs to Alkaitis only much later, a few years into his new life at FCI Florence Medium 1: Why didn't Enrico leave then? In the winter of 1999, with Ella Kaspersky's having figured it out?

In any event, in the version of history that he gives to Julie Freeman in the prison interview, he shows Kaspersky's letter to no one.

"So what happened next?" Freeman asks.

"We got a letter from the SEC. They were opening an investigation."

"Why didn't they catch you?"

"I don't know, to be honest. They were incompetent or they didn't care, or both. I assumed they'd catch us. All it would've taken was a phone call. Literally one phone call, and they could've confirmed there were no trades taking place."

"And by 'us,' you mean you and your staff."

"What?"

"'I assumed they'd catch us,' you said."

"I misspoke. I meant me."

"I see. Must have been something of a pleasant shock, when they closed the investigation without catching you."

"Very much so."

"Did you see her again?"

"Kaspersky? No."

Yes, but it isn't an evening he likes to think about. He and Suzanne were eating dinner at Le Veau d'Or, a restaurant they both loved. Well, he was eating dinner, at any rate. Suzanne was sipping chicken broth. They'd just been to see the oncologist and it was as though they'd entered a tunnel that ended in darkness.

They were being transported at high speed toward night. Alkaitis was trying to keep up his end of the conversation but Suzanne was in a different tunnel, an even darker one, she was answering in monosyllables and he could already see how they would be divided from now on, how Suzanne would be carried more and more rapidly away from him. He'd thought the evening couldn't possibly get any worse, but any given evening can always get worse. A few tables away he heard breaking glass, and when he turned to look, he saw Ella Kaspersky. She was dining alone. A busboy had dropped her wineglass and it had shattered on a bread plate.

"You know her?" Suzanne asked, seeing something in his expression.

"You're not going to believe this, but that's Ella Kaspersky."

(A difference between life with Suzanne and life with Vincent, one of many: he told Suzanne everything.)

"I didn't think she'd be elegant." Kaspersky didn't glance in their direction. She was engaged in dabbing white wine from her lapel. "All this time, I was picturing her as some kind of dishevelled crank."

"Are you going to eat any more?" He wanted his wife to eat something, to keep her strength up, and also very much wanted her to stop staring at Kaspersky.

"No, let's get the check."

He got the check and attended to the details while his wife studied Kaspersky, who'd waved off the busboy's apologies and had returned to reading some kind of document, an inch of paper held together with a binder clip. He didn't like the way Suzanne was looking at her.

"Let's just leave," he said softly, when the check was taken care of, but Kaspersky was seated at the restaurant's narrowest point, and they had to walk quite close to her table to get to the door. As they neared the table, Suzanne's face was set in a terrifying smile. Kaspersky finally looked up when they were almost upon her. She had an excellent poker face, except that her eyes narrowed slightly when she recognized him.

"Good evening, Ella," Alkaitis said. The SEC had closed the investigation earlier that week. There was no need to be ungenerous in victory.

She leaned back in her chair, considering him, and sipped her wine. She didn't speak for so long that he thought she wasn't going to say anything, and was just gathering himself to leave when she said, "You're beneath my contempt."

Alkaitis was paralyzed. He couldn't imagine what to say.

"Oh, Ella," Suzanne said. A small shard from the broken wineglass had been overlooked at the base of the bread basket. Suzanne plucked it between two fingers and dropped it delicately into Kaspersky's water glass. They all watched it drift to the bottom.

Suzanne leaned in close and spoke quietly. "Why don't you swallow broken glass?"

There was a moment where no one spoke.

"I'm sure you must hear this all the time," Ella Kaspersky said, "but you two are perfect for each other."

Alkaitis took his wife's arm and steered her rapidly out of the restaurant, out to the cold street, where the car was waiting. He bundled her in and sat beside her. "Home, please," he said to the driver. He glanced over and saw that Suzanne was weeping silently, her hands over her face. He pulled her close and held her tightly, her tears falling on his coat, and they stayed like that, not speaking, all the way back to Connecticut.

In a different life, in the library at FCI Medium 1, the visiting professor takes an uncharacteristic break from F. Scott Fitzgerald.

"I want to talk about allegory today," he says. "Any of you know the story of the swan in the frozen pond?"

"Yeah, I think I know that story," Jeffries says. He was a police officer until he tried to arrange a hit on his wife. "The one about the swan who doesn't fly away in time, right?"

Alkaitis finds himself thinking about the swan story later on, standing in line for his potatoes and mystery meat. The story was a favourite of his mother's, repeated every so often throughout childhood and adolescence. There's a flock of swans on a lake in the deepening autumn. As the nights grow colder, they all fly away. Except one, for reasons Alkaitis can't remember: a lone swan who doesn't perceive the approaching danger or loves the lake too much to leave even though it's clearly time to go or is afflicted by hubris—the swan's motivations were hazy and, Alkaitis suspects, changeable, depending on what message his mother was trying to impart at any given moment—and then winter sets in and the swan is frozen in ice, because it didn't get out of the water in time.

"I thought I'd be able to get out," he tells Freeman when she comes to see him again. "I was embarrassed. I didn't want to let everyone down. They were just so greedy, these people, the returns they expected . . ."

"You feel the investors pushed you to commit fraud," she says blandly.

"Well, I didn't say that, exactly. I take full responsibility for my crimes."

"But you seem to think the investors were partly to blame."

"They expected a certain level of returns. I felt compelled to deliver. It was a nightmare, actually."

"For you, you mean?"

"Yes, of course. Imagine the stress," he says, "the constant pressure, always knowing that eventually it would all come crashing down but trying to keep it going anyway. I actually wish I'd been caught sooner. I wish they'd caught me back in 1999, that first SEC investigation."

"And you maintain that no one else knew about the scheme." Freeman's voice was carefully neutral. "The account statements, the deception, the wire transfers, that was all you."

"It was all me," he says. "I never told a living soul."

On a different day, Yvette Bertolli circles the recreation yard, walking a little behind and to the right of an elderly mafioso whose name used to inspire terror on the Lower East Side but who now shuffles awkwardly in a slow-motion attempt at jogging. Elsewhere, Olivia and Faisal are speaking with a man Alkaitis doesn't recognize, a man who is also not a prisoner, presumably also not alive, a middle-aged man in a beautiful grey wool suit.

There were four Ponzi-related suicides that Alkaitis is aware of, four men who lost more than they could bear. Faisal was one of them; is this man another? There was an Australian businessman, if Alkaitis remembers correctly, also a Belgian. Are more ghosts even now approaching FCI Florence Medium 1? He stares at Olivia and is overcome by rage. What right does she have to haunt him? What right do *any* of them have to haunt him? It isn't his fault that Faisal chose to do what he did. If he's to be honest with himself, he supposes Yvette Bertolli's heart attack was probably Ponzi related, but she should have seen the scheme for what it was and she could've gotten out whenever she wanted, just like everyone else, and whatever happened to Olivia can't possibly be blamed on him, he's been in prison for years now and she's only been dead for a month. When Alkaitis thinks about how much money he provided, all the cheques he sent out over the years, he feels a hollow rage.

"I'm not saying what I did was right but by any rational analysis I did some good in the world," he writes to Julie Freeman. "By which I mean I made a lot of money over a period of decades for a lot of people, a lot of charities, many sovereign wealth funds and pension funds, etc., and I know that might seem self-justifying but the numbers are the numbers and if you look at investments vs. returns, most of those people/entities took out far more than they put in and made far more money than if they'd just invested in the stock market and therefore I would suggest that it is inaccurate to refer to them as 'victims.'"

"Well," he said to Suzanne, in the hospice, "at least now you won't have to go to prison when the scheme collapses."

"Think of the savings in legal fees," she said. They were like that in the last few months, all competitive bluster and stupid bravado, until she stopped talking, after which he stopped talking too and just sat silently by the bed, hour upon hour, holding her hand.

When it did finally collapse, when he was finally trapped, the wrong woman was there with him. Although Vincent impressed him, at the end, despite not being Suzanne. The tableau: His office in Midtown, the last time he was ever in that room. He was sitting behind his desk, Claire crying on the sofa, Harvey staring into space, while Vincent fidgeted around with a coat and shopping bag and then sat and stared at him until he finally had to tell her: "Vincent," he said, "do you know what a Ponzi scheme is?"

"Yes," Vincent said.

Claire, from the sofa, still crying: "How do you know what a Ponzi scheme is, Vincent? Did he tell you? Did you know about this? I swear to god, if you knew about this, if he told you . . ."

"Of course he didn't tell me," Vincent said. "I know what a Ponzi scheme is because I'm not a fucking idiot."

He thought, *That's my girl.*

In the counterlife, he walks through a hotel corridor—wide and silent with modernist sconces, the corridor of the hotel on Palm Jumeirah—and takes the stairs this time, walking slowly through the cool air. There's a potted palm on every landing. The lobby is empty except for Vincent. She's standing by a fountain, looking into the water. She looks up when he approaches; she's been waiting for him. It's different this time, he's certain that this cannot possibly be a memory, because it takes him a moment to recognize her. She's much older, and she's wearing strange clothing, a grey T-shirt and grey uniform trousers and a chef's apron. There's a handkerchief tied over her hair, but he can tell that her hair's very short, not at all like it was when they were together, and she's not wearing makeup. She's become a completely different person since he saw her last.

"Hello, Jonathan." Her voice seems to come from a long way off, like she's speaking by telephone from a submarine.

"Vincent? I didn't recognize you."

She gazes at him and says nothing.

"What are you doing here?" he asks.

"Just visiting."

"Visiting from where?"

But she's looking past him, distracted now, and when he turns he sees Yvette and Faisal, strolling by one of the lobby windows. Yvette's laughing at something Faisal just said.

"They're not supposed to be here," he says, truly alarmed,

"I've never seen them here before," but when he looks back, Vincent's gone.

Later, lying awake in his uncomfortable bed in the non-counterlife, the nonlife, he's struck by the unfairness of it. If he has to see ghosts, why not his real wife, his first companion instead of his second—his co-conspirator, his beloved Suzanne—or why can't he see Lucas? He isn't well. He's in the counterlife more often than he's in the prison now, and he knows that reality is sliding away from him. He's afraid of forgetting his own name, and if he forgets himself, of course by then he'll have forgotten his brother too. This thought is vastly upsetting, so he marks a tiny L on his left hand with Churchwell's pen. Every time he sees the L, he decides, he'll make a conscious effort to think of Lucas, and in this way thinking of Lucas will become a habit. He heard somewhere that habits are the last to go.

"A habit, like brushing your teeth," Churchwell says.

"Yes, exactly."

"See, but here's the difference. Every time you brush your teeth, your teeth aren't progressively degraded."

"What are you saying?"

"I'm no expert, but I remember reading somewhere, every time you retrieve a memory, that act of retrieval, it corrupts the memory a little bit. Maybe changes it a little."

"Well," Alkaitis says, "I suppose I'll have to take my chances." He's troubled by this new information—is it new information? There's a ring of the familiar about it—because these days he mostly only returns to one memory of Lucas, the same memory retrieved again and again, and it's terrible to think that he's chipping away at it every time, that it might even now be mutating in as-yet-imperceptible ways. When he isn't in the counterlife he likes to dwell in a green field in his hometown, in the twi-light following a family picnic. This was Lucas's last summer. Jonathan was fourteen. Lucas arrived in the midafternoon, four trains later than planned. Jonathan remembers waiting at the station for one train, then another, then a third and a fourth, Lucas finally stepping out into the sunlight, much thinner than Jonathan remembered, a wraith in dark glasses. "Sorry about that," he said, "I guess I just somehow lost track of time this morning."

"We were almost starting to worry!" their mother said with that nervous little laugh that Jonathan had only recently begun to notice. She'd spent the last hour crying in the car while their father paced and smoked cigarettes. "We thought you maybe weren't coming." The family picnic was her idea, of course.

"Wouldn't have missed it for the world," Lucas said, and their father's jaw tightened. As always, Jonathan couldn't tell if Lucas was being sincere or not. It wasn't fair that Jonathan had to be so much younger. He'd never been able to keep up.

"How's the painting going?" he asked when they were in the backseat of the car together, and decades later in FCI Florence Medium 1 he can still feel the pleasure of that moment, of hav-ing thought to ask such an adult question.

"It's going great, buddy, thanks for asking. Really great."

"You're still enjoying the city?" Mom always said *the city* in the way a preacher might say *Gomorrah.*

"I love it." Lucas's tone was a little off, though, even fourteen-year-old Jonathan could perceive that. Their parents exchanged glances.

"If you ever wanted to come home for a bit," their father said. "Take a little break from it all, even just a week or two, get a little fresh air . . ."

"Fresh air's overrated."

Later, considering the memory from afar, from FCI Florence Medium 1, Alkaitis doesn't remember much about the picnic. What he remembers is afterward: a sense of calm at the end of the long strange day, a temporary peace, sitting there in the shade with his whole family together, and then an hour or so when the sun is setting and their parents are starting to talk about driving Lucas back to the train station ("unless you'd like to stay here tonight, honey, you know there's always room . . ."), one last beautiful hour of throwing a Frisbee with his brother in the deepening twilight, running and diving over grass, the pale disc spinning through the dark.

13

SHADOW COUNTRY

December 2018

1

In December 2018, Leon Prevant had a job in a Marriott on the southern edge of Colorado, not far from the New Mexico border. It wasn't a big town but there were somehow two Marriotts, reflecting one another across the wide street and the parking lot. The Marriotts were just on the edge of downtown, but the downtown itself proved to be something of a mirage. On Leon's first day he walked there on his lunch break, past a massive mural and then up a street where he found the best café he'd seen in a while, a large shadowy place attached to a coffee roasting business. He took a coffee to go and wandered up the street. There was a huge army surplus store that seemed to have spilled into three adjoining buildings, but most of the other storefronts were empty. No cars passed by. He was standing on a corner, with long views down two streets, and in all of that, he saw just one other person, a man in a neon-orange T-shirt sitting on a bench about a block away, staring at nothing. The tables outside the café were empty. Leon walked quickly back to the Marriott, clocked back in, and resumed the work of the day, receiving a new shipment of toiletries in the supply room and then skimming drowned bugs and leaves from the surface of the pool.

"See, that's how I can tell you're from the coast," his co-worker Navarro said later, when Leon mentioned the emptiness of downtown. "You people think a place has to have a downtown to be a real place."

"You don't think a downtown should have some people in it?"

"I think a place doesn't have to have a downtown at all," Navarro said.

He'd been there six months when Miranda called. He was in the RV after his shift, doing the crossword puzzle with ice packs on his right knee and left ankle, alone because Marie had gotten a night job stocking shelves at the Walmart across the express-way, and the call was so unexpected that when Miranda said her name he almost couldn't comprehend it. There was an odd half beat of silence while he recovered.

"Leon?"

"Hi, sorry about that. What an unexpected surprise this is," he said, feeling like an idiot because obviously *unexpected* and *surprise* were redundant in this context, but who could blame him?

"Good to hear your voice," she said, "after all these years. Do you have a moment?"

"Of course." His heart was pounding. For how many years had he longed for this call? Ten. A decade in the wilderness, he found himself thinking. Ten years of travelling far beyond the borders of the corporate world, wishing uselessly to be allowed back in. The ice packs slipped to the floor as he reached for a pen and paper.

"I'm afraid I'm not calling for the happiest reason," Miranda said, "but let me just ask you first, before I get into it, would you be at all interested in coming back on a consultant basis? It would be a very short-term thing, just a few days."

"I would love to." He wanted to cry. "Yes. That would be ... yes."

"Okay. Well, good." She sounded a little surprised by his fervour. "There's been ..." She cleared her throat. "I was going to say *there's been an accident*, but we actually don't know if it was an accident or not. There was an incident. A woman disappeared from a Neptune-Avramidis ship. She was a cook."

"That's terrible. Which ship?"

"It is terrible. The *Neptune Cumberland*." The name wasn't familiar to Leon. "Listen," she was saying, "I'm convening a committee to look into crew safety on Neptune-Avramidis vessels as a general matter, and Vincent Smith's death in particular. If you're interested, I could use your help."

"Wait," he said, "her name was Vincent?"

"Yes, why?"

"Where was she from?"

"Canadian citizen, no permanent address. Her next of kin was an aunt in Vancouver. Why?"

"Nothing. I knew a woman named Vincent, a long time ago. Well, knew *of* her, I guess. Not that common a name for a woman."

"True enough. I think the important point here is, I don't need to tell you that this is the only investigation into her death that will ever happen. To be candid with you, if I had the budget I'd commission an investigation from an outside law firm."

"That sounds expensive."

"Extremely. So this is all she's going to get, just an internal investigation by the company she worked for. Companies have a way of exonerating themselves, don't you find?"

"You want an outsider," he said.

"You're someone I trust. How soon can you be in New York?"

"Soon," he said. "I just have to wrap up a few things here." He was calculating the length of the drive from southern Colorado. They spoke for a while about travel arrangements, and when he hung up he sat for a long time at the table, blinking. He checked the call log on the phone to confirm that he hadn't imagined it. *NEPTUNE-AVRA*, a 212 area code, *21 minutes*. The text on the call display seemed apt; it had been like receiving a phone call from another planet.

2

After Alkaitis, there was a different kind of life. Leon and Marie lasted a half year in their house after the collapse of the Ponzi, six months of missed mortgage payments and ruinous stress. Leon had put his entire severance package and all their savings into Alkaitis's fund, and the returns didn't make them wealthy but you don't actually need much to live well in South Florida. They'd bought the RV just before Alkaitis was arrested. In the months that followed, with Leon trying to get more consulting work at Neptune-Avramidis, which was convulsed with layoffs and had put a freeze on consultants, and Marie rendered unemployable by anxiety and depression, the RV in the driveway had at first seemed malevolent, some kind of horrible joke, like their financial mistakes had taken on corporeal form and had parked there next to the house.

But in the early summer they were eating omelettes for dinner by candlelight, the candles less a romantic gesture than a means of saving money on electricity, and Marie said, "I've been emailing with Clarissa lately."

"Clarissa?" The name was familiar, but it took him a moment. "Oh, your friend from college, right? The psychic?"

"Yes, that Clarissa. We had dinner in Toronto all those years ago."

"I remember. What's she up to these days?"

"She lost her house, so now she's living in her van."

Leon set his fork down and reached for his water glass, to dispel the tightness in his throat. They were two months behind on the mortgage. "Tough luck," he said.

"She says she actually likes it."

"At least she would've seen it coming," he said, "being a psychic and all."

"I asked her about that," Marie said. "She said she'd had visions of highways, but she'd always just assumed she was going on a road trip."

"A van," Leon said. "That seems like it'd be a difficult life."

"Did you know there are jobs you can do, if you're mobile?"

"What kind of jobs?"

"Taking tickets in fairgrounds. Working in warehouses around the holiday rush. Some agricultural stuff. Clarissa said she got a job she liked in a campground for a while, cleaning up and dealing with campers."

"Interesting." He had to say something.

"Leon," she said, "what if we just left in the RV?"

His initial thought was that the idea was ridiculous, but he waited a gentle moment or two before he asked, "And went where, love?"

"Wherever we want. We could go anywhere."

"Let's think about it," he'd said.

The idea had seemed crazy for only a few hours, maybe less. He lay awake that night, sweating through the sheets—it was hard to sleep without air conditioning, but they were keeping a careful budget and Marie had calculated that if they ran the A/C that week they'd be unable to pay the minimums on their credit card bills—and he realized the plan's brilliance: they could just leave. The house that kept him up at night could become someone else's problem.

"I've been thinking about your idea," he said to Marie over breakfast. "Let's do it."

"I'm sorry, do what?" She was always tired and sluggish in the mornings.

"Let's just get in the RV and drive away," he said, and her smile was a balm. Once the decision was made, he felt a peculiar urgency. In retrospect, there was no real rush, but they were gone four days later.

When he walked through the rooms one last time, Leon could tell the house was already done with them, a sense of vacancy pervading the air. Most of the furniture was still there, most of their belongings, a calendar pinned to the wall in the kitchen, coffee cups in the cupboards, books on shelves, but the rooms already conveyed an impression of abandonment. Leon would not have predicted that he and his wife would turn out to be the kind of people who'd abandon a house. He would've imagined that such an act would bury a person under fathoms of shame, but here on the expressway in the early morning light, abandoning the house felt unexpectedly like triumph. Leon pulled out of the driveway, made a couple of turns, and then they were on the expressway leaving forever.

"Leon," Marie said with an air of letting him in on a delightful secret, "did you notice that I left the front door unlocked?"

He felt real joy when she said this. Why not? There was no plausible scenario where they could sell their house. The whole state was glutted with houses that were newer and nicer, entire unsold developments in the outer suburbs. They owed more on the mortgage than the house was worth. There was such pleasure in imagining their unlocked home succumbing to anarchy. He knew they would never come back here and there was such beauty in the thought. He didn't have to mow the lawn anymore or trim the hedge. The mould in the upstairs bathroom was no longer his concern. There would be no more neighbours. (And here, the first misgivings at the plan, which was objectively not a great plan but seemed like the best of all their terrible options. He glanced at Marie in the passenger seat and thought: *It's just us now. The house was our enemy but it tied us to the world. Now we are adrift.*)

Marie seemed a little distant in the first few days, as they drove up out of Florida and into the South, but he knew that was just the way she dealt with stress—she evaded, she avoided, she removed herself—and by the end of the week she'd begun to come back to him. They mostly cooked in the tiny RV kitchenette, getting used to it, but on the one-week anniversary of their departure they pulled into a diner. Sitting down to a meal that neither he nor Marie had cooked seemed wildly extravagant. They toasted their one-week anniversary with ginger ale, because Leon was driving and one of Marie's medications clashed with alcohol.

"What are you thinking about?" he asked her, over roast chicken with gravy.

"The office," she said. "Back when I worked at that insurance place."

"I still think about my working life too," he said. "Seems like a different lifetime now, to be honest."

Being in shipping had made him feel like he was plugged into an electrical current that lit up the world. It was the opposite of spending his days in an RV, driving nowhere in particular.

They spent most of that first summer in a campground in California, near the town of Oceano, central coast. South of the beach access road, people rode ATVs over the dunes, and the

ATV engines sounded like bugs from a distance, a high buzzing whine. Ambulances drove down the beach to collect ATV drivers three or four times a day. But north of the road, the beach was quiet. Leon loved walking north. There wasn't much between Oceano and Pismo Beach, the next town up the coast. This lonely stretch of California, forgotten shoreline, sand streaked with black. The land here was dark with tar. In the evenings there were flocks of sandpipers, running over the sand so quickly that they gave the illusion of hovering an inch off the ground, their legs blurred like the animals in a Road Runner cartoon, comical but there was also something moving about the way they all somehow knew to switch direction at once.

Leon and Marie ate dinner on the beach almost every night. Marie seemed happiest when she was gazing at the ocean, and Leon liked it here too. He tried to keep her out on the beach as long as possible, where the horizon was infinite and the birds ran like cartoons. He didn't want her to feel that their lives were small. Freighters passed on the far horizon and he liked to imagine their routes. He liked the endlessness of the Pacific from this vantage point, nothing but ships and water between Leon and Japan. Could they somehow get there? Of course not, but he liked the thought. He'd been there a few times on business, in his previous life.

"What are you thinking of?" Marie asked once, on a clear evening on the beach. They'd been in Oceano for two months by then.

"Japan."

"I should've gone there with you," she said. "Just once."

"They were boring trips, objectively. Just meetings. I never saw much of the place." He'd seen a little. He'd loved it there. He'd once taken two extra days to visit Kyoto while the cherry trees were blooming.

"Still, just to go there and see it." An unspoken understanding: neither of them would leave this continent again.

A containership was passing in the far distance, a dark rectangle in the dusk.

"It's not quite what I imagined for our retirement," Leon said, "but it could be worse, couldn't it?"

"Much worse. It *was* much worse, before we left the house."

He hoped someone had done him the favour of burning that house to the ground. The scale of the catastrophe was objectively enormous—*We owned a home, and then we lost it*—but there was such relief in no longer having to think about the house, the vertiginous mortgage payments and constant upkeep. There were moments of true joy, actually, in this transient life. He loved sitting here on the beach with Marie. For all they'd lost, he often felt lucky to be here with her, in this life.

But they were citizens of a shadow country that in his previous life he'd only dimly perceived, a country located at the edge of an abyss. He'd been aware of the shadowland forever, of course. He'd seen its more obvious outposts: shelters fashioned from cardboard under overpasses, tents glimpsed in the bushes alongside expressways, houses with boarded-up doors but a light shining in an upstairs window. He'd always been vaguely aware of its citizens, people who'd slipped beneath the surface of society, into a territory without comfort or room for error; they hitchhiked on roads with their worldly belongings in backpacks, they collected cans on the streets of cities, they stood on the Strip in Las Vegas wearing T-shirts that said GIRLS TO YOUR ROOM IN 20 MINUTES, they were the girls in the room. He'd seen the shadow country, its outskirts and signs, he'd just never thought he'd have anything to do with it.

In the shadow country it was necessary to lie down every night with a fear so powerful that it felt to Leon like a physical presence, some malevolent beast that absorbs the light. He lay beside Marie and remembered that in this life there was no space for any kind of error or misfortune. What would happen to her if something happened to him? Marie hadn't been well in some time. His fear was a weight on his chest in the dark.

3

"How's retirement treating you?" Miranda asked. They were sitting in her office, which had previously been Leon's boss's office. It was larger than he remembered. Several days had gone by since she'd called him in Colorado, during which he'd left his job at the Marriott—an urgent family matter, he'd told his boss, in hopes of being rehired later—and driven the RV to Connecticut, where they were parked in the driveway of one of Marie's college friends.

"Can't complain," Leon said. Miranda seemed not to know that he'd been an Alkaitis investor, although the information wasn't hidden. There was a victim impact statement online somewhere, which he didn't specifically regret but probably wouldn't have written if he'd realized it was going to be available to anyone who typed his name into Google.

"No complaints at all?"

He smiled. "Did I seem ever-so-slightly overeager on the phone?"

"I didn't sense any reluctance to give up your life of leisure and take on a consulting gig, let's put it that way."

"Well," Leon said. "There's such a thing as too much retirement, if we're being honest here."

"There's a reason why I'm not planning to retire." Miranda was flipping through a file folder. *I didn't plan to retire either,* Leon didn't say, because he'd promised himself that he wouldn't be desperate or bitter, that if anyone asked, he'd spent this last decade living in an RV because he and Marie had had enough of the hassles of home ownership and had always wanted to explore the country. Miranda passed him the file, which was labelled VINCENT SMITH. Had Miranda really been his assistant once, or was that a false memory? He vaguely remembered the era when he'd spent his life on the road and Miranda had made his travel arrangements, but it was difficult to reconcile that quiet young woman with the executive across the table, impeccable in a steel-grey suit, drinking a cup of tea that someone else had made for her.

"Take your time with the materials," she said. "Obviously strictly confidential, but you can take that file home to read tonight. I know you've been gone a long time, so let me know if any questions come up. I imagine some of our procedures have changed since you left."

Gone a long time? *Yes,* he thought, *that's one way of putting it.* It was disorienting, coming back here after all this time. He'd spent the past hour walking unnervingly familiar corridors and shaking hands with people who had no idea how lucky they were.

He cleared his throat. "You mentioned on the phone that someone from the security office will be conducting the interviews," he said. "What's my role in all of this?"

"Yes, Michael Saparelli will conduct the interviews," Miranda said. "He's the one who talked to the captain on the phone last week and wrote up these preliminary notes for us. To be absolutely clear, I have nothing but respect for him. He's former NYPD. It's not that I don't think he'll do a good job, I just think with such a sensitive matter, these interviews should have more than one witness."

"You're worried about a cover-up?"

"It's more that I'd like to remove any *temptation* for a cover-up." Miranda sipped her tea. "It's not that I suspect Saparelli of being a dishonest person, nothing like that. But companies are like nation-states. They all have their own cultures." Leon suppressed a flicker of annoyance—*Is my former administrative assistant lecturing me about corporate culture?*—but on the other hand, she wasn't wrong. "I've dedicated my professional life to this place," Miranda was saying, "but if forced to point out a cultural flaw, I'd say I've noticed a certain reluctance to accept blame around here. In fairness, that's probably true of most of the corporate world, but a little frustrating regardless."

"So if whatever happened to Ms. Smith was something that could potentially have been prevented by the company . . ."

"Then that's something I want to know about," Miranda said. "Look, this is the kind of place where if I request a report into our overcapacity problems, I can pretty much guarantee I'll get twenty pages about the economic environment, and literally not one word to suggest that maybe we could've managed the fleet a little differently."

"I'll be your eyes and ears," he said.

"Thank you, Leon. You're still okay with leaving tomorrow?"

"Absolutely. It'll be a pleasure to leave this country again." Although he was ashamed later when he remembered using that word. He read through the details of the case that evening. Vincent Smith: Thirty-seven years old, Canadian. Assistant cook on the *Neptune Cumberland*, a 370-metre Neopanamax-class containership on the Newark–Cape Town–Rotterdam route. She'd settled into a pattern of going to sea for nine months at a time, followed by three months off, and had no permanent address, which wasn't at all unusual among seafarers who maintained that work schedule. She came and went between land and sea for five years, until she disappeared one night off the coast of Mauritania.

Insofar as there was a suspect in her disappearance, the suspect was Geoffrey Bell. Notes on Geoffrey Bell: From Newcastle, a name that in Leon Prevant's mind automatically summoned the wrong continent and an entire class of vessels—the fifty-by-three-hundred-metre Newcastlemax, largest ships allowable in the port of Newcastle, Australia—but Bell's Newcastle was the original, Newcastle upon Tyne. Son of a retired coal miner and a shop clerk, got his able seaman certificate and spent a few years with Maersk, switched companies twice before he landed at Neptune-Avramidis, where by the time he boarded the *Neptune Cumberland* he held the rank of third mate. His career was undistinguished and would have passed without notice, if he hadn't been dating Vincent when she died.

Two people told the captain that they'd heard an argument in her cabin on her last night on the ship. A short time after the argument, security footage captured her movements as she left her room and traversed several corridors and a staircase to reappear outdoors on C deck, even though the crew had been told to stay inside until the weather improved. There was a blind spot on the ship, a corner of C deck with no cameras. On the security footage, she turned a corner and disappeared from sight. The same cameras recorded Geoffrey Bell's route, thirty-five minutes later, as he walked the same corridors to the same corner of C deck and stepped into the blind spot. He was out of sight for five minutes before the cameras captured his return, but Vincent didn't appear on security footage again, on the ship or anywhere on earth. Bell told the captain he'd gone looking for her but couldn't find her. The captain reported that he was unconvinced by this, but there were no witnesses, no body, and no evidence. The first stop after her disappearance was Rotterdam, where Bell walked off the ship.

"It goes without saying," Miranda had said, in their initial phone call, "but of course no police force is going to investigate this."

The closest country to her disappearance was Mauritania, but she'd disappeared in international waters, so it wasn't actually Mauritania's problem. Vincent was Canadian, the captain of the ship was Australian, Geoffrey Bell was British, the rest of the crew German, Latvian, and Filipino. The ship was flagged to Panama, which meant that legally it was a floating piece of Panamanian territory, but of course Panama had neither the incentive nor the manpower to investigate a disappearance off the west coast of Africa. It is possible to disappear in the space between countries.

Leon didn't meet Michael Saparelli until he was aboard the plane to Germany. Two minutes before the cabin doors closed, a flushed and out-of-breath man in early middle age came in with the last few straggling passengers and dropped into the seat beside him. "Security was crazy," he said to Leon. "I don't mean crazy as in insanely rigorous, I mean crazy as in actually insane. They were manually inspecting sandwiches." He extended a hand. "I'm sorry. Hi. I'm Michael Saparelli."

"Pleased to meet you. Leon Prevant."

"You were a road-warrior type, weren't you?"

"I was, back in the day." *I used to barely notice that I'd crossed an ocean.*

"I couldn't do it, personally, on any kind of regular basis. Me, my idea of a perfect weekend? Not leaving my house. Anyway. What do you see as your role in all this?"

But a flight attendant had appeared to take their drink orders, so there was a pause while Saparelli ordered coffee and Leon ordered ginger ale with ice.

"Just an observer, in answer to your question. You conduct the interviews, I'll sit there and watch."

"Right answer," Saparelli said. "The only kind of partner I can stand is the silent kind."

"I get that," Leon said, as affably as possible.

Saparelli was fumbling around in his bag. He was carrying the kind of messenger-style bag that Leon associated with twenty-something men in Converse sneakers on the Brooklyn-bound subway trains, but then he realized that he'd been away from New York City for so long that the twentysomething hipsters of his memories would be middle-aged by now. They'd turned into Saparelli.

"I did some digging into Geoffrey Bell," Saparelli said. He'd produced a notebook filled with minuscule block handwriting. "Seems like no one did a background check when he was hired."

"Aren't background checks standard?"

"Yeah, they're supposed to be. Someone dropped the ball. Anyway, I got a local contact to pull arrest records, and seems there was a history of violence back in Newcastle. Nothing horribly sinister, but he had two arrests for bar fights in the year before he went to sea."

"That seems like something we should have caught," Leon said.

"Ideally, right? We can only hope that's the worst we'll find."

They didn't talk much after that. Leon spent the flight reading through the file again, as if he hadn't already memorized it.

He studied the photo from Vincent Smith's security badge. He just wasn't sure. It seemed plausible that Vincent Alkaitis and Vincent Smith were the same person, but the glamorous young woman on Jonathan Alkaitis's arm in old photos on the internet bore only a passing resemblance to the unsmiling, middle-aged woman with short hair in the security photo. It was incongruous that she could have gone from being Alkaitis's wife to being a cook on a containership, although if they were the same person, perhaps incongruity was the point. If he'd been Alkaitis's spouse, Leon found himself thinking, he'd probably have wanted to go to sea too. He'd have wanted to leave the planet. When he'd read through the file, he turned to the magazines he'd bought in the airport, purchased partly because he found them genuinely interesting and partly because he wanted Saparelli to see him as a serious kind of person who read *The Economist* and *Foreign Policy*. You could call it a performance, or you could call it presenting yourself in the best possible light, no different from putting on a suit and combing your hair. Saparelli spent the flight typing on his phone and reading Nietzsche.

A black car met Leon and Saparelli at Bremen Airport and ferried them north under low grey skies, through the pretty redbrick districts of Bremerhaven proper to the place that everyone in the shipping industry was actually talking about when they said the name of that city: a massive terminal between the city and the sea, not quite in Germany but not quite anywhere else, one of those liminal spaces that have proliferated on this earth. When he was a younger man, Leon had spent a great deal of time in these places, and now, walking with Saparelli and their security escort toward the *Neptune Cumberland*, he had a strange sense of haunting a previous version of his life. He felt like an imposter here.

It was jarring to see the ship there before them, after a week of hearing and reading its name. High overhead, the cranes were doing their work, lifting shipping containers the size of rooms from the lashing bridges and the holds. The ship was painted the same dull red as all of the Neptune-Avramidis ships, sitting high in the water now that half its cargo was gone. A pair of miserable-looking deckhands met Leon and Saparelli on shore and escorted them up to the bridge.

Morale was low, the captain confirmed. He was an Australian in his sixties, deeply shaken by the incident. He shared the commonly held suspicion that Geoffrey Bell had had something to do with Vincent's disappearance.

"Did he ever cause any trouble for you?" Saparelli asked. The three of them were at the table in the captain's stateroom, watching the movement of cranes and containers through the windows and establishing the template for every interview that would follow: Saparelli speaking with the interviewee, while Leon took cursory notes and felt utterly extraneous.

"No, he never caused trouble, as such. But he was kind of an odd duck, you could say. A little antisocial. Not great with other people. He was decent at his job, but he mostly kept to himself. I didn't get the sense he was well liked among his peers."

"I see. I understand you had heavy weather, the night she disappeared."

"Bad storm," the captain said. "No one was supposed to be out on deck."

Other interviews:

"I saw them holding hands on deck once," the first officer said. "But they didn't take shore leave together. Smith liked to go off by herself for three months. I had the impression they were sometimes a couple, sometimes not."

"They were fairly discreet," said the chief engineer. "I mean everyone knew they were seeing each other, because when you're stuck on a ship everyone knows everything, but they weren't showy about it."

"Did you know she was an artist?" asked the other third mate, the one who wasn't Geoffrey Bell. "I don't know if that's the right word. She did this video art thing that I thought was kind of cool."

"She was competent," the steward said, Vincent's former boss. His name was Mendoza. "More than competent, actually. She loved her job. I liked working with her. Never complained, good at her work, got along with everybody. Maybe a little eccentric. She liked to shoot videos of nothing."

"Nothing?" Saparelli asked, pen poised over notebook.

Mendoza nodded.

"As in, for example . . ."

"As in she'd literally stand there on deck filming the fucking ocean," the steward said. "Pardon my language. Never saw anything like it in my life. I caught her doing it once, asked her what she was doing, but . . ."

"But?"

"She just kind of shrugged and kept doing it." He was quiet for a moment, eyes on the floor. "I respected that, actually. She was doing a strange thing and she felt she didn't owe me any explanation."

"Did she ever seem at all depressed to you?" Saparelli asked. Leon had heard this question in every interview today and knew already what the answer would be. "It's difficult to know how anyone will respond to stress, but if someone told you that she'd left the ship of her own accord, if she'd jumped, would that idea seem plausible to you, given what you observed of her temperament?"

"No, she was a happy person," Mendoza said. "She'd work

nine months, then take three months off, and when she came back she'd always have these great stories. The rest of us, we mostly just go home and hope our kids remember us, but she had no family, so she'd just travel. She'd come back, I'd ask where she'd been, and she'd been hiking in Iceland, or kayaking in Thailand, or learning how to do pottery in Italy or something. We used to joke about it. I'd say, when are you going to get married, settle down? And she'd laugh and say maybe in the next life." A silence fell over the table. Mendoza wiped his eyes. "Did I say I liked working with her? I loved working with her. I considered her a friend. You know how rare it is to work with someone who loves their life?"

"Yeah," Saparelli said quietly. "I do."

Vincent's cabin was as she'd left it. The bed was unmade. Her personal effects were minimal: some toiletries, some clothes, a laptop computer, a few books. The books mostly concerned a ship called the *Columbia* (*Hail, Columbia*; *Voyages of the Columbia to the Northwest Coast*; etc.). Saparelli swiftly packed her belongings into her suitcase and a duffel bag while Leon flipped through the books and shook them over the bed. Nothing fell out. Leon wasn't really sure what he was looking for. Incriminating letters from Bell? Threatening marginalia?

"If you'll take the duffel bag," Saparelli said, "I've got the suitcase."

Leon took the bag and they stepped out onto the upper deck. The cranes were lowering new containers onto the lashing bridges. He thought he remembered having read about the *Columbia*, now that he thought about it. A ship out of Boston, eighteenth or nineteenth century. He'd look it up later. It was late afternoon, and the cranes cast a complicated shadow over the deck. In memory, these last few minutes on board took on an unwarranted vividness and weight, because they were also the last few minutes before Mendoza reappeared. In all the ambient noise, the clanking and grinding of cranes and boxes and the constant vibration of the engine, Leon didn't notice the steward until he was very close. "I'll walk you down," he said. They were near the top of the gangway stairs.

"No need," Saparelli said, but there was something about the way the steward was staring at them, so Leon nodded and let Mendoza lead the way. Saparelli shot Leon an irritated look.

Mendoza spoke quietly over his shoulder as they descended. "I saw him hit a woman once."

Saparelli visibly flinched. "Who? Bell?"

"This was a few years ago, when we were on rotation together on another ship. There was a woman on board, an engineer, she and Bell had a thing. We had a barbecue on deck one night, I heard her and Bell arguing, so I turn my back, you know, give them some privacy—"

"Wait," Leon said, "you were all out on deck together?"

"Yeah, this was back before they banned alcohol on the ships. It used to be possible to have a drink with your colleagues after work in the evening, just like a normal adult. Anyway, I turn my back, pretend I'm interested in the horizon, and then I hear a slap."

"But you didn't see it," Saparelli said.

"I know what a slap sounds like. I turn around fast, and it's obvious he just hit her. She's standing there holding her hand against her face, crying a little, they're both staring at each other, like in shock or something. I'm like, what the hell just happened, what's going on here, she looks at me and says, 'Nothing. I'm fine.' I say to him, 'You just hit her?' and she's like, 'No, he didn't hit me.' Meanwhile there's practically a handprint on the side of her face, this red mark appearing."

"Okay." Saparelli exhaled. "What did Bell say?"

"Told me to mind my own business. I'm standing there, trying to figure out what to do, but if she's insisting nothing happened, who am I to say something did? I didn't actually see it." Mendoza was walking down the stairs very slowly, so Leon and Saparelli were walking slowly too, struggling to hear him. "She looks at me," Mendoza said over his shoulder, "she looks at me and says, 'No one hits me. You think I'd let someone hit me?' And I'm a little exasperated, I mean, it's so goddamn *obvious,* but what can I say? So I leave them and walk away a little, and I hear her say to him, 'You do that again, I'll throw you overboard.'"

"Then what. What did he say." Saparelli's voice was flat.

"He says, 'Not if I throw you overboard first.'"

They'd reached the bottom of the stairs. Leon's heart was beating too hard, and Saparelli looked like he wanted to be sick. Leon was imagining the report: *Upon investigation, it emerged that Geoffrey Bell previously threatened to throw a woman off a ship.*

"When was this?" Saparelli asked.

"Eight years ago? Nine?"

"No similar incidents since then?"

"No," Mendoza said, "but you don't think that one incident is kind of bad?"

"Did you report the incident to the captain?"

"I talked to him the next day. He told me he'd keep an eye on Bell, but if the woman's insisting nothing happened, then what can we do? It's hearsay, my word against theirs, except I didn't even see it."

"Right," Saparelli said. "Where's that woman now? The engineer he was dating?"

"Raising her kids in the Philippines, last I heard." Mendoza looked away. "Keep my name out of it, will you? When you put this in your report."

"I can do that," Saparelli said, "but why didn't you tell me any of this in our interview earlier?"

"Because I liked Geoffrey. This thing I'm telling you about, it doesn't mean Geoffrey had anything to do with whatever happened to Vincent. But after I talked to you earlier, I couldn't stop thinking about it. Thought you should know."

"Thank you. I appreciate you telling me all of this."

Leon and Saparelli didn't look at one another in the car, but both wrote in their notebooks. Leon was recounting the conversation, as close to word for word as he could remember, and he assumed Saparelli was doing the same. At the hotel by the airport, they checked in and Saparelli took Vincent's duffel bag from him. "Good night," Saparelli said, when they had their room keys. It was the first thing he'd said to Leon since the port.

"Good night." Instead of going upstairs, Leon went to the bar for a while, because he was in his seventies and had no money for travel and this was probably the last time in his life he was going to have a drink at a bar in Germany, but the flattening influence of the nearby airport meant that everyone was conversing in English. He wished Marie were here. He finished his drink and went upstairs, ironed his other button-down shirt, and watched TV for a while. Trying to imagine what that last conversation would look like in the report: *An interviewee reported that Geoffrey Bell once threatened to throw a female colleague overboard. He and this colleague were involved in a romantic relationship at the time. The interviewee reported the incident to the captain. However, no mention of the incident appears in Bell's personnel file, which leads to the conclusion that the company took no action.* He lay awake all night, rose at four-thirty a.m., and drank four cups of coffee before he went downstairs to meet Saparelli and catch their car to the airport.

"Is that the same suit you were wearing yesterday?" Saparelli asked. They were sitting together in the business-class cabin, an hour into the flight. Saparelli looked as terrible as Leon felt. Leon wanted to ask if Saparelli had been awake all night too, but it seemed too intrusive.

"Short trip," Leon said. "Didn't think I needed two."

"You know what I was thinking about?" Saparelli was staring straight ahead. "The way a bad message casts a shadow on the messenger."

"Is that Nietzsche?"

"No, that's me. May I please see your notebook?"

"My notebook?"

"The one you were using in the car yesterday," Saparelli said.

Leon extracted it from the front pocket of his bag and watched as Saparelli flipped to the last page of notes, read it over quickly, then tore off the last two pages and folded them into an inside pocket of his jacket.

"What are you doing?"

"We actually have similar interests," Saparelli said. "I was thinking about this last night."

"How are your interests served by taking pages from my notebook?" Leon felt that he should be furious about the notebook, but he was so tired that he felt only a dull sense of dread.

"I know you're not retired," Saparelli said.

"I beg your pardon?"

"I know you live in campgrounds and work in fulfillment warehouses at Christmas. I know you spent last summer working at an amusement park called Adventureland. Where was that again, Indiana?" He was staring straight ahead.

Leon was quiet for a moment. "Iowa," he said softly.

"And the summer before, I know you and your wife were campground hosts in Northern California. I know you were recently employed doing menial labour at a Marriott in Colorado. I know that that's your only suit." He turned to look at Leon. "I'm not saying it's your fault. I read up on the Ponzi scheme when I came across your victim impact statement. Obviously a lot of smart people got blindsided there."

"Then what are you saying, exactly? I'm not sure what my employment history has to do with—"

"I'm saying that you want more consulting contracts, and I want to be able to walk down the hall without everyone thinking *Oh, there's that guy who wrote that awful report that leaked to the press and got people fired.* You want that too, by the way. You want to walk down the halls and have people not look at you like you're some kind of avatar of doom or something."

"You're thinking of not including that last conversation in your report."

"Anything outside of the official interviews, well, that's basically just a question of memory, isn't it? I recorded the interviews, but nothing outside of that."

Leon rubbed his forehead.

"We may or may not have heard an unsettling anecdote," Saparelli said softly. "An unsettling anecdote that proves nothing. The facts of the case are unchanged. The fact remains that we'll never know what happened, because no one else was there."

"Geoffrey Bell was there."

"Geoffrey Bell disappeared at Rotterdam. Geoffrey Bell is off the grid."

"It doesn't seem suspicious to you that he walked off the ship at the first stop after she . . . ?"

"I have no way of knowing why he walked off the ship, Leon, and we both know no police force is ever going to interview him about it. Look at it this way," Saparelli said. "No matter what I write in my report, Vincent Smith will still be dead. There would be no positive outcome whatsoever in including that last conversation. There would only be harm."

"But you want an accurate report." Everything was wrong. The sunlight through the cabin windows was too bright, the air too warm, Saparelli too close. Leon's eyes hurt from sleep deprivation.

"Let's say, theoretically, the report includes every conversation we had on that ship. Will that bring Jonathan Alkaitis's girlfriend back?"

Leon looked at him. Upon inspection, he was certain Saparelli hadn't slept either. The man's eyes were bloodshot.

"I just wasn't sure," Leon said. "I wasn't sure if she was the same woman."

"How many women named Vincent do you know? Look, I was a detective," Saparelli said. "I look into everyone and everything, just as a matter of professional habit. Seems like a bit of a conflict of interest, doesn't it? Your accepting this consulting contract involving the former companion of a man who stole all your money? Does Miranda know?"

"I've never hidden anything," Leon said. "It's all publicly available—"

"Publicly available isn't the same thing as recusing yourself. You didn't tell her, did you?"

"She could have looked. If she just typed my name into Google—"

"Why would she? You're her trusted former colleague. When was the last time you Googled someone you trusted?"

"Gentlemen," the flight attendant said, "may I offer you something to drink?"

"Coffee," Leon said. "With milk and sugar, please."

"Same for me, thank you." Saparelli leaned back in his seat. "If you think about it," he said, "you're going to realize that I'm right."

Leon had the window seat; he gazed out at the morning Atlantic, vastly upset. There were no ships below, but he saw another plane in the far distance. The coffee arrived. A long time passed before Saparelli spoke again.

"I'm going to tell Miranda that you were extremely helpful to me and I appreciated having you along, and I'll recommend that we bring you on board for future consulting gigs."

"Thank you," Leon said. It was that easy.

4

After Germany, Leon began to see the shadow country again, for the first time in a while. For the past few years he hadn't noticed it; after the initial shock of the first few months on the road it had faded into the background of his thoughts. But a few days after he returned from Germany, at a truck stop in Georgia, Leon happened to be looking out the window when a girl climbed down from an eighteen-wheeler nearby. She was dressed casually, jeans and a T-shirt, but he realized what she was at the same moment he realized that she was very young. She disappeared between trucks.

At a gas station that night, he saw another girl climb down from another truck, a hitchhiker this time, wearing a backpack. How old? Seventeen. Sixteen. A young-looking twenty. He couldn't say. Dark circles under her eyes in the harsh blue light. She saw him watching her and fixed him with a blankly appraising look. You stare at the road and the road stares back. Leon knew that he and Marie were luckier than most citizens of the shadow country, they had each other and the RV and enough money (just barely) to survive, but the essential marker of citizenship was the same for everyone: they'd all been cut loose, they'd slipped beneath the surface of the United States, they were adrift.

You spend your whole life moving between countries, or so it seemed to Leon. Since the collapse of the Ponzi, he'd often found himself thinking about an essay he'd read once by a man with a terminal illness, a man who wrote with gratitude of the EMTs who'd arrived when he woke one morning and found himself too sick to function, kind men who'd ferried him gently into the country of the sick. The idea had stayed with Leon, and after Germany, in the long quiet hours behind the wheel of the RV, he'd begun formulating a philosophy of layered and overlapping countries. If a medical misfortune sends you into the country of the sick—which has its own rituals, customs, traditions, and rules—then an Alkaitis sends you into an unstable territory, the country of the cheated. Things that were impossible after Alkaitis: retirement, a home without wheels, trusting other people besides Marie. Things that were impossible after visiting Germany with Michael Saparelli: any certainty of his own morality, maintaining his previous belief that he was essentially incorruptible, calling Miranda to ask about other consulting opportunities.

A week after he returned from Germany there was an email from Saparelli, with a link to a password-protected video. The email read, "We examined Ms. Smith's laptop and reviewed hours of video. Several videos like this one, some shot in very bad weather. Thought you should see it; supports our conclusion that her death was most likely accidental. Remember weather was bad the night she disappeared."

It was a short clip, five minutes or so, shot from a rear deck, at night. Vincent had recorded several minutes of ocean, the wake of the ship illuminated in moonlight, and then the camera angle changed: she stepped forward and peered over the railing, which on this particular deck wasn't especially high. She leaned over alarmingly, so that the shot was straight down at the ocean below.

Leon played it twice more, then closed his laptop. He understood that Saparelli was doing him a kindness, sending him evidence to assuage Leon's conscience and support the narrative of the report. Leon and Marie were in Washington State that night, in a private campground that was almost deserted in the off-season. Night was falling outside, the branches of fir and cedar silhouetted black against the fading sky. The video proved nothing except a certain recklessness, but the video also made it easy to fill in a narrative: rough seas, high winds, a distracted woman on a slippery deck, a low railing. Perhaps Bell had walked off the ship because he'd killed his girlfriend, but on the other hand, perhaps he'd walked off the ship because the woman he loved had disappeared.

"This is such a beautiful place," Marie said one night, a year after Leon returned from Germany. There had been no more consulting contracts. They'd just spent the pre-Christmas season at a warehouse in Arizona, ten-hour days of walking quickly over concrete floors with a handheld scanner, bending and lifting, and had retreated to a campground outside Santa Fe to recuperate. Difficult work, and it got harder every year, but they'd made enough money to get the engine repaired and add to their emergency fund, and now they were resting in the high desert. Across the road was a tiny graveyard of wood and concrete crosses, a white picket fence sagging around the perimeter.

"We could do a lot worse," Leon said. They were sitting at a picnic bench by the RV, looking at a view of distant mountains turning violet in the sunset, and he felt at that moment that all was well with the world.

"We move through this world so lightly," said Marie, misquoting one of Leon's favourite songs, and for a warm moment he thought she meant it in a general sense, all of humanity, all these individual lives passing over the surface of the world with little trace, but then he understood that she meant the two of them specifically, Leon and Marie, and he couldn't blame his chill on the encroaching night. In their late thirties they'd decided not to have children, which at the time seemed like a sensible way to avoid unnecessary complications and heartbreak, and this decision had lent their lives a certain ease that he'd always appreciated, a sense of blissful unencumbrance. But an encumbrance might also be thought of as an anchor, and what he'd found himself thinking lately was that he wouldn't mind being more anchored to this earth.

They sat watching the sunset fading out behind the mountains, they stayed out well after dark until the sky blazed with stars, but they had to go in eventually and so they rose stiffly and returned to the warmth of the RV, performed the various tasks of getting ready for bed, kissed one another good night. Marie turned out the light and was asleep within minutes. Leon lay awake in the dark.

14

THE OFFICE CHORUS

December 2029

"Most memorable job?" Simone hears herself say at a cocktail party in Atlanta, where she lives with her husband and three children and works for a company that sells clothes on the internet. "Oh, that one's easy." She's in a circle of colleagues, holding court. "Any of you remember Jonathan Alkaitis? That Ponzi scheme, way back in 2008?"

"No," her assistant says. Her name is Keisha. She was three years old when Alkaitis went to prison.

"*That* Jonathan Alkaitis?" An older colleague. "He stole my grandpa's retirement savings."

"Oh my god, that's terrible," Keisha says. "What did he do?"

"My grandpa? Spent the last decade of his life in my mother's guest bedroom. You never met a more embittered man. Simone, you had some connection with Alkaitis?"

"I was his last secretary before he went to prison."

"You *weren't*."

"Oh my *god*," Keisha says, looking at her boss in the way administrative assistants do when it's just dawned on them that the boss was once an administrative assistant.

"I'd just moved to New York," Simone said, "so I was approximately twelve years old, and the city had a kind of sparkle to it. I got a job pretty quickly, at this financial place in Midtown, receptionist duties with some light secretarial work. Three weeks in, I'm just about ready to die of boredom, and then one day I walk into a meeting with a tray of coffee—"

"You had to get coffee?" Keisha has to get coffee twice a day.

"That wasn't even the most boring thing I had to do," Simone says, choosing to ignore Keisha's tone. "Anyway, Alkaitis is having a meeting with his staff, and he calls for coffee, so I bring it in on a tray. When I walk into the room, there's just this very fraught atmosphere. Like everyone was scared. I don't know that I can really explain it, it was like . . . help me out here, Keisha, you're the poetry major."

"An atmosphere of dread?"

"Thank you, yes, exactly. An atmosphere of dread, like someone had just said something awful or something. I'm just leaving with the tray, and as I'm closing the door, I hear Alkaitis say, 'Look, we all know what we do here.'"

"Wow. This was just before he was arrested?"

"Literally the day before. Then he comes to me an hour later and asks me to go buy paper shredders." She's honed the story over the years, made it sharper and more entertaining, and now, as always, she has to carefully suppress the vision of Claire in the back of the black SUV that carried her home the next night. What became of Claire? She doesn't want to know.

"Which were you, though?" Keisha asks, toward the end of the story. "His secretary, or his receptionist?"

"Bit of both," Simone says. "More the latter. Does it matter?"

"Well, probably only from a word-derivation sense," Keisha says with the hesitance of people who know no one else is nearly as interested in the topic as they are, and the conversation moves on, Simone forgets to ask what she means, but she looks it up later in the quiet of her bedroom, her husband sleeping beside her. She was never Alkaitis's secretary, she realizes now, when she looks up the word. A secretary is a keeper of secrets.

By then, when Simone is in her mid-forties, the rest of us have served our sentences—four years, eight years, ten years—and have been released from prison, although Oskar was released and then sent back in for a different crime. We're released in different years and from different facilities. We emerge into an altered world in various states of disarray, clutching our belongings in our hands. Harvey is the first, because in light of his invaluable assistance to the prosecution he was sentenced to time served—four years of shuttling between the orderly hell of the Metropolitan Correctional Center in lower Manhattan and the opulent offices of the court-appointed asset trustee uptown, four years of acting as a tour guide to the Ponzi by day and lying alone in his cell at night and on weekends—and after the sentencing he obtains permission from his probation officer to leave the state and move to New Jersey, where his sister owns an ice-cream shop. He serves ice cream near the beach and lives in her basement.

Ron avoids conviction but not divorce. He lives with his parents in Rochester, in upstate New York, and has a job taking tickets at a movie theatre.

Oskar and Joelle are dropped off at bus depots, in different years and in different states: Joelle travels from Florida to Charlotte, North Carolina, where she sits for a long time in the Greyhound waiting room, watching mothers with their children, until finally her sister arrives, late as always, chattering about traffic and weather and the spare room where Joelle's welcome to stay until she gets back on her feet, whatever that means; Oskar stands for a while in front of an information board at the Indianapolis bus station and eventually boards a bus bound for Lexington, the destination chosen because the bus is leaving soon and he can afford the ticket. He drifts off to sleep and wakes in the mountains under cloudy skies, pine trees rising into mist on steep hillsides, and the sheer beauty of the world brings tears to his eyes. This is a landscape that he holds on to when he's arrested on drug charges a year later, handcuffed on the sidewalk at two a.m. and shoved into the squad car, where he closes his eyes on the way to the station and takes himself back to this moment on the bus on the way to Kentucky, a vision of steep slopes, pine trees, mist.

Enrico has two small daughters and a wife who thinks his name is José. It isn't an especially happy marriage, but they have a nice house by the beach. The rest of us are united by our obsession with Enrico. In our imaginations he has become a heroic figure, leading a life of verve and mystery beyond the southern border. But in his actual life he watches his daughters and his wife chasing one another on the beach in the twilight, and thinks about how they will fare if—not if, *when,* surely when—he is finally apprehended and taken away. He can't escape the dread. Once he was proud of himself for evading his fate, but more and more lately he feels it moving toward him, his fate approaching from a long way off. He is always waiting for a slow car with dark windows, a tap on the shoulder, a knock on the door.

15

THE HOTEL

1

On a late spring night in the Hotel Caiette, in 2005, the night houseman was sweeping the lobby when a guest spoke to him. "You missed a spot," she said. Paul forced his face into a semblance of a smile and hated his life.

"I'm kidding," the guest said, "I'm sorry, that was a terrible joke. In all seriousness, though, can you come over here for a moment?" The woman was standing by the window, a Scotch in her hand. She was old, or so it seemed to Paul at the time—in retrospect, she was probably only about forty—but there was something striking about her. She conveyed a general impression of having her life together, which was a state to which Paul could only aspire. He carried the broom over awkwardly and stood near her.

"Can I help you with something?" He was pleased with himself for thinking to say this. It sounded very butlerlike, which was more or less the model he was going for. Every now and again he caught a glimpse of, if not exactly the pleasures of the hospitality industry, at least the pleasure of professional competence. He could see how there might be a certain satisfaction in being good at a job, the way Vincent was good at hers. He'd always been an indifferent employee. At that moment Vincent was at the other end of the lobby, laughing along with a guest who was telling her a story about a fishing trip gone hilariously awry.

"I wonder if I might speak with you in confidence," the woman said. Paul glanced over his shoulder at Reception, where Walter was applying his considerable powers of soothing to an American couple who were furious that the room with the Jacuzzi they'd paid for was, in fact, a room with a Jacuzzi, and not a suite with a full-size hot tub. "I'm Ella Kaspersky," she said. "What's your name?"

"Paul. Pleased to meet you."

"Paul, how long have you worked here?"

"Not long. A few months."

"Are you going to stay much longer, do you think?"

"No." He hadn't exactly thought this through before he said it, but the answer rang true. Of course Paul wasn't going to stay here. He'd come here from Vancouver in order to get away from friends with bad habits, and because Vincent was already here and had told him it was a decent place to work, but he knew it was a mistake by the end of his first week. He hated being back in Caiette. He hated living in the same building as his co-workers, the claustrophobia of it. The waiter who lived in the next room had sex with a sous-chef every night, and Paul, who was extremely single, could hear every noise they made. He didn't like his boss, Walter, or Walter's boss, Raphael. He missed his father, who'd died months ago but whom Paul somehow still expected to see every time he walked into the village. "Actually," he said, "I've been thinking about leaving soon. Maybe very soon."

"What do you want to do instead?"

"I'm a composer." He'd thought that saying it aloud might make it more real, but saying it aloud only made him feel like a fraud. He was composing music that he showed to no one. He'd fallen into a territory between classical and electronica and had no confidence in his work.

"Tough line of work to break into, I'd imagine."

"Extremely," he said. "I'm just going to keep working in hotels while I work on my music, but I want to get back to the city."

"It's one thing to rest and recharge in the middle of nowhere," Ella said, "but something different to live out here, I'd imagine."

"Right, yeah, exactly. I hate it." It occurred to him that he probably shouldn't be talking this way with a guest—Walter would be furious—but if he was leaving anyway, what difference did it make?

"I'd like to tell you a story," Ella said, "which will end with a business proposition, something that would involve you making a bit of money. Are you interested?"

"Yes."

"Keep standing here, and we'll look out the window together, and if that uptight manager of yours asks about it later, I was asking you about fishing and local geography. Deal?"

"Deal." The intrigue was wonderful and solidified his desire to leave, because even if she stopped talking at this moment and said nothing further, this was still the most interesting thing that had happened in weeks.

"There's a man named Jonathan Alkaitis who lives in New York City," she said. "We have exactly one thing in common, and that's that we're both regulars at this hotel. He'll be here in two days."

"Are you some kind of detective or something?"

"No, I just give extravagant tips to burnt-out front-desk employees. Anyway. When he arrives, I'd like to convey a message to him."

"You'd like me to deliver it?"

"Yes, but we're not talking about slipping an envelope under a door. I'd like it to be delivered in an unforgettable way. I want him to be shaken by it." Her eyes were shining. He realized for the first time that she was actually quite drunk.

"I knew a girl who once wrote graffiti on the window of a school with an acid marker," he said. "Something like that?"

"You're perfect," she said.

When Paul wrote the message, it felt like stars exploding in his chest. It felt like sprinting in a summer rainstorm. On the appointed night he left for his dinner break and crept around to the side of the building, where he'd hidden an oversized hoodie with an acid marker in the pocket, then crept into position near the front terrace, just outside the pool of light cast by the hotel. There was a breeze that night, which made it easier to move undetected, his footsteps disguised by all the small forest sounds, the creaking of branches and rustling of wind. For a long time the night porter stood by the door, too close, and Paul almost despaired of completing the mission, but then Larry glanced at his watch and stepped back, disappeared into the lobby, walking in the direction of the staff room. Coffee break. A cloud passed over the moon and it seemed like a sign, the night conspiring to hide him. He uncapped the marker and stepped out quickly onto the terrace, heart pounding, head down. *Why don't you swallow broken glass.* He wrote the message backwards, the way he'd been practising in his room, and then slipped back into the forest, and like choreography the cloud slid away from the moon and the message was illuminated. He crept around the side of the hotel and back toward the staff quarters. It was impossible to move in perfect silence but the night forest was full of noises anyway. In the staff lodge there was some kind of party happening, light and music spilling out of a suite on the second floor, the day staff getting wasted to dull the agony of customer service.

He stripped off the hoodie and gloves, balled them up and shoved them into the bushes at the base of a stump, stepped out onto the path connecting the staff lodge with the hotel, and came walking out of the woods into the bright pool of hotel light so that if anyone happened to be watching from the hotel, it would look like he'd just gone back to his room for a moment. He glanced at his watch and opted for a slow walk around to the side entrance, nothing to see here, just enjoying some fresh air, high with the twin pleasures of action and secrecy, and the elation lasted until the moment he stepped into the lobby and saw the tableau: the guest standing in the middle of the lobby, stricken; the night manager stepping out from behind the desk; his sister looking up from the glass she'd been polishing behind the bar; all of them were staring at the words on the window, and the look on Vincent's face was unbearable, a look of naked sadness and horror. The guest turned and Vincent looked away while Walter sailed forward on a wave of efficiency and reassurance— "May we offer you another drink, on the house of course, I'm so sorry that you had to see this," etc.—while Vincent stared hard at the glass she was polishing and Paul stood just inside the side door, unnoticed. It somehow hadn't occurred to him that anyone else would see the message. He slipped back out into the cold night air and stood for a while just outside, eyes closed, trying to get ahold of himself, before he made a second, more obvious entrance, closing the door loudly behind him, trying to act casual but his gaze falling immediately on the philodendron that someone—probably Larry—had pushed in front of the window.

Walter was watching him from behind the desk.

"Something happen to the window?" Paul asked. To his own ears, his voice sounded wrong, high-pitched and somehow off.

"I'm afraid so," Walter said. "Some extremely nasty graffiti."

He thinks I did it, Paul thought, and felt inexplicably affronted.

"Did Mr. Alkaitis see it?"

"Who?"

"You know." Paul nodded toward the guest, the man in his fifties who was staring into his drink.

"That isn't Alkaitis," Walter said.

Oh god. Paul found some excuse to extricate himself and went to the bar, where Vincent had finished polishing glasses and had moved on to wiping imaginary dust from bottles. "Hey," he said, and when she looked up, he was shocked to see that there were tears in her eyes. "Are you okay?"

"That message on the glass," she whispered.

He wanted to walk away now, just leave all his stuff behind, just call a water taxi from the lobby and walk to the pier and get a ride to Grace Harbour and keep going. "It's probably just some drunk kid."

She was dabbing surreptitiously at her eyes with a cocktail napkin. "Excuse me," she said, "I'm too upset to talk right now."

"Of course," he said, miles deep in the kind of self-loathing that he'd been warned against in rehab. He sensed a gathering of attention in the lobby; Walter was stepping out from behind the reception desk, and Larry was retrieving a luggage trolley from the discreet closet by the piano. Vincent was drinking a quick shot of espresso. In the glass wall of the hotel, the lobby was reflected with almost mirrorlike fidelity, but now the reflection was pierced by a white light out on the water, an approaching boat. Jonathan Alkaitis was just arriving.

2

Three years later, in December 2008, Walter read the news of Alkaitis's arrest at Reception and the blood left his head. Khalil, the bartender on duty that night, saw him drop out of sight and was at his side within seconds with a glass of cold water. "Walter, here, take a deep breath ...," and Walter tried to breathe, tried to drink the water, tried not to faint, stars swimming in his vision. Walter's colleagues were kneeling around him, asking what was wrong and making noises about calling the water taxi to get him to a hospital, and then Larry caught sight of the *New York Times* story on the computer screen and said, "Oh."

"I was an investor," Walter said, trying to explain.

"With Alkaitis?" Larry asked.

"He was here this past summer, you remember?" Walter felt like he was going to be sick. "He and Vincent. I had a conversation with him one night, we got to talking about investments, I told him I had some savings ..."

"Oh god," Larry said. "Walter. I'm sorry."

"He acted like he was doing me a favour," Walter said. "Letting me invest in his fund."

Larry knelt and put a hand on his shoulder.

"It can't be *gone*," Walter said. "It can't just be gone. It was my life savings."

Here, a gap in memory: how did Walter get back to his apartment? Unclear in retrospect, but some time later he was on his bed, staring at the ceiling, fully clothed but with his shoes off, a glass of water on the bedside table.

It was somehow almost eight a.m., so Walter went to see

Raphael in his office. "I don't know anything," Raphael said. He was spinning a pen on the knuckles of his left hand, a quick nervous motion whose mechanics eluded Walter's grasp. How did the pen not fall? "We have to wait for word from the U.S."

"Word of what?" Walter was staring at the pen.

"Well, word of our fates, at risk of sounding melodramatic. I just got off the phone with head office, and there's an asset trustee in New York, apparently, some lawyer appointed by a judge to manage Alkaitis's entire mess, so what happens to the hotel, I guess that's the trustee's decision."

As it happened, the suspense was short-lived. Toward the end of the next week, word trickled down to the hotel that the trustee had decided to sell the property, to recoup the greatest possible gain for the investors in the shortest possible amount of time. There were rumours for a while that the hotel management company might buy the property, but Raphael was skeptical.

"Let me tell you a secret," Raphael told Walter. "This place hasn't turned a profit in four years. If there's a buyer, it likely won't be a hotelier."

"Who else would buy it?"

"Exactly," Raphael said.

When their fate became clear—the property for sale with no immediate buyers on the horizon, the hotel scheduled to close in three weeks—Walter was seized by a strange idea. Everyone was leaving, but did that necessarily mean that Walter had to leave too? On one of his quiet mornings at Reception, just before the shift change, he made his fourth attempt to reach the asset trustee on the phone, and finally got past Alfred Selwyn's secretary.

"This is Selwyn."

"Mr. Selwyn, it's Walter Lee calling. I hope you'll forgive my persistence," Walter said, "but I'd hoped to speak to you about something quite pressing, for me at least . . ."

"What can I do for you, Mr. Lee?"

Walter wasn't sure what he'd expected. Something out of a legal drama, he supposed, some duplicitous sharklike person with an obnoxiously American accent, but Alfred Selwyn was soft-spoken and courteous, and conveyed an impression of listening carefully while Walter delivered his pitch.

"From what I understand," Selwyn said, "the property's quite remote, isn't it?"

"Not impossibly so," Walter said. "I can get to Grace Harbour within the hour if I call a water taxi."

"And Grace Harbour, is that a fair-sized population centre? Forgive me, just one second—" A faint commotion as Selwyn cupped the receiver with his hand. "Mr. Alexander," Walter heard him say, muffled by the hand, "if you'll please have a seat, I'll be right with you. Lorraine, may I have some coffee, please, for me and Harvey." More rustling, and Selwyn's voice regained its normal volume. "I apologize. What I'm trying to get a handle on, at dire risk of being overly blunt, is whether you'll lose your mind if you live by yourself in an empty hotel in the wilderness."

"I understand your concern," Walter said, "but the truth of the matter is, I love living here." He heard himself talking about the pleasure of living in a quiet place with immense natural beauty, the friendliness of the locals in the nearby village of Caiette—an exaggeration, most of them hated outsiders—and all he could think was *Please, please, please let me stay.* There was a beat of silence at the end of the monologue.

"Well," Selwyn said, "you make a good case for yourself. Could you send me a few references by the end of the week? Including your current supervisor, if possible."

"Of course," Walter said. "Thank you for considering this." When he hung up, he felt lighter than he had in some time, since the night he'd read the news of the arrest. He looked around the lobby and imagined everybody gone.

"You want to do what?" Raphael asked when Walter came to him. There was an open binder on his desk. Walter saw a chart labelled *RevPAR 2007–2008*, spanning two pages. Revenue Per Available Room. Raphael was transferring to a hotel in Edmonton and was spending his days reading up on his new property.

"The hotel needs a caretaker," Walter said. "Selwyn was in agreement that it's in no one's best interests to let it fall into ruin."

"Look, it would be my pleasure to give you a glowing reference, Walter, but I can't believe you want to stay out here by yourself. Do you have an end date in mind?"

"Oh, of course I wouldn't stay here *forever*," Walter said, in order to be reassuring, but that wouldn't be the worst thing, he thought on the walk back to the staff lodge. Caiette was the first place he'd ever truly loved. There was nowhere else he wanted to go. *Give me quiet,* he thought, *give me forests and ocean and no roads. Give me the walk to the village through the woods in summer, give me the sound of wind in cedar branches, give me mist rising over the water, give me the view of green branches from my bathtub in the mornings. Give me a place with no people in it, because I will never fully trust another person again.*

3

A decade later, in Edinburgh, Paul accepted a glass of wine from the bartender and turned to slide back into the crowd, and there she was before him.

"You," he said, because he couldn't remember her name.

"Hello, Paul." She was exactly as he remembered—a small, well-put-together person with a very precise haircut, dressed this evening in an elegant suit, wearing a necklace that seemed to involve a mosquito trapped in a walnut-sized piece of amber—but who was she? He was jet-lagged and slightly drunk, also so bad at remembering faces and names at the best of times that lately he'd started to wonder if it was maybe some kind of *thing*, either borderline sociopathy—*Am I so self-absorbed that I can't see other people?*—or some mild variant of facial blindness, that neurological situation wherein you won't recognize your wife if she gets a haircut, not that he had a wife. He ran through all of this while the mystery woman waited patiently, whisky in hand.

"Not to rush you," she said finally, "but I was about to head up to the terrace for a cigarette. Perhaps you'd like to join me while you think about it?"

She had an American accent, but that brought him no closer to placing her. The party had drawn a cross-section of the Edinburgh Festival, and a fair percentage of the guests had American accents. He mumbled something ineloquent and followed her through the crowd, but her identity didn't come to him until they'd been alone on the terrace for a moment and she'd lit her cigarette.

"Ella," Paul said. "Ella Kaspersky. I'm so sorry. I'm a little jet-lagged . . ."

She shrugged. "You see a person out of context . . ." She left the thought unfinished. "And it's been a long time."

"Thirteen years?"

"Yes."

It was cold on the terrace and he wanted to go back in. No, not back in, back to his hotel. The cold wasn't really the problem.

Practically speaking, flying economy from Toronto to Edinburgh meant that he'd been awake for two days, which fell into that increasingly vast category of things that were doable when he was eighteen but less so as he slid into middle age. Seeing Ella Kaspersky only made him feel worse. Something of this must have shown in his face, because Ella seemed to soften, just a little, and she lightly touched his arm.

"I've wanted to apologize to you for thirteen years," she said. "I was angry in Caiette, and I'd been drinking too much, and I let both those things get the better of me. I shouldn't have asked you to do that."

"I could've said no."

"You should've said no. But I should never have asked you in the first place."

"Well," he said, "you were right about Alkaitis, at least." He'd never been particularly interested in the news, but he had read a book about the Ponzi that came out a few years later, looking for news of his sister. In the book, Vincent was a marginal figure, her quotes confined to excerpts from a deposition transcript. It was obvious that the writer hadn't managed to secure an interview with her, although there was a great deal of speculation about the material opulence of her life with Alkaitis.

"Yes. I was right."

"Did you know he lived with my sister?" He was smoking a cigarette, although he couldn't quite remember Kaspersky's having given it to him. Lately time had been stuttering a little.

"Are you serious?"

"She was the bartender at the Hotel Caiette," he said. "A man walks into a bar, one thing leads to another . . ."

"Extraordinary. I saw pictures of him with a young woman, but I never made the connection back to the hotel."

"Do you remember a pretty bartender with long dark hair?"

She frowned. "Maybe. No. No, if I'm being honest, I don't remember her at all. What became of her afterward?"

"We're not in touch," Paul said. For Paul, Vincent existed in a kind of suspended animation. On the first night of his run at the Brooklyn Academy of Music, back in 2008, he walked out onto the stage and saw her. She was in the front row, at the far end; his eyes fell on her and his heart sped up. He got through the opening somehow, and when he glanced up again, no more than ten minutes later, she was gone, an open seat yawning in the shadows. That night he procrastinated for two hours before he left the theatre, but she wasn't waiting for him outside the stage door. She wasn't there the next night, or the next; he expected to see her every night when he exited the theatre, and she was never there, but he imagined the confrontation so many times that it began to seem like something that might actually have happened. *Look, all those years you lived in Vancouver, you left the videos boxed up in your childhood bedroom,* he'd tell her. *Obviously you weren't going to do anything with them. You didn't even notice they were gone.* And you thought that meant you could take them? she would ask. *At least I did something with them,* he'd tell her, and after days of imagining this conversation he almost began to long for it. It turned out that never having that conversation with Vincent meant that he was somehow condemned to *always* have that conversation with Vincent. It had been exactly a decade since the performances at BAM and he was still talking to her, the imagined Vincent who never materialized outside the stage door. Do you mean to tell me, she'd ask, that you've built a whole career on my videos? *Not a whole career, Vincent, but composing soundtracks for your videos led to collaborations with video artists, live performances at art fairs in Basel and Miami, the residency at BAM, my fellowship, my teaching position, all of the success that I've found in this life.* Does that justify it? she'd ask. *I don't know, Vincent, I've never known what's reasonable and what isn't. But for whatever it's worth, after the BAM performances I never did another public performance with your tapes.* Do you think that redeems you? *No, I know it doesn't. I know that I'm a thief.*

"Still with me?" Ella said, and he realized that he may have been staring into space for a while.

"Sorry, yes. I'm a bit wrecked from travelling all night."

"Parties are a bit much under those conditions," Ella said. "Let's get out of here, and I'll buy you a drink somewhere." Ten minutes later they were at a pub around the corner, an old-time kind of place with a bright red door and a forest's worth of wood panelling inside.

"So," Ella said, when they'd slid into a booth. "Forgive me, but you look terrible."

"I've been awake for two days."

"That'll do it, I suppose." But she was giving him a certain kind of look. He had trouble with names and faces but didn't have trouble recognizing the question she was refraining from asking. It was a look he'd been seeing more and more of lately.

"How did you end up at that party?" he asked, to distract her. He was acutely aware of the little plastic bag in the inside pocket of his jacket.

"My husband's a theatre director."

"Small world."

"The smallness of the world never ceases to amaze me."

A waitress took their drink orders, and Paul excused himself to shoot up in the men's room, not a lot, just enough to bleed a little chaos out of the world. He stood very still in the stall for five deep breaths before he returned to the table. He was calmer now, the sharp edge of the jet lag a little blunted. Everything was fine. No one needs to sleep *every* night. He could save a lot of time from now on, if he just slept every second night.

"So," she said, "you've been busy since I saw you last."

"Very. It's been extraordinary." He hadn't expected success and still found it disorienting. "I stepped through the looking glass into a strange new world where people actually listened to my music," he said. *I couldn't possibly have seen this coming,* he told Vincent, in his head, *I just took the opportunities that arose, I was hustling just like everyone else . . .* The opportunities that arose, like you had no choice in the matter? *I couldn't have anticipated this life,* he told her, and actually, why didn't he ever try to contact her after they'd both left the hotel? Because of his guilt over upsetting her with the graffiti and stealing her videos, obviously, but maybe he should try to find her now? Maybe enough time had passed? The condition of having landed in an unimaginable life was something he thought she might know something about.

"It was such an interesting angle you came up with," Ella was saying. He'd been half following along while she told him that she liked his work. "One sees so much video art, but that collaboration you did, the programmable soundtrack console, that was a wonderful innovation." For two separate works of video art, Paul had composed twenty-four hours' worth of music, arranged as a collection of thirty-minute pieces that could be programmed to play in whichever order the buyer preferred: a night owl might prefer something fast and sharp at three in the morning, for instance, segueing into calm around a five a.m. bedtime, while the early risers might prefer to walk into their living room and hear something bracing as the sun rose.

"Some of those video art projects need a soundtrack to be

even halfway interesting, if we're being honest here," Paul said. The beer in front of him was a terrible idea. If he drank it, he would lay his head on the table and fall asleep.

"I was curious about your musical influences," she said.

"Baltica," he said. "Everything I do sounds like an electronica group called Baltica that used to exist in Toronto in the late nineties."

"Oh, I didn't realize you'd been part of a group."

"I try to compose stuff that sounds different," he said, "I mean I'll really try in a concentrated way, and then I get to the end, I play it back, and it somehow always sounds like . . ." He stopped talking, and looked over his shoulder to cover his unease. "Do you think they have coffee here?" He was deeply shaken. He'd never told anyone about Baltica, and here he'd just blurted it out to her without hesitation.

"I'd imagine so." She waved, and a waitress appeared at the table.

"A coffee, please."

"Our coffee's terrible," the waitress said. "Fair warning."

"I think I might want it anyway."

"If I could possibly dissuade you," she said. "I mean, if you insist. But I promise that you'll send it back."

"Do you have black tea?"

"You're in Scotland."

"Something extra-strong," Paul said. "The strongest tea you've got. A lot of it. The more caffeine, the better."

"I'll bring you a pot, then," the waitress said, "and you can let it brew for as long as you'd like." Paul had the impression he often had in the United Kingdom, of just having been subtly insulted in an obscure way that would take too much energy to parse, and as always he couldn't tell whether the insult was real or just a typically Canadian case of postcolonial insecurity. *Damn it, I know how tea works,* he wanted to say, but it was too late, the waitress had departed and he was alone with Ella, who was giving him that look again.

"Do you still play music with that group? Baltica, was it?" She'd misunderstood, but he couldn't possibly explain.

"We've all gone our separate ways," he said. "I only see them on Facebook now. Annika's always on tour with like five different bands. Theo's a family guy. Is the hotel still there?" he heard himself ask, desperate to change the subject.

"It closed after Alkaitis was arrested," she said.

4

Eight time zones to the west, Walter was standing by the window of his room in the old staff quarters of the former Hotel Caiette. There was still no cellular service here, but some years ago he'd splurged on a cordless phone, in order to wander around his apartment while he talked with the outside world.

"I can't believe it's been almost ten years," his sister said. "Good lord. You're still not lonely?"

"I'm not sure *lonely* is exactly the word. No, I wouldn't say lonely."

The last guest checked out of the Hotel Caiette in early 2009, two months after Jonathan Alkaitis was arrested, and the rest of the staff left shortly thereafter. Is a hotel still a hotel without guests? Walter was there on the pier when Raphael departed. "Keep in touch," he said to Walter, and the men shook hands with the mutual understanding that they'd never speak again. Raphael climbed aboard the boat with his overnight bag—his belongings had gone on ahead to Edmonton—and the chauffeur, Melissa, started the motor. She was being paid through the end of the day but hadn't bothered with her uniform. She was leaving the boat in Grace Harbour and returning home by water taxi. "I'll stop by next week," she said to Walter. "Just to check in on you."

"Thanks," he said, moved and a little surprised by this. She cast off from the pier and the boat pulled out into the water, arced around the peninsula and out of sight. It was a muted day, the sea reflecting a pale grey sky, the forest dark and dripping from the morning's rain. Walter stood on the pier until he could no longer hear the boat and then turned back to face the empty hotel. He walked up the path and unlocked the glass doors of the lobby, locked them behind him. Raphael had ceremoniously switched off the lights as he left, but now Walter switched them back on. The dark wood of the bar gleamed softly. His footsteps echoed. The furniture had all been sold off except for the grand piano, which was too costly to move. Walter played a few notes, unnaturally loud in the silence. It was true silence, he realized, not at all like being in the forest, which even at its quietest was alive with small sounds. He walked past Reception, past the bar, to the staircase.

The largest suite, the Coast Royal, was where Jonathan Alkaitis had always stayed. Walter had thought to move in here—it had a splendour that the staff quarters lacked, and surely the hotel caretaker should live in the actual hotel—but the thought of sleeping in the bed where Alkaitis had slept was repulsive, and Walter liked his apartment. He wandered through all of the guest rooms, left the doors open behind him.

What was strange was that he didn't feel alone in all this space, all of these empty corridors and rooms. It was as though the hotel were haunted, but in the most benign sense: the rooms still held an air of presence, a sense of occupation, as if at any moment the boat might pull in with new guests and Raphael might walk out of his office complaining about the latest staffing problem, Khalil and Larry arriving for the night shift. He walked out onto the terrace. It provided a view of the empty pier, shadowy in the early winter twilight. He stood there for a while before he realized that he was waiting, by habit but completely without logic now, for a boat to come in.

"I can't quite believe it myself," he said to his sister, on the phone in 2018, "but I woke up this morning and realized, in February I'll have been here as the caretaker for ten years." Difficult to believe, but there it was: ten years of living alone in the staff quarters and playing tour guide to the infrequent potential buyers who arrived by water taxi, a decade of weekly trips to Port Hardy for supplies, cleaning the hotel, mowing the grass, meeting with repairmen when necessary, reading in the afternoons, teaching himself to play piano on the abandoned Steinway in the lobby, walking to the village of Caiette for coffee with Melissa; ten years of wandering by himself in the forest, watching the first pale flowers push through dark earth in the springtime, swimming by the pier in the hottest days of summer and reading on a balcony under blankets in the clear autumn light, sitting alone in the lobby with the lights out for the thrill of winter storms.

"But it seems like you still like it," she said.

"I do. Very much."

"Solitary, but not lonely?"

"That's a fair way of putting it. I wouldn't have expected this," he said, "after working in hotels all my adult life, but it turns out I'm happiest when I'm away from other people."

When he hung up, he left the staff quarters and followed the short path through the forest to the overgrown grass behind the hotel. He let himself in through the back door, making a mental note to sweep and mop the lobby today. Without furniture, the lobby was like a shadowy ballroom, a vast empty space with a panorama of wilderness beyond the glass: inland waters, green shorelines, a pier with no boats.

5

At the pub in Edinburgh, Paul's tea wasn't working very well. "I was always ambitious," he heard himself say, "but I never thought anything would come of it." Ella nodded, watching him. For how long had he been talking about himself? Did he just fall asleep for a second? He wasn't sure. It was difficult to stay awake. "All the videos are either beautiful or interesting, but not beautiful or interesting *enough,* without music added to them." Did he say this already?

"You seem tired," Ella said. "Shall we call it a night?"

He glanced at his watch and was startled to find that it was almost one in the morning. She was settling up with the waitress.

"Well, good night, then," she said, "and good luck, Paul."

"Do I seem like I need it?" he asked, honestly curious, but she only smiled and wished him good night again. He hated her in that moment, as he rose and left her alone in the bar—the unbearable smugness of the non-addicted—but of course she wasn't wrong, he knew he needed luck, he'd OD'd a month ago and woken up in the ER. ("Welcome back, Lazarus," the doctor had said.) He'd been perfectly functional for nearly a decade on heroin, not just functional but miraculously productive, just a matter of knowing his limits and not being stupid about it, but the problem now was that sometimes the heroin wasn't heroin anymore, sometimes now it was fentanyl, seeping into the market by mail and by ship, fifty times more potent than heroin and cheaper to produce. He'd been hearing rumours lately of carfentanil in the supply line, which terrified him: one hundred times stronger than fentanyl, approved for the sole purpose of tranquilizing elephants. The other night he'd read about a new rehab facility in Utah, and he'd spent some time on the website, looking at pictures of low white buildings under a desert sky. In a distant, logical way, he knew that going back to rehab wouldn't be the worst idea. Just do it, get it over with. Outside on the street, the rain had that diffuse quality that Paul associated with both the U.K. and British Columbia, a gentleness about it, coming from all directions at once.

He was almost certain that his hotel was back in the direction of the Royal Mile, which he was almost certain was a left turn at the end of this next street. He was thinking about the Hotel Caiette again, which led to thoughts of Vincent. The street he was on now looked vaguely familiar, but he couldn't be sure if that was because he was close to the hotel or if it was just that he was going in circles. He stopped walking and sat in a doorway, because he was tired and in his current state the rain wasn't a problem, sat on the step and rested his head on his arms. Should he try to find Vincent, contact her somehow, offer to share some of his good fortune? No, he needed the money. All of it. *I've never been able to completely grasp what my responsibilities are,* he told her. Sometimes when he spoke to Vincent now, he was the only one talking, while she just watched and listened to him. The doorway was unexpectedly comfortable. He'd just take a little nap, he decided, he'd just rest for a minute and then find his hotel and sleep properly.

But he wasn't alone. He sensed someone watching him. When he looked up, there was a woman standing just on the other side of the narrow street. She was wearing some sort of uniform, with a long white apron and a handkerchief tied over her hair. She must be a cook from a local restaurant, he decided, perhaps someone who'd just stepped out on a late-night dinner break, but if she was taking a break, she was spending her time very strangely, just staring at him instead of getting something to eat or smoking a cigarette. She looked familiar, she couldn't possibly be Vincent but—

"Vincent?" he said, and perhaps he'd imagined her, in any event she was gone, but for the rest of his life he would tell the story as if she'd really been there, he'd pull it out like a card trick whenever the subject of ghosts came up—"I was sitting on a step in Edinburgh, and I saw my half sister standing there on the other side of the street, and then she was gone, like she just blinked out. I started looking for her, and what I found out weeks later was that she'd actually died that night, maybe even that minute, thousands of miles away . . ."—and he would always play it as the real thing, as if he wasn't hallucinating and the woman he saw was really Vincent and Vincent was really a ghost and the ghost was really there on the street with him, whatever that means—what does it mean to be a ghost, let alone to be *there*, or *here*? There are so many ways to haunt a person, or a life—but uncertainty would always pull at him and he could never be sure; later he would wonder if he actually saw her standing there in an apron or if he added the apron to the memory in retrospect when he found out she'd been a cook; and always the question that pulled at him even at that moment, sitting in a doorway in the rain, drifting at the edge of sleep: Did he really see her, standing there on the street? Or was he just drunk and high, lost in a foreign city far from home, delirious with exhaustion and seeing things in the dark?

16

VINCENT IN THE OCEAN

1

Begin at the end:
> Plummeting down the side of the ship
> The horizon flipping once, twice, camera flying from my hand
> It felt like plunging into shards of ice.

2

No, begin twenty minutes earlier:

"Where were you last night?" Geoffrey asks. "I was looking for you after my shift." It is December 2018, and we've been together for years now, on and off, coming together and then agreeing to be apart. There are certain frictions: he wanted to marry me once, but I decided long ago that I will marry no one and will never again be dependent on another human being; he talks about quitting the ocean and living together somewhere, but I have no desire to return to land. Tonight we're together, although we were fighting earlier, and he lies beside me in my bed. We've been watching my suitcase slide back and forth across the room. This is the third night of heavy weather.

"I went for a walk."

"Where? The engine room?"

"On deck."

"We're not allowed on deck," he says, "you know that. Confined to interior until the weather eases up."

"Are you going to tell the captain?" I smile, but then I realize that he's angry.

"It's dangerous," he says. "Please don't do that again."

"I just wanted to film the ocean."

"What? Vincent. Please don't tell me you were hanging off the railing filming things in a storm."

"Can you not talk so loudly, Geoff? The walls are thin. Look, I know going on deck was questionable, but it was worth it. It was beautiful." I'd felt immortal, up there on deck. There was such power and magnificence in the storm. Only through the convergence of storm and ocean could a ship like the *Neptune Cumberland* feel small.

He's sitting up in bed, pulling on his clothes, still talking too loudly. "*Questionable* is not exactly the word I would use for this, Vincent. For Christ's sake, don't do that again."

The one thing in my life I have hated the most, out of a long list of things, is being told what to do. I can tolerate it in a kitchen but not in the bedroom, and I tell him that.

"I'm not telling you what to do for the sake of telling you what to do. I'm telling you to not go out in storms because I don't want you to die."

"I'm not going to *die*. You're being melodramatic."

"No, I'm being sane, and I wish you'd return the bloody favour," he says, and he slams his way out of my room.

I lie there for a long time, seething, watching my suitcase slide back and forth with the rocking of the ship. The thing with heavy weather is that it's impossible to sleep, at least for me, because it's impossible to lie unmoving in the bed; when the ship rolls, I roll with it, and it makes for a restless twilight kind of night. Finally I rise and get dressed, take my camera, and slip out into the corridor, then walk out onto C deck to meet the storm.

The fresh air is a balm, even the rain is wonderful, after an entire day of stale industrial interiors. Lightning flashes and the ship is illuminated. It's difficult to walk—I stumble against the railing—but I feel the old quickening that's always come over me when a beautiful shot is somewhere near. I will film just a few minutes, I decide, then I'll go back in. I make my way to the back corner of C deck, where the barbecue is clanking against its chains. I switch on the camera as I hear the thunder, and I record the most beautiful thing I've ever seen, lightning flashing over the roiling ocean. In a storm, the waves are like mountains. Cold rain in my face and I know it's on the lens but this, too, will be beautiful, the blurring and the raindrops. I stand by the railing, but with one hand on the railing I can't keep the camera steady, so I let go—just for a moment—and in an instant of calm between towering waves, I lean forward so that the shot describes an arc from sky into water, the shot pointing straight down at the ocean.

The light on the wall behind me begins to flicker. When I look over my shoulder, I realize there's someone here with me, at the other end of the deck.

"Hello!" I call out, but there's no response.

No, I was mistaken. I'm alone. I must be alone, because I thought I saw a woman, but I'm the only woman on board.

No, she's there. I can see her, almost. The light is still flickering, the deck intermittently illuminated. The horror is that this other person is somehow intermittent too, less a human figure than a disturbance in the air, a shadow that appears on the railing and then fades, a presence approaching. She is very close now. There's an impression of a hand on the railing, a silhouette, and then Olivia Collins is standing beside me at the bow, looking down at the water. She looks much younger than she did the last time I saw her, also less substantial. The rain falls through her. I'm still holding my camera over the railing. I can't breathe. She turns as if to say something and the camera falls from my hand; I reach for it without thinking, leaning too far, the ship lurches

I am over the side

I am weightless

the camera flying away into the rain,

the blue square of the viewfinder flipping through the dark—

3

The cold is annihilating—

4

I am holding hands with my mother. I am very small. We are in Caiette, picking mushrooms in the woods. A memory, but it's a memory so vivid that there's a feeling of time travel, of visiting the actual moment. What a pleasure to be here again! "Oh look, my lamb," she says, stooping to pluck a fluted little orange shape from the dark earth, "this one is a chanterelle."

5

It's like the moment just before sleep, when you're not quite unconscious—you're awake enough to realize that you're falling asleep—but your thoughts and your memories begin unspooling into narrative and you realize that you've already started to dream: one last moment of waking, choking on seawater, surfacing for an instant in a valley between waves, out of air, out of time, the ship an indistinct mass of shadow and lights, and then Olivia pulls me aside to apologize. She was thinking of me, she says, as she often thinks of me, and thinking of the ocean, that trip in Jonathan's yacht, so she sought me out and found me there on the ship, filming the storm. She didn't think I'd see her. She's pulled me aside to tell me this, but pulled me aside from where? We're in some in-between space, or so it seems to me, between the ocean and something I don't want to think about—

6

Sweep me up: words scrawled on the window of the school when I was thirteen years old, the letters pale on the glass—

7

A memory I wish I could stay in for longer: Kissing Geoffrey on C deck, beside a wall of shipping containers at the rear of the ship. His hand on the side of my face.

"I love you," he whispered, and I whispered it back. I'd said it before, but it seemed to me I'd never known what the words meant until that moment—

8

But now Geoffrey Bell and Felix Mendoza are standing on deck by the gangway stairs in a light rain, the orange cranes of the Port of Rotterdam overhead. Geoffrey is unshaven and has dark circles under his eyes. This isn't a memory.

"You know it makes you look guilty," Felix says.

"I swear to god I don't know what happened to her." Geoffrey's voice cracks; he swallows hard and closes his eyes for a second, while Felix stares at him, "But I'm afraid if I stay I'll get blamed for murder." Felix nods, they shake hands, then Geoffrey turns away and descends the stairs, shoulders squared in the rain. He looks so alone and so bereft, and I wish I could go to him and touch his shoulder and tell him I'm all right, I'm safe now and nothing can hurt me, but there's some confusion, some distance, he's receded—

9

I'm in a hotel that I recognize. I think this is Dubai, but this place isn't like the other places and memories I've been visiting. There's an unreality about it. I'm standing by a fountain in the lobby.

I hear footsteps, and when I look up I see Jonathan. We're in some nonplace, some dream-place, a place whose details keep shifting. No one else is here. I feel more solid here than elsewhere; Jonathan can see me, I can tell by his surprised expression, and it's possible to speak.

"Hello, Jonathan."

"Vincent? I didn't recognize you. What are you doing here?"

"Just visiting."

"Visiting from where?"

I'm visiting from the ocean, I almost say, but I'm distracted just then because I think I just saw Faisal walk by the window with a woman who looks vaguely familiar—is that Yvette Bertolli?— and in any event the ocean isn't exactly where I am, or if I'm there I am also somewhere else—

10

Some time has passed. I've been drifting through memories. I visit a street in some distant city where my brother sits in a doorway, because I heard him talking to me, but when he looks up and sees me he has nothing to say; I move for a while through Vancouver, walking the neighbourhood where I lived when I was seventeen, although *walking* isn't quite the word for the way I travel now; I search for Mirella and find her sitting alone and pensive in some beautiful interior, a loft of some kind, staring at her phone, she looks up and frowns but doesn't seem to see me there—

11

In memory I'm back at Le Veau d'Or, in the interior of gold and red, listening to my least favourite of Jonathan's investors talk about a singer. No, not a singer, a Ponzi scheme. "Couldn't recognize an opportunity," Lenny Xavier said, talking about the singer. "Whereas me, when I met your husband? When I figured out how his fund worked? That right there was an opportunity, and I seized it."

I watched Jonathan's look of alarm, the way he leaned forward as he spoke, his obvious desperation to stop Lenny from talking—"Let's not bore our lovely wives with investment talk"—and Lenny's smirk as he raised his glass: "All I'm saying is, my investment performed better than I could've imagined." He knew, but of course I knew too, if not the details of the scheme than the fact that there *was* a scheme, because I'd been pretending to be Jonathan's wife for months by then, it was just that I'd chosen not to understand—

12

I look for Paul again and find him in the desert, outside a low white building that seems to shine in the twilight. He just stepped out of the door, and he's lighting a cigarette with shaking hands. He looks up and sees me, drops the cigarette and then retrieves it.

"You," he says. "It's you, isn't it? You're really there?"

"I don't know how to answer either of those questions," I tell him.

"I was just talking about you," he says, "in my session just now. I was just telling my counsellor all the things I've never told anyone." I can't see his face clearly in the fading light, but he sounds like he's been crying. "Vincent, before you go again, can I just tell you."

"Tell me what?"

"I'm sorry," he says. "I'm sorry for all of it."

"I was a thief too," I tell him, "we both got corrupted," and I can tell he doesn't understand but I don't want to stay here and explain it to him, there's somewhere else I'd rather be, so I move away from the desert and away from Paul, all the way to Caiette.

I'm on the beach, not far from the pier where the mail boat comes in, and my mother is here. She's sitting some distance away, on a driftwood log, hands folded on her lap, with an air of waiting calmly for an appointment. Her hair is still braided, she's still thirty-six years old, still in the red cardigan she was wearing the day she disappeared. It was an accident, of course it was, she would never have left me on purpose. She has waited so long for me. She was always here. This was always home. She's gazing at the ocean, at the waves on the shore, and she looks up in amazement when I say her name.

Acknowledgements

I would like to thank the kind people at *Lloyd's List* for granting me a trial subscription to read more about shipping, and would also like to thank Rose George for her fascinating book on the industry, *Ninety Percent of Everything*. While all of the characters in this book are entirely fictional, the financial crime in the narrative is modelled on Bernard L. Madoff's Ponzi scheme, which collapsed in December 2008. I am indebted to two excellent books on the subject: Erin Arvedlund's *Too Good to Be True* and Diana B. Henriques's *The Wizard of Lies*.

With thanks to my wonderful agent, Katherine Fausset, and her colleagues at Curtis Brown in New York; my editors—Jennifer Jackson, Sophie Jonathan, and Jennifer Lambert—and their colleagues at Knopf in New York, Picador in London, and Harper-Collins Canada in Toronto; Anna Webber and her colleagues at United Agents in the U.K.; Lauren Cerand and Kevin Mandel for reading early drafts of the manuscript; and Michelle Jones, my daughter's nanny, for taking excellent care of my daughter during the time I spent writing this book.